# 7 SECONDS

BY

RACHEL DEFRIEZ

TWO CENTS PUBLISHING



ISBN 978-0-9893459-4-1

*for Janie and Josh*

*and for Dany, in memoriam*

# CHAPTER 1

Feeling like a stalker with nowhere to hide, I groped for a strand of hair to twist. No luck. Spencer, my best friend and personal style guru since seventh grade, had decreed this the year of the pixie cut. Too short to get a grip.

From time to time, I checked my cell. The hours and minutes were still legible through the splintered cracks in the screen. Tapping my heel in the gutter, I wondered if I should have invented some pretext for bringing him with me. Probably not. I didn't have enough friends to risk losing one in the crossfire. Losing Spencer would rip away a part of me—the part that had friends.

Very few trees broke up the concrete and asphalt jungle of West Derby Street. Splotches of shaggy grass checkered the bald dirt and weeds. Rusted car skeletons littered most of the front lawns. Across the street, loomed the brick and stucco duplex I'd seen in my 7-second glimpse of the future.

From the house behind me, an elderly woman squinted at me through her front window. On one side of her yard, a wooden fence, sagging and weathered, separated her lawn from the neighbor's drive. On the other, in the public park strip, an overgrown monster of a juniper spilled into the street. For lack of a better plan, I sat on the curb next to the shrub in front of the old woman's house and waited to catch up with my future.

Nothing happened.

At 3:28 p.m., after I'd gnawed off most of my thumbnail, a tiny drop of sweat dribbled down my temple to my ear. The unfiltered sun—or more likely the stress of thinking up all the ways altering the future could go royally wrong—had boiled up a mist of perspiration across my forehead.

If I managed to prevent this tragedy, how did I know the change wouldn't trigger a bigger disaster somewhere else? Maybe I should have just walked away and let the events happen, but I couldn't live with that choice. A little girl's life was at stake.

Two elementary-sized boys, backpacks slung over their shoulders, appeared from the other side of the juniper hedge. I hadn't thought about other kids showing up in the middle of the coming fray. This could get ugly—well, uglier. What if all I could do was shuffle around the damage? Who was I to decide who got screwed and who got saved?

Two houses up, the boys parted ways and disappeared through front doors on opposite sides of the street. A tepid breeze chilled the sweat on my arms and neck. Where the hell were the little girl and her brother? Around 3:30 in the afternoon. That's what the reporter said in my drift—pretty sure there is no scientific term for passing out in the present and flashing forward into the future for 7 seconds. I call it drifting. Sounds less freakish, more daydreamy.

Last year, my sophomore year in high school, I blacked out and my consciousness surfaced in my junior self while I was watching a news report. For that particular 7 seconds, a blond woman in a blue blazer outlined the essential details of a shooting. With that much information, I couldn't live with myself if I hadn't done something, even though I had no idea how, or when, or why it would happen.

Normally, the peripheral vision around a drift is unreliable, to say the least. The trouble with 7-second doses of the future is that they don't reveal enough details to make planning an intervention feasible. This time though, I had just enough info and what I saw was dire enough that I'd have felt like a barnacle on the butt of humanity if I didn't show up and try to do something—anything.

That's why, instead of catching a ride home with Spencer after French 3, I walked to the station and caught the light rail north to West Valley. I was old enough to drive, but that would require a car and a license. Most of the time, Spencer drove me around because my mom's job at Wal-Mart couldn't pay for a *working* car and the Utah Department of Motor Vehicles doesn't issue a license to drivers prone to "seizures." So, I didn't have a license to drive, and I sure as hell didn't have a permit to alter the future.

At 3:33, a black SUV turned down the street and parked in front of the driveway directly across from me. I grabbed the edge of the curb. This was it. The future was about to happen—or not if I could help it.

The driver, a lanky but toned kid about my age, hopped out of the car and left the engine running. He was the brother, Shafiq. I'd had an entire year to look up the address and stalk the victims. The news report supposed Shafiq was the target. He jogged up the drive, leaving a little girl seatbelted in the back. Yana. Somehow it seemed like alarms should be going off and Shafiq should be glancing over his shoulder, ready for an ambush. But he had no idea this was the day his five-year-old sister would get shot in the head.

From the SUV, Disney's "Let It Go," filtered into the street. Yana's mop of curly black hair bobbed as she belted out her best karaoke version.

Before Shafiq reached the front door, a white sedan rounded the corner. I jumped to my feet, heart pounding. The shooters! 3:34. Yana was completely oblivious. I had to do something. But what? I had no idea how the shooting would unfold. Before I could race across the street, the blue and black letters on the sedan rolled into view. A patrol car. The part of the news report I'd watched hadn't mentioned an officer on the scene. Either the timeline had already shifted or, more likely, my measly 7 seconds had failed, once again, to give me the whole picture.

As Shafiq disappeared into the house, the police car passed me and then turned into the neighbor's driveway behind the juniper. The old woman opened her front door and stepped onto the porch, arms crossed.

The patrol car door opened. A couple seconds later, the officer emerged onto the sidewalk behind me. He hiked up his utility belt and pushed up his aviator sunglasses. "Hello, miss. What's your name? What are you doing here?"

I glanced back at the Neighborhood Watch Nazi on her porch. A stranger camping out on her curb—duh, of course, she called the cops. But…rude!

Now what? How was I supposed to tell a cop I knew a kid was going to get shot without looking like I was in on it? "I…uh…" What was going through my head was that I had no cover story. Thank Goddess for theater class. "I'm, uh, I think I'm lost. Dude, it's hot. I just sat down to rest. Is that illegal or something…" I glanced at his name badge, "…Officer Knighton?" He was tall, not too much older than I was, and really attractive—in a cop sort of way that made total sense for a movie but not at all for real life. The stuttering might not have been all due to my lack of an explanation.

"Nope. Can you tell me where you were?"

"On the train; I think I got off at the wrong station. There's no mall around here, is there?" I scratched my neck and scrunched my eyes.

"That would be the West Valley Central station—last stop on the green line." While Officer Knighton responded, I kept an eye on Yana. Once her song finished, she didn't wait a hot second before she unfastened herself. The cop nodded and hitched up his belt.

"Well, that would explain it. I got off one stop too early."

He pulled a notebook and pen from the little pocket on his black shirt and flipped to a new page. I was on the verge of spilling my guts with everything I knew and letting a certified professional handle the situation, but I couldn't come up with a plausible explanation for knowing what I knew, at least not one that wouldn't land me in the psych ward at the university hospital. It occurred to me that I should have phoned in some anonymous tip or something. Late is not always better than never.

"Name and address?"

The urgency of a five-year-old floating free in a running car occupied all my brain space. "Uh, yeah…um. Officer, you should really…" My hand swiped nervously across my nose and I pointed toward the car death trap.

"Just your name, miss."

"Uh, yeah, but, uh…" I sighed, "…yeah. Ivy. Ivy Leif."

Eyes narrowed, he glanced down at my face to see if I was messing with him.

Sadly, I was serious. I met his stare straight on, shrugging. "It wasn't *my* choice. I think a bottle of Jack Daniels had something to do with it."

Yana tumbled over the console into the driver's seat, grabbing the steering wheel to catch her fall. Scrambling to her knees to see out the windshield, she pretended to steer. Asphalt crackled under shifting wheels. "Uh, officer…" I pointed across the street.

The old woman shook an accusatory finger at me. "She's wearing them gang colors. Don't listen to anything she says!"

Officer Knighton squinted doubtfully. I glanced down at my purple t-shirt with the big yin yang logo across the front and at my thrift store canvas shoes sporting rainbow peace signs.

Yana's brother still hadn't reappeared when another white car rounded the corner at the end of the street. Its Nissan logo flashed in the spring sunshine just as the door locks clicked on the SUV. I barely heard the sound over the pounding of blood in my ears. My breath hitched.

"Excuse me, officer—I... " The white car crawled past the house two doors down. From my spot on the curb, I could make out the driver's grey baseball cap. His passenger wore a blue bandana around his head. If either had been able to see the cop car hidden behind the juniper, the whole tragedy probably would never have happened. But they were busy looking for an address and, thanks to the paranoid old woman's landscaping, they couldn't see the police car. The passenger shoved a gun out the open window.

# CHAPTER 2

Officer Knighton's expression jerked to attention when his line of sight caught up with mine. "Get down!" He shoved me to the ground. Flipping up the strap on his holster, he ripped out his gun and targeted the oncoming car. "Drop the weapon!" The driver spotted him and yelled something at his passenger but just kept coming. Yana danced and rocked, oblivious.

"No! Oh, shit!" Without stopping to think about what I was doing, I jumped up and sprinted across the street to the SUV. I already knew what was going to happen if I didn't derail this fate train.

The policeman hollered, "Drop the weapon and stop! NOW!" The Nissan sped up like it was going to mow him down.

For a split second, the shooter's eyes met mine and death stared back at me from the wrong side of the barrel. Having seen snapshots of my future, I lived in a comfortable bubble of an assured life expectancy. I'd never even imagined the pull of a trigger could erase it in a fraction of a second. My heart skipped and I couldn't breathe.

Whirling around, I banged my fists like a rabid zombie on the SUV's window. "Get down! Hide!"

I'd never heard a live gunshot before. My knees jerked. The window exploded and a shard pierced my eyebrow as I sank to the asphalt, covering my head with my arms.

At the crack of a second shot, my body tensed for a sudden blast of pain. *Oh, Goddess! Please just nick my arm or something.*

Instead, metal pierced metal and the Nissan's tires squealed. The cop was returning fire. A third shot shattered plastic from the Nissan's brake lights. Red chunks peppered the street.

Yelling into his radio, the cop requested backup and rattled off a license number as he ran for his car. He slammed the door and swerved into the street.

Shafiq raced down the drive just as the Nissan and the cop car squealed around the corner. He rattled the locked passenger door. "Yana! Yana? Open the door!"

I hauled myself to my knees. Pebbles of grey asphalt stuck to the back of my arms. For seconds, I bit my lip, fearing that the future was written in Sharpie and couldn't be erased. Dreading what I might find, I peeked through the shattered window. The curly black top of Yana's head emerged from below the dash. She was fine! She ducked! No bullet holes. No blood. Not a scratch.

Shafiq sighed loud enough for me to hear across the car.

Yana stared at me, wavering between fear and confidence, as her brother leaned over his knees and sucked in relieved breaths. Tears smeared the little girl's cheeks. The blood trickling around my eye from the glass in my brow couldn't have been terribly reassuring.

"I'm so sorry, kidlet. I didn't mean to scare you. Are you okay?" I petted her hair. For the first time in my life, my blackouts and trips to the future actually meant something more than that I was a freak. A little girl survived because I saw a news report in the future. In my brain, astonishment and gratification shimmied up a little happy dance.

Yana's hand, only half the size of mine, reached for my arm. She opened her mouth to say something, but the moment her skin touched mine, her whole body stiffened. From her fingers, an intense wave of heat and energy burned up my arm and pounded into my head. Her eyes fixed vacantly on the sky and she chanted exactly what was in my head. "Ivy's drifts can save."

Ripping my hand out of her grasp, I clutched the burn and stared, stunned, at Yana, who looked as if she'd just woken from a dream. A drop of blood trickled from her nose. Her eyes rolled back and she crumpled into an unconscious heap on the front seat. My mouth gaped open. *What the hell was that*?

I'm not really one to see coincidence as divine, but something surreal had happened between me and this little girl. I saw her future and she read my thoughts. We clearly had some kind of connection.

Unfortunately, I didn't get the chance to investigate because, just then, a backup cop arrived, pulled up in front of us, and got out of the car. Shafiq stood, exhaling noisily, and walked to the front of the car.

From across the street, the old woman gestured emphatically at my back and hollered at the brother and the police officer. "She was with them! She was sitting here the whole time! I called the police!"

Shafiq's expression morphed from relief to rage, and he charged around to the driver's side, flimsy pink ballet clothes flopping in his hand. In his mind, I held the holster to a smoking gun. He had no idea I'd just gifted his sister a longer lease on life. In fact, not a soul on the street, except me—and maybe Yana—knew about the tragedy that should have happened. Good—but…not good!

Coming up on my side, he ignored my sputtering explanations and shoved me away from the door. My ankle rolled as I tried to catch my balance. I tumbled onto the asphalt again. Pain shot up my leg. Groaning, I put up my hands to plead my case. "Wait! You don't understand. I was trying to help…"

"Whoa, whoa, whoa!" The cop put a hand on the brother's shoulder. The kid shirked him off and pulled the door open. "Yana?" He bent into the car, unlocked it, and scooped her out. "Yana, sweetie, are you okay?"

Holding my breath, I waited. Finally, her curly black lashes flickered. I sighed, relieved that fate hadn't corrected its course and found an alternate route to her death.

Shafiq turned on me, vengeance in his eyes. "I know you! That was Gabe's car. You're his slutty girlfriend. You were standing lookout for that bastard!" Rage darkened his face as he nodded back at the SUV. "He almost shot my sister!" A sharp kick to my ribs punctuated his accusation.

Pain ripped across my chest. I yelped and winced. "But he didn't!" Although that fact made me feel better, it did nothing to douse the brother's fury.

The officer stepped between us. "Take your sister inside. Someone will be here in a few to take your statement."

Beneath Shafiq's glare, I scooted back to lean on the SUV. I was screwed here. All I wanted to do now was find out what had just happened between Yana and me. I'd just come here to help.

A nudge from the cop sent Shafiq up the drive.

The cop turned to me. "Ivy Leif?"

"That's me." Oh, the joys of having a memorable name. Thank you very much, Officer Knighton.

"I'm going to have to ask you to come with me."

He helped me up and I hobbled on his arm over to his car as another officer pulled up. His hand on my head, he stuffed me in the back seat. Well, I definitely hadn't seen *this* coming. Like Spencer always says, "No good deed goes unpunished."

# CHAPTER 3

It wasn't my first time in a police station. On a sporadic basis, I collected my mom from the one a couple blocks from our apartment. West Valley precinct was cleaner and quieter than I expected. It was a bit early, I guess, for the usual suspects to have shuffled in during the evening rush. A sweaty, hairy guy in a muscle shirt and another teen with gauges in his ears and a black mohawk lounged in plastic chairs near the window. The air conditioner purred over the ring of distant telephones. The policeman who brought me in escorted me to a chair near the front desk, spoke to the attending officer, and left. I'd pulled the shard from my brow in the cop car and the blood trickling down my cheek had dried and scabbed. It was my ankle that really hurt.

My phone was dead—as usual. Let's just say my cell and I had a dysfunctional relationship. 95% of the time, the phone wasn't functional. The other 5%, I wasn't. The cracked screen made it more of a must-have high school accessory than functional technology. Much easier to explain that my phone was broken or out of battery than that I couldn't afford one.

Left alone with my thoughts, I churned the post-shooting events on rewind. *Yana read my thoughts! Is she like me? I mean like me with different symptoms?* My arm still burned. *Are there other freaks with odd psychotic episodes like us out there? Are we all connected somehow?*

The desk officer wore her ponytail so tight and scratched notes so ferociously on her clipboard that I sat there for 20 minutes too intimidated to limp over to the counter.

"Excuse me, ma'am. Would it be okay if I made a phone call?" I wasn't sure if the one phone call was even a thing. But it was in all the movies. Apparently, it's not—at least, that's what I read on Reddit afterward.

She flipped through the papers while my fingers groped nervously for a lock of hair to twist. Glancing up through her bottle-thick, black-rimmed lenses, she sized me up and then jerked a thumb at the phone on the end of the counter. "Collect calls only. Cell phones and VOIPs don't accept them. You'll need to call a landline." From the box at the corner of the counter, she handed me a tissue to wipe the blood from my face and nodded at the drinking fountain.

A landline? Who has a landline? I only knew one person on the planet with a landline. My Great Aunt Grace. Plus, all my other numbers were safely stored in my cell phone—which was now dead. The only number I knew by heart—because my mother taught it to me before I could count—was Grace's.

I never knew my grandmother. She died before I was born, but her sister, my Great Aunt Grace, was a substitute grandma only a Disney dream could rival. She owned a bath boutique downtown and a Queen Anne cottage with a fairytale garden in the backyard. Her house smelled perpetually of roses and lavender.

The hitch was that I hadn't spoken to her in over four years, not since the drift that landed me face down in my Tater Tots at lunch. I can't really describe the awkwardness of flashing into a future self lip-locked to Amr, Autumn Hills Middle School's most eligible bachelor, and then reemerging into my present, ketchup-smeared face opposite Mr. Gorgeous himself. Spencer had recently scooped me out of the social gutter, hosed me down, and launched me into the select group that merited a seat at Pretty Boy's table. When I surfaced from my mini time travels, I imagined my condiment facial would douse my acting career before it caught fire. While concerned administrators were hauling me into the nurse's office to notify my mother, Spencer declared my performance of the narcoleptic from Moulin Rouge incomparable and dared anyone else to match it.

The fallout from that drift was pivotal. It was the first time Spencer covered for me and the last time I saw my Great Aunt Grace. As she often did before the Tater Tot drift, my mother called Grace for help with the medical bills. They argued. Not about the bills, Grace was loaded, and she would have helped more if mom let her. No, it was something else. Something my mom went into the bathroom to discuss in hushed tones that escalated into camouflaged shouting. When she came out, she was a little red in the face and threw her phone across the kitchen. The corner hit the wall next to the window. A shower of drywall sprinkled the linoleum. After that, I never spent another lavender-laced spa weekend at my aunt's. That's when, with Spencer's help, the "seizures" magically stopped—at least as far as my mother knew.

Of course, I still tried to sneak in a clandestine visit to Grace's shop here and there during the summer. But I had to take the train, and it got harder and harder to cover my tracks—*Goddess, I love a great pun*! Finally, though, Grace said it wasn't fair to my mother to meet behind her back. Personally, I thought it was more unfair for my mother to cut off our meetings. But I respected my Aunt Grace and, by the time I was in high school, theater had swallowed up all my free time anyway.

The phone rang three times before she picked up. I wondered what happened if no one answered your one phone call.

"Hello?" Grace's phone was so old she didn't even have caller ID.

"Aunt Grace…"

The operator cut me off. "*Collect call for Grace Sedona from Ivy Leif. Will you accept the charges*?"

"Well…yes, of course, I'll accept them."

"*Thank you. You're connected. Go ahead.*"

"Hello?"

"Hi, Grace, it's Ivy."

"Ivy! What a pleasure to hear from you!"

"Well, maybe not…" I turned to face the corner and lowered my voice, twirling my finger in the old-fashioned cord.

"Oh, dear. What's up?"

"Uh, I'm at the police station…"

"Are you dating a police officer now?"

"No, Grace. I'm only 16."

"Then I hope you were having some real fun before you ended up there. I want to hear all about it."

"Actually, I was just kinda in the wrong place at the wrong time. There was a shooting…"

"Dear Goddess! Are you all right?"

"Oh, I'm fine. It's just there was this little girl, and she needed to duck, and I happened to be there…"

Silence.

"Aunt Grace?"

I can't say I wasn't shocked when my aunt's voice shifted from her signature "Miss Honey" to Head of MI6. "I'll send someone immediately. Which station are you in? Have they arrested you? Put any information in the computer?"

Astonishment dammed up my thought processes. "Uh…not yet. I gave my name to the officer at the scene. The policewoman at the desk has been too busy to talk to me. I'm at the West Valley station."

"Ivy, listen to me. This is important. You say nothing to anyone until Mr. Brattweiler arrives. Nothing. Do you understand?"

"Yes, but…Mr. Brattweiler?"

"Barry Brattweiler. He's my lawyer. He'll be there in 30 minutes. Remember, Ivy. You don't have to tell them anything. No fingerprints, nothing until your lawyer arrives."

"Okay, nothing. But Grace, my mom…uh, she doesn't know. I don't really think it's a good idea…"

"Don't worry about that. I won't mention it, and Barry will take care of everything."

Within 30 minutes, the tallest man I had ever seen in real life walked through the glass front doors. He bent a little to make the clearance. Briefly, I imagined that a forest had spontaneously grown up around the station and that one of the tree elders had come to file a report. The man who towered above me looked a lot like the portrait on the front of my copy of Crime and Punishment. Thick black hair matched his ebony eyes. I was the only female my age in the lobby, so he walked right up to me and extended a pale, long-fingered hand. "Ivy? Barry Brattweiler, your Great Aunt Grace's attorney."

"Hi, thank you for coming. I'm so sorry…"

"Don't mention it. Grace and I go way back. It's a pleasure. Wait here just a moment while I sort this out."

Barry strode to the front counter and spoke with the attendant. "Good evening, officer. I'm Ms. Leif's attorney Barry Brattweiler."

Apparently, she knew the name. She looked up immediately from her clipboards and stood at attention. "How can I help you, sir?"

Barry spoke in subdued tones, but I overheard the words "heroic actions," "mayor," "minor," and "wipe her name." Then the desk phone rang.

The officer listened intently, nodding her head periodically and scratching off notes on a yellow pad. "Yes, ma'am. Yes, of course. I'll take care of it, ma'am." When she hung up, she gazed a little wide-eyed and speechless at Mr. Brattweiler.

"Thank you very much, officer. We appreciate your service. I believe we're finished here."

"Ms. Leif," the officer leaned around my attorney to make eye contact, "you can go. Thank you for your cooperation."

Astonished, I stood but crumpled when my ankle gave out. Mr. Brattweiler caught me, and I hobbled out on his arm. "You'll have to see to that ankle."

"I'll be fine. I've had worse. My mom's gotten pretty good at playing nurse. She's not going to be happy about it, though."

A car drove up to the curb and stopped. Barry opened the door for me. "I trust you'll make up an appropriate explanation?'

I nodded.

"The Uber will drop you at Spencer's house. From there, you can walk. Easier to avoid awkward questions that way."

"How do you know about Spencer?"

"There's very little that concerns your Aunt Grace that I don't know."

Bewildered, I ducked my head and climbed into the seat. "Wait! The little girl—Yana. Is she all right?" I'd learned young to keep secrets from my mom, from her bosses, from my friends, but something about Barry inspired confidence. He reminded me of the 100-year-old sycamores lining Grace's street. The residents would come and go, but the trees would always be there, standing sentinel. I didn't know how I could ever show my face again on West Derby Street, and I needed to know what happened to Yana.

"It would be best if you remained anonymous in this situation."

"But she…she," I rubbed my arm, still pink and tingling from the encounter.

"I'm aware of Yana's psychological profile. We're keeping an eye on her. Don't worry. You, yourself, should take whatever precautions you deem necessary to guarantee your own psychological profile remains untraceable."

"My psychological profile? How do you know about that?"

He nudged me into the seat.

"I told you. I'm your Aunt Grace's attorney." The door swung shut, and the car pulled away from the curb.

# CHAPTER 4

Obviously, time and I have a complicated relationship. I tend to jump forward, so I'll just back up a bit. It's hard to pinpoint my earlier 7-second field trips into the future. I think I was about three, though, the first time I figured out what was really going on. Well, I didn't really figure it out. A blue-eyed boy showed up during a 7-second drift and explained it to me.

Dora chattered on the television while I colored at the coffee table. One hand scribbled across the page while the other covered my nose. My brain connects smells and sounds to traumatic memories; it helps me sort and catalogue them. Once again, my mom had failed to make it off the couch to puke in the bathroom. Curdled chunks nestled in the ratted strands of her peroxide hair. Her natural blonde changed colors like a mood ring.

Moaning, she smeared vomit across her cheek. I covered her with my ratty blanket and then, using the wobbly three-legged stool, climbed up on the cracked kitchen counter to pour her a cup of coffee. By the time I was three, I already suspected that the magical potion exterminated the hangover worm crawling around in her head and munching away at her motherly instincts.

On the shelf below the coffee cups, the empty box of generic O's reminded me I hadn't eaten for a while. My stomach growled and my head puffed like a popcorn kernel as I stretched one leg backward, off the counter. My toe barely brushed the wooden stool top. I lowered the other foot. The stool wobbled.

My baby hands didn't quite complete a circle around the coffee cup as I slid it towards the edge and pirouetted on my precarious perch. A black hole erupted in the center of my vision, blocking out the view of my mother sprawled on the grey couch. Sighing, I braced for the looming blackout. Like walks in the park or trips to the zoo, the 7-second drifts into my future were not far from routine.

Just before the darkness swelled over me, I wondered if my mom would be angry about the spilled coffee.

*Second 1: Fluorescent light flickers. Medical waiting room. Numbness recedes. Antiseptic in the air. Red-headed mother sipping steaming coffee.*

*Second 2: Nurse. Ring in nose. Tattoo of a fish slithers up her neck. "Ivy Leif?"*

*Second 3: My mother gathers up her purse and stands.*

*Second 4: "Where are we, mommy?" My three-year-old voice doesn't fit the teen-age body in the chair.*

*Second 5: "Oh God, Ivy, not again. This never ends..." My mother turns exasperated eyes to the nurse.*

*Second 6: Blue-eyed, dark-haired boy in the seat next to me. His eyes meet mine. "They have you now, Ivy. Don't take...*

*Second 7: ... the medication. I won't be able to find you in time..."*

Of course, I had no idea what he was talking about. I was three. But, that's why I never took the seizure pills—well, that and they tasted like dirt—yes, I did try dirt. Probably for the best, too. I mean, I didn't really have seizures. I just checked out to visit my future from time to time. Mostly, I wanted to meet the blue-eyed boy. I hoped he'd come back, and he did.

In my lonely, sometimes scared, childhood, I clung to the idea that I had a guardian angel looking out for me. It gave me a sense of security in the unpredictable world of a child with a mentally absent mother. Don't get me wrong, I'm not complaining about my mom. It can't have been easy for her, alone, after my father left. No wonder she drank—sick kid, lousy job. No wonder I sometimes fantasized that I wasn't sick, that I had fairy blood, and the blue-eyed boy was my supernatural mentor.

My fantasy bubble popped when I went to high school and learned that magic is just science we don't understand yet, and everything human is chemical. My drifts probably had a very simple scientific explanation. I just hadn't found it yet.

# CHAPTER 5

Much simpler than pinpointing the first time I figured out what was going on is pinpointing the first time my mom actually realized what a freak her daughter was. September 11, 2001. I was four.

"You're burning it! You're burning it!" I tugged at my mother's sleeve from the bar stool that I had dragged up to the stove. The pancake passed the bubble in the batter stage while the burning building on the TV captivated my mom's attention.

A smoking tower smoldered on the screen across the room as its twin looked mournfully on at the hole spewing smoke and ash at frantic people running through the streets. I recognized the scene. I had a drawing of it taped to the closet next to our bed. I started scribbling out my visions after I met the blue-eyed boy. How else was a kid, with minimal experience and even fewer words, supposed to make sense of what she saw in her 7-second jaunts into the future, a future that was more complicated, more sophisticated—more messed up? The world was much broader and deeper than my toddler brain.

"Shush, Ivy!" Mom waved me away with the spatula, flipped the dirt-brown pancake over, gulped from an already half-empty glass of wine on the counter, and then wandered mesmerized to the couch that separated us from the fuzzy screen. "Oh my God…this is…this is…how does someone accidentally fly a plane into a skyscraper?"

The pancake was as doomed as the tower.

Sighing, I maneuvered off the barstool and padded in my bare feet to the closet by the bed. Jagged globs of masking tape plastered my drawings to the closet door. The one I was looking for was at least a year old. In the same way that I connected the smell of spilled coffee to the smell of coffee in the doctor's office, I connected the smell of a burning pancake to what was happening on the TV. A little of the eggshell paint pulled away from the closet door and clung to the ragged strip of tape hanging from the drawing.

Wandering back into the kitchen, I contemplated my time-yellowed masterpiece. In the bottom corner of the drawing, an abandoned pancake shriveled to black on the grill. It looked a bit more like a turd than anything. Little curly cues of grey smoke illustrated the burnt smell. The large primitive stick figure sitting on the sofa was obviously my mother because of the mop of violent red hair topping the warped circle of her head. The smaller blob of yellow-brown on the stick child sitting next to her on the grey sofa was my best rendition of me. The little girl was showing her mommy a picture of two towers, one smoking grey like the pancake and the other frowning as a smaller plane flew from the top corner on a collision course with its belly. On the drawing of the television screen that sat in front of the stick figures, I had drawn the exact same drawing that the stick figure girl was waving in front of her mother's face. It was a little like a drawing within a drawing within a drawing...pretty complicated for a three-year-old, but understandable under the circumstances—and considering the look my mother gave me when I reemerged from the drift.

She hardly noticed me as I climbed onto the grey cushion beside her, so I held the picture up to her nose and waggled it there until she shook her head and batted it away like an annoying little fly buzzing through the enormity of the terror she was witnessing. "Oh, my God! Oh, my God! There's another one!" My eyes riveted themselves to the red band that marched relentlessly across the screen. A brilliant flash of light doused the entire scene. Before the second plane collided with the second building, the empty void of an incoming drift engulfed me and locked my consciousness in some basement of my mind while my three-year-old self popped into my four-year-old body for a visit—for 7 seconds.

When the world refocused around me, my mother was standing above me gripping the drawing. Her wide-eyed horror darted from the yellowed paper to the artist and back to the live broadcast. She looked at me as if I had hundreds of spiders crawling all over my face. The voice coming out of me during the drift had probably been some gibberish from my three-year-old self, judging roughly by how long the picture had been hanging on my closet. I was chronology challenged. Time jumbled together for me.

So, did watching 7-second trailers of my future make me a prophetess? Hell, I had no idea. I just saw things—some kind of hyper déjà-vu. Honestly, I didn't really see any divine calling in it. I mean, a prophet should have a purpose and a vague idea of what the visions of the future mean. I didn't. What I really thought was that my drifts were a side effect from when my mom dove head first off the wagon while I was developing brain cells.

# CHAPTER 6

After bingeing on Ibuprofen for a couple weeks until my ankle healed, I returned my school elevator key. I worried that the analgesic might interact with my "condition." Okay, I was a little OCD about tracking my drifts. Who wouldn't be? I mean, if I didn't know what triggered them, I couldn't control them. The biggest suspects, at that point, were hunger and fluorescent lighting—especially if it was flickering, or really strong. I'd been tracking triggers since that first time I was old enough to actually realize a "seizure" was coming on and remember the circumstances. I was three and an artist in embryo.

At least, I could cross Ibuprofen off the list of possible triggers. I was back in full stomping form when the next drift slammed me during AP Chemistry. Fortunately, Spencer was my lab partner because instead of a younger version of myself popping in for a quick look around, I exited the stage for a field trip to my future.

*Second 1: Ears pop. Prism-ringed black hole fades from my vision. Nausea recedes. Sensation trickles into my right arm. Hum of an engine. Blur of leaves, brick, and cobblestones.*

*Second 2: Silver car, black leather. Small village shops. Narrow road. French on the signs.*

*Second 3: France? Oh, I hope it's France, but half the world speaks French.* Boulangerie Artisanal—*a bakery.*

*Second 4: Who the hell is the man driving the car, mumbling into his cell? Long black hair, slicked back curls. Square jaw. Sunglasses. Olive skin. Coat gaps open. Gun holster strapped to his side.*

*Second 5:* "On arrive dans cinq minutes..." *Yank down the visor to see myself in the mirror. Only gaping brackets where my reflection should be.*

*Second 6: I grab the rearview and twist it in my direction. Red hair, chin-length, long bangs. Yellow shirt—Saturday.*

*Second 7: The back of the driver's hand flies across the center console and slaps me.* "Merde*!* Elle a fait son truc...

My consciousness crash-landed back into AP Chem. A headache pounded so fiercely behind my left eye that I wanted to grab scissors, jab them through the socket, and murder the nail-gun wielding alien in my skull.

I wasn't sprawled on the floor. Spencer must have caught me when I fell. He had this sixth sense about my drifts. I owed him big time and, one of these days, now that I'd figured out a way to track the lottery numbers, I'd pay him back in hard cash.

Instinctively, I wiped the back of my hand across my mouth to eliminate the unsightly strands dangling there. Above the counter, the classroom buzzed. When Spence saw that I'd returned from my accidental mind vacation, he announced, "Here it is! I found it!"

I didn't bother to ask; I just went along with it. "Oh, thank Goddess! I can't see a thing without my contacts."

Spencer pretended to hand it over for the benefit of the gawkers in our row and offered me a hand up. We both knew the drill.

My radar nose picked up the acrid scent of burning chemicals. Our line of sight reached the countertop just in time to confront Ms. Tucker charging our lab station. During the "seizure" chemicals spilled, Bunsen burners tipped, and lab notes ignited.

Fortunately, our chem teacher had the flame under control before the alarm had time to detect it, but not before a dozen phones caught it on camera to preserve for all posterity.

"What happened here, Ivy? Spencer?" A few curls had escaped her ponytail. She was visibly restraining her temper. Why? Because next to my name in her electronic grade book a little blue medical alert square flagged me as a freak to be handled with care.

"She lost her contact." Spencer peered solicitously into my left eye and, for a brief instant, his eyebrow twitched, reminding me I had a role to play. We'd attracted an audience. My mother could *not* get a call from the school alerting her that my "seizures" had started up again. It would make things…difficult.

The chatter hushed. A few cell phones still recorded the incident for global electronic distribution. Ms. Tucker shooed the onlookers back to their lab stations. "You only have twenty minutes left to finish your assignment, people. Let's get going." Eyes narrowed and fists on hips, she turned back to me and Spencer.

Now it was my turn to improvise. "I think maybe I should go to the office and have the nurse look at my eye." Occasionally, freak status offered benefits. Yin Yang. I'd learned to live by it.

Spencer nodded sympathetically. "Do you want me to go with her, just to make sure she gets there okay?"

Ms. Tucker sighed and shook her head, trapped, against her better judgment, by the little blue square next to my name. "Ivy, you can't keep ducking out of class like this and making up the work later. Eventually, all the late work is going to catch up with you and then your grades are going to suffer."

At this point, the script called for saying nothing and looking mortified. The truth was, my drifts all caught up with me eventually, but missing class never did. Spencer and I had matching 4.0s.

Ms. Tucker didn't really give us permission as much as wave us away with her hand. "You have two days." She stalked away to police a couple of chatty 2.0s across the room.

Spencer grinned conspiratorially. I had 20-20 vision—well, I wasn't sure how an optometrist would classify the ability to see into the future. This wasn't the first time we'd pulled off an act like this. The two of us were matched accomplices, inseparable and complimentary, the perfect couple—if it weren't for Amr.

# CHAPTER 7

"You okay, Drifter?" Away from the prying eyes, Spencer was all concern. He's the one that first coined the term "drift" for my "seizures." Very P.C. of him. He peered into my face and then dropped his arm around my shoulder. "You're shaking. I think the drifts are getting worse. You've never been this pale before. Maybe you should rethink taking the medication." For Spencer to suggest medication, he had to be seriously worried. A childhood of enabling a single mom opioid addict had soured him on the whole pharmaceutical industry. While other kids were trading Pokémon cards, Spence and I traded mommy addiction stories.

The 7 seconds of my future that I'd just witnessed freaked me out enough to want to break my vow of silence. In my gut, I was 99% sure Spencer wouldn't abandon me if I revealed the true depths of my oddity, but then again, there was that 1%—and I was already dangling precariously on the fringe of the social network. Without Spencer to cling to, I'd fall right off.

Maybe I was just tired of the loneliness or maybe the violence of my most recent drift—and the discovery that I could actually change the future and make a difference for someone—made me feel like I needed to grow up and take charge of my life. Or maybe it was staring into the wrong end of a gun and realizing that life could be shorter than I expected. Either way, I needed backup and moral support. Whatever the reason, after six years of silence, I breathed in a healthy dose of courage, grew a backbone, and took the plunge. "It's not the drift making me pale, Spence."

"Then what? Because, girl, you look hammered."

As we passed Ms. Hardman's AP Biology class, Amr Jafari caught sight of us through the open doorway. His hand went up. Ten to one he was asking to use the hall pass. We weren't five paces beyond the classroom before he matched his step to ours. "Did it happen again? Oh, my God! Spencer, is she okay?"

No big mystery that I also hung with the only Muslim in our white-washed high school. Our school was as homogenous as a gallon of organic whole milk. He was also the only other student in our theater clique that knew the details of the blue flag next to my name in the roll book.

Amr had his own social challenges. For one, his name was unpronounceable. Everyone called him AJ. I didn't get it. It wasn't that complicated. Separate the two consonants, roll the "r" a bit, and *voilà*. Maybe it was because I took French. Safe to say it was his undecipherable name that secured Amr his spot on the fringe, even though he was brilliant, in a witty, sexy sort of way, and drop-dead gorgeous—at least I thought so. I would never admit it out loud, though. He was more like a step best friend. Kindergarten made him and Spencer inseparable. For me, having Amr as a close friend was mostly an eye-candy perk of being Spencer's go-to-girl—and maybe, if I was honest with myself—which I wasn't most of the time—a secret aspiration. Why? Because I'd seen things.

So, here's the deal with Amr. He was the co-star of the Tater Tot drift. I passed out, face-planted into a pile of ketchup, and surfaced into my future self staring deep into the mocha eyes of the most gorgeous kid in school—only he wasn't a kid anymore and neither was I. He had one hand in my hair and the other around my waist. My lips were parted, and I gasped when his touched mine. Our lips moved in slow, sensual waves for nearly 7 seconds. A flurry of hormones and chemicals billowed like butterflies and vodka in my veins and my head floated in a starry, starry night. Goddess! My first kiss! In the last second, his lips dragged mine with them as he pulled away without breaking eye contact. His forehead leaning on mine, he looped a lock of hair around his finger and whispered, "shoulder-length lavender."

And then I plummeted back to my middle-school reality and the ketchup plastered to my face. So maybe now, my ambivalence around Amr makes senses. I mean, how do you act after that? My impulse was to just ignore him completely. I couldn't risk doing something utterly asinine that would jeopardize that future. But that was just the female ADHD talking. How would we ever get to point C if I never traveled through point B? Should I flirt? Should I be friends? Should I be best friends? Should we be enemies? All the Rom-Coms start with the love interests as enemies. Maybe he only ended up liking me because I never let him know I liked him. Oh, Goddess. I just didn't see enough! Thus, my adamant and awkward ambivalence about Amr.

"Ivy, did you have another seizure? Are you all right?"

"I'm not saying, Amr. You're on my no-tell list." Deflection. It was my go-to strategy with Amr. "Jillian Jefferson? Does that name mean anything to you? Because there are like 50 text messages on my phone from her from last weekend, when you freakin' fell off the planet and left me to clean up the pieces of her shattered heart."

He threw his arm around my shoulder and squeezed. "That's why I love you, Ivy. You're a great listener." His pearly white smile would slay a bitch. With no warning, I raised my left knee a little higher than I needed to and jammed the heel of my combat boots down on the toe of his canvas *Vans*.

"Ow! God! You bitch!" Amr hopped about trying to grab the traumatized toe, but then knelt down to apply pressure.

Spencer's brow went up, but neither of us slowed our pace.

About half a minute later, AJ caught up, limping slightly. "What the hell, Ivy?"

"Sorry, boy. I just wanted to make sure you were human…you know, with actual feelings."

"God! It wasn't me. It was her. The girl never shuts up! I needed, like, two days of solitude just to recover. It was never going anywhere anyway. It needed to die—quietly." In the theater clique, Amr's air of forbidden fruits, obscenely long eyelashes, and general tall, dark and charming gorgeousness had landed him the role of player.

Poor Amr. He couldn't help but have this driving need for acceptance in our monoculture fishbowl. He was the guppy sloshing around outside the bowl, suffocating in isolation, dying to get into the water. He was integrating himself one girl at a time—the most logical way for someone with those smoky eyes and spring-blush lips.

"Seriously?" Spencer viewed Amr's relationship MO less forgivingly than I did. "No text? No Facebook status change? No heart-wrenching DTR? You're brutal, dude."

"It's not my fault." Spencer and I responded with synchronized eye-brow tilts. "It's your fault, Ivy. You've totally ruined every other girl for me. You've got this freaky…otherworldly…vaguely threatening air about you."

He was referring to my rather eccentric invitation to a girl's choice affair that year. I'd lured him into a dark empty field, surrounded him with seven or so chanting, hooded accomplices in a circle of red candles, and threatened to murder him if he didn't agree to accompany me. That was actually the only time Amr and I had gone on a date—the only time Spencer was unavailable because he'd been trapped into going with Jillian. They were friends, but everyone knew Jillian wanted to be more.

"Besides, you're a 4.0 in a flock of 2.8's."

I rolled my eyes, but Spencer couldn't resist. "Which means she's not dumb enough to end up on your fling of the month list." If only brains had anything to do with it. My act of prickly indifference to Amr's charms was probably the magnum opus of my entire high school theater career.

We were headed toward the office, but when we reached the door, I pushed them farther, across the cafeteria toward the rape hall. Don't get me wrong. The isolated hallway to the art complex had sketchy lighting and moldy overtones and rarely got monitored; pretty sure no one got raped there.

"I have to show you something." I twisted out the code on my locker…yes, the random assigning mechanism had located my locker in the rape hall. More fringe material. I pulled out a sketch pad and hugged it to my chest to steel myself against the high probability that, in choosing to reveal my mutation, I could lose my best friend and my first kiss all in one blow.

"If this is about your art grade, you really have to chill. You always do this." Spencer's hands flew to his hips, kind of like my mom's. "You get one B+ and you flip. You're not going to fail, it's…"

"It's not about my art grade. Come with me." We headed out the doors and escaped to the grassy hill between the seminary building and the faculty parking lot. The moment was here. The AP Chem drift tipped my hand. I was going to need help. Spencer was an obvious choice. Amr was a wild card. At some point, he would know about me anyway. After that kiss, he took the time to tell me the color of my hair. He knew exactly what was happening.

The heavy papers of my collection of 7-second glimpses slapped against each other as I flipped through them.

"What are we looking at?" Amr squinted. Adorable.

"The future."

They checked my eyes to spot the joke. Didn't find it. Spencer folded his arms. "Seriously, I think we should go see the nurse. You need to get some help before you fry your brain. Hiding your seizures from your mom is one thing, but you've got to tell someone what's going on…."

"I am. I'm telling you."

"I'm not a neurologist."

"I'm going to be a neurologist." Amr wagged his eyebrows and grinned.

Spencer rolled his eyes. He'd learned to tolerate Amr's self-inflation.

On the other hand, I—no, I knew better than to wake that sleeping puppy. "I'm telling you now because I'm not actually having seizures."

Spencer's eyes crinkled as he tried to figure out what the hell I was talking about. "What? It's all an act?"

"No! Who would do that?" I think both Spencer and I thought "Amr" at the same time. But neither one of us said it. I saw it though, in the sidelong glance of Spence's eyes and the arch of his brows. "No. I am not pretending to have epilepsy. Doctors have officially diagnosed me—but that's not what's really going on. What really happens is…" The words stuck in my throat. A random kid shuffled down the stairs from the seminary building.

"What?" Amr nudged my shoulder.

I waited for the kid to disappear behind the cars before I hissed out the truth. "… my consciousness checks out of my present self for 7 seconds and drifts into my future self." Gulping, I waited. Visions of the horror that disfigured my mother's face on the day she realized what was really happening weighed heavy on the seconds ticking by.

# CHAPTER 8

Spencer's brow furrowed. "So…you don't have seizures. You pass out and 'drift' into the future? For 7 seconds?"

Both Spence and Amr folded their arms and squinted—almost in perfect sync like they were doing a scene. Amr leaned over to look closer at my pupils. "Did you hit your head when you fell? Maybe you have a concussion."

"No! I did not hit my head and I'm not crazy. Look!" I shoved my sketchpad at Spencer.

Frowning, he took it and flipped slowly through the pages. He paused on the stick figure of a girl with lavender, shoulder-length hair being robbed at knifepoint. When he came to a black pixie cut sketch with more recognizable facial features, he pointed to the hair. "Is this why you make me choose you a new hairstyle on Jan. 1 every year?"

I nodded, holding my breath. My heart pounded as the jury deliberated on the future of our relationship. I thought if I explained, it would give Spencer time to figure out that this was unusual but okay—very scientific, not at all an improbable fantasy. "It's like this. I'm not always somewhere where I can tell the date and time. I try to wear my watch every day, but even then, it's not reliable."

"And you never have your phone on you." My epically irresponsible phone handling drove Spencer nuts. It never worked, and I could never remember where I left it. But then, unlike him, I had no entourage of friends texting me 24/7.

"Right. That's why I needed a better source of info so I wouldn't have to waste my 7 seconds figuring out the day and year. You've never seen the sketches. If you choose my hair color at the beginning of each year, then, when I drift forward,

I can make a note of what my hair looked like in the drift. That way, when you randomly choose that hairstyle in the future, I have the sketches that tell me what's going to happen that year. Get it?"

Amr's eyes crinkled up. In a shift of the eyebrows, the player disappeared and the future neurologist took the stage. "That's not really a precise method—points for creativity, though."

"Obviously, but I was in elementary school when I started noticing the changing hairstyles in my drifts and wanted to know when some of them…"—the kissing one with Amr, for instance— "…would happen. It's actually pretty reliable. I can tell the day of the week it will happen by the color of shirt I'm wearing."

"You day code your shirts?" Amr nodded, warming up to my methodology.

"Yep." I pulled out my t-shirt to illustrate. "Today's Tuesday, a red-shirt day." Bowing my head, I pointed to my roots. "Sometimes, if I can see them, the length of my roots tells me how many months into the year I am. Hair grows about half an inch per month."

Spencer pursed his lips and inhaled. Over his shoulder, Amr observed the data in the sketches, weighing the possibilities. My thumbnail found its way between my front teeth. Spencer flipped the notebook closed, a stern frown on his brow. My heart sank. My gamble was a bust. He clearly thought I was certifiable. Oddly enough, Amr, the scientific one, seemed much less inclined to judge. That was his MO, though. I was the new target. I could have told him I danced with fairies in the moonlight and he'd have gone along with it—until he got bored of me.

I could see Spencer rethinking his social choices. His frown creased into anger. I really should have learned my lesson from the first time I tried to share the truth with someone close to me—with my mother. "Why didn't you tell me about this? I thought we were friends."

"I didn't tell you because you're my ONLY friend."

"Hey!" Amr objected.

"You don't have friends, Amr. You have conquests." I didn't really worry too much about hurting his feelings, I wasn't all that sure he had any. Besides, I already knew at some point he'd come to embrace my anomaly.

It was Spencer's reaction that had me biting my nails. "Yeah! I am your friend, so you could have told me. We could have...like...I don't know...won the lottery." Ah! The Spencer I knew and loved! Maybe he wasn't completely lost to me. "You could keep the winning numbers in your pocket and then one day..."

"Oh, my Goddess, I was just thinking that when you dragged me up off the floor today." Reaching in my pocket I pulled out a folded sticky note with the week's numbers. "One of these days, we're gonna win big." I waggled it in front of his face, hoping to lure him with cash away from his anger at my silent betrayal and the utter improbability of what I was claiming.

"What about me? I want in on this."

"You don't need money, Amr. Your parents are rich, mentally stable, socially adjusted doctors." Spencer shook his head. "All these years, Ivy! Really? Imagine what we could have done."

"I'm sorry. Really, I am. It's not that simple. I mean it's only 7 seconds, and then, think about it. 'Hey, Spence, when I passed out in the middle of chem lab, I saw myself get abducted in the future.' It's bad enough that..."

"Wait! Wait! Stop right there!" Spencer grabbed my shoulder. "You got...WILL get...abducted? Is that what you saw?"

"Yeah." My fingers groped for a non-existent lock of hair to twist. "I'm kind of scared...the guy had a gun. He knew I could see the future, and he backhanded me when I checked the mirror to date the drift."

Spencer shook his head and then hugged my shoulders. "Damn it, Ivy. I wish you'd told me sooner. We're friends. Friends have each other's backs...and futures." He handed me the notebook. "You'd better draw what you saw. Maybe we can at least figure out where you were."

Relief allowed me to breathe again. If I'd known my only friend wouldn't freak, I'd have broken the news a lot sooner.

But I could never really be sure of the future, even if I got a random glimpse. Spencer slid a thin grass blade from the root and gnawed on it.

"This is totally legit!" Amr's shoulder nudged mine. On a clean page, I sketched the silver car. It was a Mercedes—somewhere in my mind, I'd noticed the emblem. Spencer turned away.

My hand stopped sliding across the page. "Are you still mad?"

"No," he snapped and then fidgeted with his collar. "I'm just feeling guilty."

"Guilty? Why? You've saved my butt more times than I can count."

"Yeah, but you didn't know you were saving mine—because I didn't tell you."

My pencil stopped scratching against the paper. "Tell me what?"

The building doors opened, and the smell of freshly baked bread from the cafeteria wafted out into the parking lot. My stomach gurgled. If I hurried, I'd finish the main pieces of the sketch in time to grab food—most likely the only meal I'd get today. Free school lunch—damaging to the psyche, essential to survival. Another thing Spencer and I had in common.

"Ivy…" he leaned over my knees, "…Amr. You two are the only people in my life I trust enough to tell the truth."

My hand stopped briefly. Spencer and I locked eyes. He was as worried about my reaction as I'd been about his.

"I'm gay."

The seminary doors opened behind us and a crowd of students poured down the steps. The cacophony of voices filled the silence between us.

Finally, my eyebrows went up and I shrugged, not really sure what words were required in this situation. I put my arm around Spence's shoulder. "I know."

"You know?"

"Spencer, we've been best friends since 5th grade. Obviously, I know."

Amr leaned across me. "We all know, Spence—well, maybe not Jillian."

Spencer's mouth dropped open.

I shrugged off the revelation and kept sketching while I narrated. "The name of the bakery we passed was a play on words. *LE CHO'PAIN.* It sounds like Chopin the musician. But, in French, those words are homonyms with Chaud Pain (hot bread). Get it? Artisanal bakery?" Blank stare. "Yeah, well...whatever keeps it in my head."

"I'll Google it." Spencer leaned over to make out the name. "Let's see if I can find out an address. The place might give you some clues about what you're doing there. Maybe they have a website with an address...a photo of the storefront if you're lucky."

"Lucky? She goes to France but gets kidnapped." Amr watched, mesmerized, as a blond with long legs sauntered past. He just couldn't help himself. "I wouldn't exactly call that lucky," he muttered when his brain returned to working order.

"You're going to Narbonne." Spencer flashed me a picture of the bakery I'd just seen in my drift.

"Hmm! Pretty! Provence. Maybe I go to Paris, too. No one should die before they've seen Notre Dame."

"You're so full of shit, Ivy. Don't make a joke out of this." Spencer's index finger smacked the pad. My hand jerked and sliced a black streak across the page. "This is serious."

Fortunately, my pencil had an ample eraser. "Maybe. Maybe not. It was only 7 seconds. Can't really tell."

"The guy is a stranger..." Amr started counting off the facts on his fingers.

"...to me, now. But maybe not then."

"He has a gun..."

"...maybe he's protecting me."

"He backhands you!"

I didn't really have a response for that one. I'd have to concede it.

Spencer lay back, his head thudded against the lawn. He was processing a considerable amount of new input. When he looked at me, I could see the concern—unsettling, serious, genuine concern. "I don't like this, Ivy."

"Well, I'm starting to think sometimes you just have to look the future in the face and say, 'I'm not going there.'"

# CHAPTER 9

The ding of the doorbell rushed me out of my shower. Spencer had an awkward habit of showing up early—even in summer. A towel turban on my head, I opened the door, ready with a lecture on social skills, but then stopped cold. Barry Brattweiler stood on my porch. Behind him, heat wafted up in rippling waves from the faded parking lot. A silver Jaguar flanked my mom's rusted Pontiac.

"Hello, Ivy."

"Uh, hello." My terry robe suddenly struck me as highly inappropriate. "Come in, uh, excuse me, uh, just a minute." I gestured to the vomit-stained grey couch and scurried to the bathroom to throw on some jeans and run a brush through my wet hair.

When I padded barefoot back down the hall, he was still standing, contemplating a photo of me and my mother taped to the fridge. Embarrassed, I swiped the coffee mug off the counter of the otherwise immaculate, but woefully worn, kitchen and tucked it away in the dishwasher. "You don't take after your mother. But you certainly resemble your grandmother Sabrina…and Grace." He turned and smiled. "Is your mother here?"

"Uh, no. She's at work…I hope." My nervous chuckle revealed more than I intended.

He nodded knowingly. "Ivy, may we sit?"

The grey couch sagged beneath the weight of this giant of a man. My nose tickled at a lingering scent of pine and oak when he leaned close. "I'm afraid I have bad news. Grace passed away last night."

I didn't see that coming.

My hand flew to my mouth and tears welled up. One of the few people in existence who gave a damn about my happiness had exited life without even a curtain call. My *phenomenon* didn't even bother to give me a heads-up about the passing of the woman who brought bath bombs and bubbles into my mess of a life.

"Was she sick? Why didn't she tell me?" My eyes stung and the words stuck.

"Please don't resent Grace for not keeping in better contact. I know she and your mother had their differences, but her only motivation was your well-being. At some time in your life, you may come to understand that she kept you at a distance because she loved you."

"That doesn't make any sense."

"Much of life doesn't until you have more information. And then it does." He squeezed my hand, and I sniffled. Barry spoke as if he might actually be the spokesman for the trees—solid, reliable, enduring. He inspired an uncanny urge to lean back and drift off to sleep under the shade of his watchful boughs.

"My mom used to take me to Aunt Grace's bath store." The memory of those outings into the wonderland of smells brought a sad chuckle to my throat. My chest felt oddly empty in the place that usually warmed when random memories of my Aunt Grace blanketed my mind. "Her shop was better than a candy store. I love bath bombs! She used to send me home with a box full and a little note explaining when I should use each one…"

"Believe me, she cared for you, more deeply than you know. I don't believe she loved anyone more than you, unless it was her sister Sabrina."

"Mom and Aunt Grace argued about my…condition. I…"

"Yes, I know. Grace wanted to protect you from the implications of being able to see the future, help you to adapt to it, but your mother preferred to ignore your gift and suppress it. I'm sorry."

Mr. Brattweiler inspired confidence, a sense of reliability like an ancient oak. My Aunt Grace trusted him, why wouldn't

I? In fact, a sense of relief that someone with such an air of dependability shared my secret with me washed over me. "I didn't see Aunt Grace much after she and mom argued. My mom would never talk about it and, well, I couldn't drive…so…" The tears stung my eyes and dribbled down my cheek.

"She wanted me to tell you in person how much she cared for you." Barry let me mourn for a while before he sighed, squeezed my shoulders, and stood to leave.

"Thank you for coming. Will you tell us about the funeral arrangements? I'm sure that my mom…despite everything…I mean…we'd like to come."

My tentative self-invitation puzzled him. "Ivy, your great aunt left her entire estate in trust for you: the house, the bath boutique, everything. That's why I'm here. I'm the trustee. My office will handle the business for you until you're old enough to take over."

My mouth gaped open. Without any warning, my whole future had changed. The sketch of me planting bulbs in my Aunt Grace's garden promised that one day the relationship between my aunt and my mom would mend. I never imagined that it forecast her death. Yin Yang, I guess.

# CHAPTER 10

The utterly random nature of my drifts depressed me. Deep down, I harbored a secret hope that some unknowable purpose drove them, something I was meant to do to make my time on earth useful. But, no. One of the few people in existence who had some minor motivation to care about me exited life and the phenomenon didn't even bother to give me a heads up.

Maybe there was just nothing I could have done.

In July, my mom and I moved out of the subsidized rent apartment in the suburbs and into Aunt Grace's house in this charming, chic neighborhood in Salt Lake City. Barry set me up to manage her bath boutique *Indulgence*.

As a trustee, Barry lived up to his hard-ass lawyer reputation. My mother despised him for a tight-fisted tyrant, but I liked him. He bankrolled all my gardening, drove me up the canyon to buy my golden retriever puppy, Dany, and bought me a TRAX pass so I wouldn't have to change schools my senior year. On the outside, I looked like a regular rich girl from the city. On the inside, I knew it was all just a mask.

In April, we competed in the state theater competition at a high school several hours to the south. Spencer and I performed a scene as Hotspur and Lady Percy from *Henry IV*. Amr performed a scene from *Twelfth-Night* with Jillian. When he ripped off his shirt in the middle of the scene, the girl next to me gasped—actually gasped, a single breath in the wave that rippled through the auditorium. During the critiques, one judge leaned over on his elbows and pointed at Amr, "I have no idea how to pronounce your name, honey, but *you* are gorgeous!"

Spencer and I killed our scene—Superior all around—except for the new guy. He didn't know how the scoring worked and knocked us all out of the finals. Only Eric took home a first place. The day, suffused with anticipation and dampened by disappointment, stretched long. On the bus ride home, shoulders sagged, conversations rumbled in low, disgruntled tones.

By ten p.m., none of us had eaten for hours. Our teacher promised us a stop at the first fast food joint on the road. A string of nameless, floundering towns scrolled by. A gas station, a few forlorn homes with broken farm equipment adorning the lawn, the odd hardware store. Nothing civilized enough to merit sidewalks. And then, a back wheel of the bus rumbled and flapped. The bus driver swore and cranked the steering wheel with two fists to maneuver us off the road in the middle of nowhere. When the bus was safely on the shoulder, he asked us all to exit while he changed the flat tire.

Spencer's usual entourage, Jillian, Eric, and Matt, swept him away in their wake. It's only fair to interject that he was seriously crushing on Matt at the moment. I mean, who wasn't? But I also suspected he blamed me for our dismal standings. I opted to give him a little space.

My foot hit the pebble-strewn asphalt. My stomach grumbled, my right arm and lips buzzed, melting into empty vibrating shells of sensation. Outside in the dark, in the dry, dusty dirt at the side of the road, the faint smell of diesel dissipated on the breeze. Familiar sparkling rings flickered and then invaded my vision. "Not now." I pressed my fingers to my temples and scanned the tumbleweeds for a quiet, hidden place to perform my freak show.

A boulder blocked my path, but, in my emergency, served nicely as a rest stop. Before my hand reached the rough contours of the rock to steady my fading self, another hand intercepted it.

"Are you drifting?" The hand was dark in the fading glow of the school bus headlights. Amr wrapped his other arm around my waist. He lowered us to the ground in front of the boulder and wrapped his arms around my waist, seatbelts for the coming rollercoaster ride.

Above the buzz of teenage chatter, the bus driver swore. Metal clanked against metal.

To our right, several pockets of thespians camped under the shelter of sporadic cedar trees, the only verdure hardy enough to survive this water-forsaken land. To the left, a makeshift, crumbling wire fence pretended to protect an abandoned shack with shattered windows and no door. The dryness in the air tingled with salt on the tip of my thickening tongue.

"I apologize in advance for any awkward drooling or twitching."

"Is it outgoing or incoming?" His breath tickled my ear. "Have you already seen us here in front of this rock?"

"No, Amr. To be honest, I've never experienced your arms hugging my waist while the half-moon glares down on us. This is a first. I'll be senseless in a minute, and you'll see the side of me I hide from everyone but Spencer because no one else wants to see the…" What was the word? In my brain, words were dissolving into puzzles. The normal neuro paths of recall melted into muddy swamps, "*…abnormality*. It's unsettling."

"Don't worry, Ivy." His lips brushed my temple. "There's no side of you I don't want to see. Sometimes, I wish you would let me see more."

His sheer lack of sarcasm, his hopeless honesty, unnerved me. *Now? He's revealing raw, unguarded truths about his feelings? Seconds before I'm about to check out of my skin?* The pounding in my bloodstream challenged the pounding in my skull. "Take a good hard look because your wish is about to come true. You know, you have very bad timing, Amr."

"Actually, it's perfect. I have sides of me that no one else wants to see. It's only fair that I should be here now. You're the only one I would trust to hold me."

The words were symbols that didn't match the pictures they were supposed to convey. When I turned to see his face, the void in my vision obscured all but his left ear. "What are you saying, Amr?"

I didn't hear his answer.

*Second 1: I can't breathe! Edges of my vision fade into twilight. Something is wrong! The light! Fluorescent! Too bright. Spasmodic blinking. Light penetrates my eyelids.*

*Second 2: Urge to turn my head away from the beams. Arms and legs bound. Body sloshes listlessly to brain's commands to kick and thrash.*

*Second 3: "Oh, thank God!" Squinting. Blue-eyed boy. Ivy, you're dying!" Lips barely open. Throat gurgles.*

*Second 4: "Only the past is set. We can change this." He bends close to my chest.*

*Second 5: "Blink if you can hear me." Blinking is all I have left. "521! Say it!"*

*Second 6: Lips solid lead. Rasping. "521."*

*Second 7: "Tell me that number!" He lassos a lock of my hair. "Red. Chin length. Long b..."*

From this nightmare of my future, I woke sweating. My blood, whipped to a frenzy, stampeded to my heart. Gasping, I sucked at the air all around as if I'd just emerged from too long a stay at the bottom of the pond. My head throbbed to the beat of my pulse. "521!"

"Hey, Ivy. You all right?" Amr brushed a hand across my crown. His *Axe Fire*, tainted with a musky boy smell from too much close air in a bus, welcomed me back to our time.

I startled, running my hand across my mouth. An elegant strand of saliva smeared my clammy palm.

"521, Amr. Don't let me forget that! 521. I need my sketch pad." I tried to stand, to respond to the urgency of what I'd just seen. The sudden disequilibrium when I pushed away from Amr's chest wobbled the world on its axis, knocking me back into his lap. Inhaling, I held the air in my lungs.

The night was just as I'd left it: dark, empty, and tainted with bus exhaust. But, everything had changed. "I think I just saw myself dying, Amr." His shoulder pillowed my head as it sank back in utter exhaustion.

"Oh, my God, Ivy!" He squeezed me tighter.

# CHAPTER 11

"When? How does it happen?" Amr's lips brushed my ear.

"I don't know. Wait, yes, I do. He told me about my hair." *Red. Chin length. Long Bangs*. The clouds shrouding my recent drift parted and regathered, exposing and catching the details. "He knew how I keep track of the time." The anesthetized body I had drifted into had dulled my senses and restricted the number of details I retained. My fingertips pressing against my temples, I struggled to reconstruct the scene of my death in my memory. "Uh…thick straps around my arms and legs, a metal chair, bright florescent lights. I couldn't breathe, I couldn't struggle, I could barely speak."

Reliving the scene strangled me. The loss of agency frightened me more than the actual relinquishing of breath. I did not want to die strapped to a chair. "He promised, Amr. The blue-eyed boy promised he'd find me. Why didn't he find me in time?"

The red, chin length, long bangs year unhinged me. Hyperventilating, I allowed the scene to rewind over and over, gathering more and more details from my subconscious each time until I squeezed my eyes shut and pounded the dirt with clenched fists. A violent abduction and death, I couldn't just bow to this inevitability. What would happen to all my dreams and aspirations? Even if they meant nothing to the universe, impacted no master plan, changed no pattern in the tapestry of existence, to me, they were my meaning—to touch, to taste, to smell, to love, to know what it was to be human—this was purpose. Why be alive if not to revel in living? My eyes stung at the loss of savory moments dissolving untasted into non-existence. My hand covered my mouth, forbidding the uttering of the end. To say it might make it real. Pivoting at my waist, I threw my arms around Amr. "I need more time."

The warmth of his arms encircled the loss of the future and banished it from the wealth of the present. Now that all the gory details were imprinted in my memory, I tore my thoughts from the scene. The boy's words still rang in my ears. *Only the past is set. We can change this possibility.* The future is fluid. If I'd learned anything from Yana, it was that the secrets of the future unveiled themselves, not to be guarded like cold marble statues, but to be chiseled and molded, as best I could, into something more beautiful—or less terrifying—than I'd begun with. My breathing slowed; my muscles relaxed.

Amr's embrace conjured up memories of the moments before I drifted, and I planted my thoughts there to stop the horror from growing. He kissed the top of my head, and in that moment of human contact, the fears of the future fled before the face of the pressing present. My nose nearly touched his chin as I tilted my head back to look in his eyes. "Amr, talk to me." I needed the calming reassurance of his voice to coax me into the here and now. "What did you tell me just before I drifted?"

Our distance from the overshadowing aura of the city illuminated tiny sparks of light in the roof of the world. Always on the edge of the circles that encompassed the people we called friends, Amr and I stood apart, literally and figuratively, from the laughing theater cliques. They lived in a bubble where theater was a reality and a future. For us, it was just another role we played to fit in somewhere. "You know, my parents want me to play soccer." His gaze wandered ruefully toward the huddled silhouettes beneath the gnarled limbs of the cedars near the bus. "My mom wants to pull me out of theater. She thinks it's too feminine."

How the mind wanders along meandering paths. Taking his cheeks in my hands, I tilted his face back to mine. "Those days are over, Amr. You can do whatever you want to." The intense knowing in my eyes needed to penetrate the doubt in his. This was just post-performance depression. All the adrenaline was gone.

He snorted and nodded. "Yeah, it's all good to say that, but, what if it's all an act?"

"It IS all an act. We're theater nerds."

"Funny." His lips formed the word. His eye roll denied it.

My headache drifted toward a gentle throb. Running my fingers through my long black hair, I twisted up one of the white streaks framing my face and scooted to his side. His shoulders drooped under the weight of my arm.

"The thing is…" he glanced over at the students wandering in waves toward the bus as the driver stowed his tools, "…ah, God, it's so stupid."

"I just drooled on your arm, passed out, and saw myself dying. Nothing you say now will sound stupid."

"No," his index finger scribbled indiscriminate lines in the dirt between his knees, "no, it's really lame."

"What is it, Amr? You know, all the bullshit aside, you and I, we're—"

I looked away. The wire between the gnarly grey fence posts sagged, but the barbs on the wire, probably rusty from years of weathering, still posed a silent threat.

"We're what?" He looked up from the ground, to watch my lips finish the phrase.

What was I going to say? Tell him I'd seen us kissing? Tell him we were meant to be a couple in the year of lavender shoulder-length? I didn't even know if that was true. A kiss, in 7 seconds, could mean anything, especially to a twelve-year-old with virgin lips. God! I wanted to tell him! But, as far as I knew, we were only practicing for some romance scene in a play when my younger self popped in for an unannounced visit.

Maybe I should just tell him about the other one. The one that compelled me to keep him close. The one where we're running side by side before— "Whatever. The name we give it doesn't change the connection." And yet, it was a legit question. One I didn't have an answer for. Maybe Amr and I, we were just pin cushions to absorb the sharp points that life stuck in us and not pop. "Tell me."

Silence sat between us, a cat on the fence.

"Hey, AJ! Ivy! We're leaving! Get your butts on the bus. I'm starving." Spencer. Best not to annoy him when he was hangry. I stood up, leaning heavily on Amr's shoulder for balance.

"It's totally shallow. You won't understand." He banged the back of his head against the boulder.

"You're talking to me, right? The girl who randomly blacks out for 7 seconds."

He nodded. His lips begrudged every word that slipped through their grasp. "You heard that judge. He didn't say 'you're a brilliant actor' he said 'YOU are gorgeous.' That's what I am, Ivy. That's how I hang on the fringe of this society where I don't fit in the holes. My name doesn't have enough vowels. I'm a Muslim in Salt Lake City, for God's sake, and I'm hardly that."

"Hey! You are so much more than a name, or a look, or a religion for that matter. You are a unique being, with distinctive thoughts and feelings and rare intelligence. Look at that line." My finger drew his attention to the theater herd. It was dwindling to nothing as they took their seats on the bus. "There's no one like you there. Spencer and Jillian, maybe they're really going to be actors. But, look through the fishbowl to what's on the other side. For you and me, this drama world we orbit liberates us so we can be someone else and escape the stereotypes that brand us. It doesn't define us. It's not who we are. You're going to be a neurosurgeon, Amr, and I'm going to study Bio-Chem and Biology so I can unlock the healing properties of plants and figure out what the hell is wrong with me. That's our contribution. Don't park yourself at a rest area on the highway and think you've reached your destination."

"Nice monologue!" He clapped slowly, staring up at the myriad stars twinkling obliviously down upon our pain, mocking our drama. The chill of the spring evening prickled his arms with goosebumps. Hugging himself, he rubbed them away, and then reached over and entwined his fingers in mine, covering the bond with his other palm and contemplating the sculpture of our mingled hands. "But don't you feel like a pretender? I get the grades, I go through the motions, but in the end, I feel like I'm just playing a role, being what everyone expects me to be."

"We're all just playing a role. Nobody knows what they're doing. We act our part until one day, we are what we're pretending to be."

The massive headache receded like a storm cloud drifting sluggishly past the eastern mountains. I hauled Amr to his feet.

The side of his face reflected the half-moon. My tug on his hand pulled us toward the bus. Our streams of thought flowed into each other as we walked, a couple of fingers loosely linking us.

The narrow entrance into the bus only supported one lane of traffic. The quiet night air gave way to unsettled and disgruntled murmurings—humanity in search of food. I reclaimed my hand from his and walked the narrow stairs.

# CHAPTER 12

Yes, there was marijuana in the back corner of my garden near the garage. No, I did not plant it, and I never smoked it—well, not much, just enough to get a scientific idea of how it worked. Did I let it grow because I'd seen it in my future, or would I have done it anyway? Hard to say. Technically, a stray marijuana plant would succumb to Utah's arid, desert conditions without some serious caretaking. Just the improbability of its survival was worth letting it grow.

"You're an idiot to be growing it in your garden in the first place." Spencer cocked a disapproving eyebrow my direction as he sank his teeth into a monster burger. Spencer, Amr, and I haunted this burger joint even though the menu offered literally nothing for a vegetarian. Spence's idea of compromising was tossing me his tomato slices. "For someone who sees the future, you have very poor foresight. You're going to jail. Why don't you take 7 seconds and think about that future?"

"Give a bitch a break. I'm not going to jail. Barry is the best lawyer in the city. Besides, marijuana has medicinal applications."

"The drugs my mother OD'ed on last month had medicinal applications."

"Chill, Spence. I'm conducting an experiment. Did you know studies show that cannabis can actually inhibit epileptic seizures? I just want to try it out."

Amr pointed his fork at me. "You don't have epileptic seizures. You drift into the future." Future neurologist speaking.

"Most doctors diagnose my drifts as seizures. They must be related. Besides, the violence I've seen in the future since I saved Yana makes me want more control."

"So, experiment in the privacy of your own home where the vice principal won't turn you over to the school cop." Spencer started stacking everything on the tray. Amr tossed his plate on top.

The clock on the wall glowered down at us: 12:57. The open campus policy only provided half an hour for lunch. We were going to be tardy—again. Who cared? We were seniors, already accepted to the university, finished with our AP exams, awarded scholarships. Of course, I was going to study Bio-Chem. I needed to know what the hell was happening in my head and how, if at all, I could control it. These last couple of weeks of high school were only token seat time.

"I can't. I'm experimenting with its effects on my drifts and the only one I can pinpoint at school this year is the marijuana one. Today is a green shirt day." I exhibited ostentatiously the color of my shirt. "The marijuana drift only has today and next Thursday to play itself out this year. Spencer and I exchanged furtive looks. He'd dubbed this year black with white streaks around my face. Inadvertently appropriate for the nasty break-up with Amr I was now expecting in late fall during my freshman year at the university—based on the length of my natural honey-blonde roots.

Spencer's ten-year-old, white Chevy Impala waited for us in the parking lot. The hubcaps were gone, it spewed exhaust fumes, and lurched with a sickening clunk when the engine shifted gears—but it got us to lunch.

Amr's hand bumped mine, intentionally. My cast iron armor against his charms had been slowly melting. Originally, I didn't want to do anything stupid that would mess with the natural timeline leading up to the drift of the kiss during the lavender shoulder-length year. Dating Amr in high school fell into the "something stupid" category. He was a psychopathic heart slasher. And yet, my fingers brushed his noncommittally. I was a fool.

"Okay." Spencer stopped short. "You two are killing me. Ivy and I are now officially NO LONGER an item…but we're still best friends." The whole school assumed that since Spencer and I were inseparable, we were a couple. Suited both of us just fine.

"What?" Amr played dumb as if he had no idea why Spencer and I would be *breaking up*.

"I'm gay not blind." Spencer unlocked the car door and motioned me into the back with Amr, who looked like he'd just stolen the crown jewels with the approval of the queen. "Tough love, girl. If you insist on engaging in epic stupidity," his sideways glance at Amr confirmed that he meant more than just my weed experiments, "despite all my perfectly legit nagging, you're on your own."

"C'mon, Spencer! It'll be fun—and scientific."

Amr squeezed my hand and clapped Spencer's shoulder over the seat. "Dude, have a brownie!"

Pursing his lips and shaking his head, Spencer glared at us in the rearview mirror, turned the key, and pumped the gas. The car rumbled pathetically and finally choked out an ignition.

"If I never try it out, how will I know if marijuana has an effect on my drifts? What if it turns out to be the magic potion that helps me control them?"

"I'm totally supportive, girlfriend. I'll visit you in Juvie." Spencer would not bend. Too many opioid-mom issues?

"Seriously, I'm not stupid. I know what's going to happen. I'm prepared." *Was I? Was that even possible?* Less confidently than I looked, I dug in my purse and handed Amr a brownie. I hadn't really eaten anything but a pale, hardly ripe excuse for a tomato slice since breakfast. I was starving and devoured mine.

Only one class followed late lunch. The bell had already rung and the teacher's lounge was deserted. I slipped in and stowed the box of marijuana-laced brownies in the fridge. Bold? Not really. Just smart. Who would ever, in a million years, think to look in there? The door to the faculty room was always closed but unlocked. Slipping in unnoticed was actually pretty simple.

Eighty minutes later, Amr was waiting outside my AP Gov class. When I walked out, he grabbed my hand like it was a new toy. I sort of wondered when he'd tire of playing with me.

Obviously, whatever was going on between us couldn't last. Amr couldn't help himself—he didn't have any staying power. One day, he would, most certainly, go silent and then move on, as if there'd never been anything more than friends between us. His MO was well-documented. Maybe it was the brownies talking, but all I could think was *Carpe Diem, baby! Let the heartbreak begin!*

"Oh, my Goddess! Mr. Thornton was a hoot today." Overcome with giggling, I stumbled a little over the metal border between the carpet and the tile hallway but caught myself on Amr's shirt. He steadied me in a lusty bear hug. His eyes, slightly bloodshot, grinned. The two of us chuckled out into the main hallway, past the drinking fountains and the library.

"You know, you ARE gorgeous, Amr."

"Why haven't we ever dated?" he wondered aloud.

I knew the answer but didn't care. A vacated tributary hallway presented itself to our left. I dragged him in, dove for his lips, missed, and planted a warm, sloppy kiss on his ear instead. We laughed until our sides split.

"I've been wanting to do that…well, not kiss your ear, I mean, you know… for three years now."

Finding my response supremely comical, Amr could barely speak until, without any warning, his face stiffened into utter seriousness. "Are you starving? I'm starving."

"I'm ALWAYS starving!"

We both found that hilarious.

Fortunately, there were no stairs between history and the rape hall. We would have tumbled down them, laughing all the way.

My fingers stumbled through the combination to my locker, and the door popped open. "We should go outside and enjoy the sunshine. It's so dark in here." I turned to find Amr less than six inches from my chest, his signature, musky *Dior* scent embracing me.

"It's not dark; you're here." Amr looped his arms beneath mine and clasped his hands behind me. A gentle nudge and my back was up against the lockers. His eyes savored in advance the forbidden fruit in my lips. All of its own accord, my head tilted back, offering.

Pressed to mine, the rose-petal velvet of his lips zinged across the neurons of my brain. Memories of another kiss sizzled to the surface. 7th grade. I face-planted into my Tater Tots at lunch and drifted into what I always assumed would be my first kiss with Amr in the year of the lavender shoulder-length hair. But that year hadn't caught up with reality yet—and here we were. Our lips answered questions with more questions. I stopped to catch my breath and we stood, a little embarrassed, the THC in our blood mingling with oxytocin. My forehead lounged against his.

At 2:45, locked in Amr's arms, in front of my locker, the odds of the marijuana drift happening that Thursday slipped quietly away.

"I don't feel any symptoms. I think the drift isn't going to happen. Do you think the marijuana worked—stopped it?"

"I think it was the kiss."

"You're so full of yourself."

He stifled my giggles with his mouth. Technically, he might have been right. The oxytocin swimming in my blood may have been the crucial agent inhibiting the phenomenon. My experiment results were now tainted.

"Ivy!"

We both started, swiveled, and unchained our arms. Ms. Miller, my vice principal, growing larger with each of my heartbeats, cast a shadow in the light at the entrance to the dark hallway.

# CHAPTER 13

"Hey, Ms. Miller." Amr and I greeted her in unison and then exchanged looks. Did this mean the drift was going to happen after all? I had no symptoms. What if the cannabinoids only blocked the symptoms? That would be disastrous. I'd have no advanced notice to brace myself.

"AJ, how are you? Congrats on the scholarships, you two. I saw the lists." Of all the vice principals, Ms. Miller was the one to draw. It wasn't her idea to sidestep his name, he told her he preferred AJ—part of the act. Ms. Miller's professional philosophy was that she worked in a school where children learned from their mistakes, not hell where they suffered for them. Ms. Miller was pretty young for a VP, never looked tired, always smiled, and often called students down to her office just to tell them what a great job they were doing and reward them with a candy bar.

"Thanks!" We both nodded and Amr slipped his hand into mine, squeezing.

"Ivy, you don't by chance have a box of brownies in your locker, do you? Mind if I take a look?" Stepping toward us, she leaned sideways to see past the door.

At least I was prepared. Not knowing how the hell Ms. Miller knew I'd brought marijuana-laced brownies to school, I'd baked a second box of perfectly yummy, untainted brownies and stowed them in my locker. What I hadn't planned on was Amr holding my hand. During the 7-second vision, when I drifted out and my elementary school self drifted in, the VP asked me to hand over the brownies in my locker, which, for some unknown reason, I had voluntarily confessed were laced with marijuana. Yielding to the temptation to kiss him before the timeline of that first kiss in the lavender-hair year might have irrevocably changed the future. I was supposed to black out while my elementary consciousness took control, but my present drifted to the future while my past drifted to my present! That had never happened before.

*Second 1: Beach. Sunshine. Azure blue everywhere. Breeze sifts through my hair. Toes immersed in smooth pebbles and shallow water. Child splashes toward me.*

*Second 2: Blue-eyed boy peers into my eyes. He's holding my hand. "Ivy? Are you okay?"*

*Second 3: I pull strands of my damp matted hair forward to see it. Shoulder-length lavender.*

*The dark, curly-haired toddler trips over the boy's feet.*

*Second 4: The boy helps the toddler scramble away. I glance down at my bathing suit. It's green. Thursday.*

*Second 5: "521, Ivy? What does that mean?"*

*Second 6: "Is that the Mediterranean? Where did we meet?"*

*Second 7: He nods, pointing up the beach toward the restaurants dotting the port.*

And then the drift was over.

And then I drifted again.

*Second 1: "Forget him, Ivy." The television blares.*

*Second 2: Spencer squished up next to me. Grey couch in my basement. "You knew this would happen, you told me you could deal with it."*

*Second 3: "What color is my hair?" Purple shirt. I dig a paper with the week's Powerball numbers from my sweats.*

*Second 4: "Black shoulder-length layers. January."*

*Second 5: I read aloud to improve my chances of remembering: "4, 16, 17, 38, 63 and 25.*

*Second 6: ...4 squared is 16, 17, 38 is 17 doubled plus the 4...*

*Second 7: ...63 was the age of my Aunt Grace when she died, 25 is..."*

And then the drift was over.
And another began…

*Second 1: Jet engines hum just outside my round window. General darkness. Morning light pierces an open portal. Screen in front of my seat depicts the arc of a flight path to France.*

*Second 2: White shirt. Lavender shoulder-length hair. Balding man with a large beer belly blocks my view of the aisle...*

*Second 3: Boy with blue eye leans across the woman in the aisle seat. "6:30, June 17th…*

*Second 4: ...hotel La Fiancée du Pirate, Villefranche-sur-Mer..."*

*Second 5: "... a boy drowns in the pool."*

*Second 6: The bald man walks right through the boy. Astonishment. "Save him. You sent me because…"*

*Second 7: I reach to touch his hand and mine passes right through. "...they're coming for you, Ivy."*

# CHAPTER 14

Somehow the ceiling above glided past my blurred vision. Amr's arms cradled me as we rushed through the hallway. I blinked and then focused on Ms. Miller's face peering into mine. "Oh, thank God, Ivy. You really gave us a scare. What can I get for you? Let's go to my office. I'll call your mom."

"No!" Swinging my arm around his neck and straining my toes toward the ground, I commanded Amr to set me down. "I'm totally fine."

Ms. Miller laughed skeptically. "I don't think so. You just experienced acute disorientation and then blacked out for at least a minute."

"Fourteen seconds," I mumbled. My mother thought I'd outgrown this. Nothing but tears and accusations could come from her finding out she thought wrong. And things had been going so well.

"Besides," she held up the box of brownies, "you and AJ informed me that the ingredients in these brownies aren't exactly kosher." AJ's eyes grew wide with guilt and surprise. "Yes, AJ, I heard you whisper."

Ms. Miller responded to the indistinct static issuing from her walkie-talkie as I shot Amr a look of daggers and hissed, "You told her about the marijuana? What the hell?"

"It's not my fault. It's yours. I was just protecting our interests. Your junior high self looked like she was going to hand them over. All I did was whisper quietly in her ear that the brownies contained a little marijuana. She practically yelled the info back at Ms. Miller. And what the hell, yourself? That seizure dragged on way longer than 7 seconds. You were gone for at least…"

"…twenty-one seconds. 7 while my junior high self drifted in and 14 while I drifted to the future."

Ms. Miller stopped and pointed to the main office door. "I'm going to ask your mom to come down here, Ivy. AJ, would you make sure she gets into my office safely? I'll be there in two minutes. I have to handle some things."

Amr's head lolled back and he sighed in agony as I opened the door. My mind churned. I was pretty expert by now at processing my drifts. My consciousness only sipped up essential info in the 7 seconds, but my subconscious drank in gallons. I just had to regurgitate it all in a drawing. The neural input from three consecutive drifts was crashing my brain's hard drive.

"It wasn't *a* drift." I shoved him through into the attendance office. "I bounced. There were three in a row. That's never happened before. I think it was the marijuana."

"I think it was the kiss."

"Goddess! Are you seriously so…" Was I seriously asking? "Nevermind."

The other startling development was that I had actually drifted into my future while my past was drifting into my present. That had never happened before either. And, for the first time, Spencer played a part in one of my drifts. It was one of those awkward moments where I dutifully suppress the urge that wills me to cuddle up under his arm. Although Spencer is gay. It isn't like my female hormones make any sexual preference distinctions.

Suddenly, the marijuana drama exited stage left while the Powerball scene took center stage. "Oh, my God! I need paper and a pencil. I have to write down some numbers."

To reach Ms. Miller's office, we paraded past the hallway leading to the teacher's faculty room, where Mr. Benson, the aging, but extremely gifted, calculus teacher sat at the lunch table enjoying a brownie as he read the paper. My mouth dropped open.

"Are you insane? Paper and pencil ? We're in deep shit, Ivy. My parents are going to bust my balls for this. Spencer was right. We're going to jail." He wiped his hands across his face and through his hair.

"Relax, stress boy. I've got this covered. There's nothing in those brownies. I knew this was going to happen. I made two boxes. The brownies in my locker were clean. I put the box from my bag in the faculty refrigerator."

"You what?"

"It's fine." Leaning back, I peeked into the faculty room to check on Mr. Benson. He was no longer reading the newspaper. He was now swaying and humming to a beat only he could hear. Hopefully, he was so old that anyone who saw him would conclude senility was setting in. "Just let me do the talking. What really worries me…"

"You mean more than going to jail?" Amr crossed his arms and watched my face twist.

Piles of paper, a computer monitor, and folders littered Ms. Miller's desk. Retrieving a writing instrument and sticky note required shuffling. "4 squared is 16, 17, doubled plus the four is 38, 63 was the age of my Aunt Grace, 25 is easy."

"What's that? Are you delirious?"

"No…no…um, it's nothing. It's a Spencer thing." Success! Having dug up a Sharpie and scratch paper, I jotted down the numbers to the Powerball in the year of the black layered hair. Spencer would be ecstatic. The years he'd invested in befriending a freak were about to pay off.

"Okay, Ivy…" Ms. Miller swept back into her office and shut the door.

"Look, Ms. Miller. You don't have to call my mom. I can explain about the brownies. They're completely fine. You just happened to catch Amr and me in the middle of a conversation. We were talking about the beneficial effects of…"

"…of marijuana on epilepsy." There was a reason Amr hung with the theater crowd. He was a natural. And his puppy dog eyes were irresistible—at least I thought so. Ms. Miller was still on the fence.

"Yeah! Did you know that research shows that marijuana can reduce the frequency and duration of seizures? Do you know what that could mean for me?"

The blue flag beside my name was working its magic. Ms. Miller mulled over our story. Her eyes scrunched up, she scrutinized the situation. The toe of her comfortable, but professional, pumps tapped beneath her desk. She flipped open the lid to the suspicious box, sniffed, and sniffed again.

"Really, Ms. Miller. There's nothing wrong with those brownies. They're just brownies. You can take them home, feed them to your kids, or give them to the police—they're just the mix kind. If I'd eaten them sooner, I probably would have been fine. Low blood sugar. It triggers the seizures."

Taking a deep breath, she glanced at the clock. The vague sound of far off singing seeped beneath the door—Mr. Benson's baritone had added words to the beat he was grooving. The telephones rang at the attendance secretary's desk.

Ms. Miller exhaled. Nodding her head, she slapped her hand on her desk. "Okay. This is what we're going to do. I'm going to ignore the marijuana thing. I can't smell anything in there but brownie." Her open palms brushed the air, erasing the whole scene. She dumped the plastic container in the trash. "The phone tip was obviously some senior prank. I'm assuming that two intelligent, motivated, over-achievers like yourselves are not stupid enough to ruin your bright futures with an idiot move like bringing drugs to school. Despite the research—and I am aware of it—marijuana is still a controlled substance and we have zero tolerance here—even in the last week of school."

Amr exhaled noisily.

"That said, what really concerns me, Ivy, is the seizure. I want to make sure you get professional care. This is a serious medical condition. I'd like to have a conversation with your mother."

"That's not really a good idea, Ms. Miller. It'll just upset her. Can we please not say anything? I haven't had one of these for years." At least not one that I'd told my mother about.

"I'm sorry, Ivy." She leaned across the desk. "You blacked out. If AJ hadn't been there to catch you, you could have seriously injured yourself. You really need to monitor this. You two can go ahead and go, but I *will* contact your mom and make sure you have some medical resources before I go home today."

I nodded, resigned. This would mean another round of doctors who would diagnose me and prescribe pills that the government would pay for and I wouldn't take.

"You don't drive, do you?" She put her arm around me and chauffeured me out the door.

"No. I have a TRAX pass."

"Great. AJ, would you make sure she gets home safely?"

"Yes, ma'am."

We held sober faces until we reached the hallway that led into the faculty room. I ushered AJ after me. The coast was clear. Hopefully, Mr. Benson was not driving. The box of loaded brownies in the fridge slid nicely into my backpack. Waste not; want not.

# CHAPTER 15

Ms. Miller had her nice conversation with my mom. I couldn't get an appointment to see the neurologist until a few days after graduation. I recognized the waiting room when we walked in. I'd finally caught up to the future I glimpsed the day I fell from the counter while making my mother coffee. The fluorescent light in the waiting room flickered. My stomach growled—it was summer, so I'd slept in and missed breakfast. My fingers tingled.

My mother sipped a cup of coffee in the seat next to mine.

The sense of déjà-vu overwhelmed me. I knew what was about to happen. Nausea set in, churning the acids in my empty stomach. The flashing prisms invaded my vision and the tingling traveled up my arm. My five-year-old self was about to hijack my life as I waited, silently crumpled, in the wings of my subconscious. Just about now she was stepping off the stool, a mug of coffee cupped in her hands.

And then I was gone—for 7 seconds.

The room refocused sluggishly. My mother's annoyed, embarrassed face peered over mine and the view of the fish tattoo on the nurse's neck blocked my vision as she supported my weight. The boy had just warned me not to take the medication. He'd also told me the Guild had me now. I remembered this drift vividly.

My head pounded. The nausea receded. Deliriously, I groped for the empty chair beside me. "Where is he? Where'd the boy go? He was sitting right here."

"Ivy, I don't know what you're talking about. That seat has been empty the whole time we've been here." My mother looked crushed. Now, I wasn't just having seizures, I was seeing things that weren't there.

For the first time, it occurred to me that I was the only one who could see this boy who appeared in my drifts. And yet, when I saw him in the marijuana drift to the beach in Villefranche, I was almost certain he was there physically. He had to be because the little girl tripped over him…or would when that actually happened. Maybe that meant that I would first meet the blue-eyed boy in the flesh in France in the year of the lavender, shoulder-length hair—the year he would beg me to show up and rescue a drowning boy.

# CHAPTER 16

"Is it time, yet?" It took a few months for my present to catch up with the lottery drift in the year of black layers. The rumble of battle and gore from episodes of GoT rocked the basement while we waited for the Wednesday evening Powerball numbers. Dany dozed on the floor, completely oblivious to the tension of the moment.

Since the home I inherited from my Aunt Grace was only blocks away from the University of Utah, Spence practically lived on the grey couch in the basement. In his wallet, lay what could be the winning lottery ticket. It was a purple shirt day, a Friday in January, when I memorized the two-day-old numbers in my pocket during the marijuana drift. But since they draw the numbers on Wednesday, we were actually watching for the winners two days before I was set to discover them in my drift. Weird! In the first two weeks of January, Spencer had made the trek up to Idaho to buy tickets with the numbers I'd memorized, along with the multiplier, but neither of those had won.

The remnants of my junk food dinner littered the coffee table. "Do you think I ruined the future, you know, by going out with Amr in high school instead of waiting for college?"

"I told you that was a bad idea—not just for high school, for any time." He licked his fingers, grabbed the last hot wing, and ripped into it. A tiny trail of fluid trickled down his chin.

"Yuck! Animal blood!" I swiped it away with his greasy napkin. "This is exactly why I'm vegetarian."

"What? This?" He waved the bone in front of my nose. "This isn't meat. It's chicken!"

"Goddess!"

Blank stare.

Can't tell if he's acting or not. "Seriously? Never mind."

My black fleecy sweats marked the day a Wednesday and also fit nicely the pre-mourning phase of my yet-to-happen second breakup with Amr, the serial heart slasher. Along with the lottery numbers, I'd seen myself crying on Spencer's shoulder next Friday.

"I never should have kissed Amr in the hallway. Damn brownies!"

"Won't argue with that."

"That first kiss I saw in 7th grade—I know it was a first kiss, I could feel it in my gut. Kissing him in high school changed the future."

"Hey, Ivy," he pulled me across the couch and tucked me up under his arm. "Relax! You're going to fry your brain if you keep thinking like that."

My index finger twisted in the black strand that leaked from my messy bun as I contemplated the implications of sabotaging my own timeline. "Don't you get it, Spence? I ruined everything!"

"Okay, you have to chill, girlfriend."

"How can I chill? If I screwed up the years, then maybe we're not even going to win the lottery this month. Maybe…"

Squeezing my shoulders, he put the straw from his shake up to my mouth. Spence didn't share his food with just anyone. It was a gesture of ultimate love and concern. I took a sip. "This is my take on it. Your actions can change some outcomes, but they can't possibly affect which numbers come out of the machine. So, even if you did screw up your personal life, the patterns in the big scheme of things keep going. And if they don't, you just keep stuffing those numbers in your pocket until we get it right. It happened once, it's bound to happen again."

"But what if…?"

"What if what? That's the problem. You can't live like that. No one else glimpses the future. None of the rest of us know what would have happened 'if.' Embrace normalcy, girl. Live like the fish—never knowing, always up for a surprise…"

"…or disappointment."

"Geez!"

"Yin yang." I stole another slurp and handed back his cup.

He sucked up the rest and tossed the empty cup on the table. "Look. I have this vision of myself as an actor, so I do what I have to in order to get there. I don't just sit back and hope it happens. It's no different for you. This could just be one of the setbacks that inevitably leads up to the moment in your vision." Spencer could afford to be optimistic. He'd just landed a role in a university production of *The Crucible*. His future was right on track, while I was pretty sure marijuana had derailed mine. "Forget about Amr. He was high school. Move on, girl. The guy from your drifts with the dark hair and the blue eyes sounds much more interesting."

The clock chimed.

"Oh, my God! Check the numbers, check the numbers!"

Dany glanced up at me, vaguely interested in my enthusiasm.

Spencer refreshed the page on the Powerball website. His scholarship had included some perks like a free laptop for students in need. He read the numbers aloud. "4…" My heart skipped; the first number was correct. My breath caught in my lungs.

"16, 17, 38…"

"Oh, my Goddess!" I jumped up and crammed my thumbnail between my teeth, bouncing on my toes. The first four numbers matched. Dany nudged my leg and I bent to scratch her ears absent-mindedly.

Spencer stopped and shut the laptop, not disappointed, but not exactly ecstatic. "Four out of five isn't bad. I think there's a pretty good prize for that."

"What? Is the last one wrong? Oh, shit. I knew it! I changed the future. We could have been set for life, Spence!" I clasped my palms to my head, lamenting. "We're never gonna catch a break. Oh, well," I tried and failed to mimic his lack of disappointment, "I carry the numbers with me all the time now. I jumped into a future once where I had them, I'm bound to do it again. We can wait."

Spence just stared at me.

"What? What were the other numbers? How far off was I?" I grabbed for the computer.

He swiped it out of my reach and lifted the lid. It took a while to reload the page.

"You're killing me, Spence."

"The Powerball is worth $588,000,000.00, Ivy. We can't even IMAGINE how much money that is. Do you have any idea what that would mean? What that kind of money can do to people? Maybe it's better if we never win."

"No! We just won't be stupid. When we win, we'll get Barry to handle the cash for us until we know what the hell we're doing. Now read the damn numbers!"

"588 million, Ivy!"

"Spencer, I'm going to kill you. Just read the last number!" I crowded the screen. Spencer scooted away, tipping it out of sight.

His eyes fell, then rose to meet mine. His lips pursed and he sighed, shaking his head.

"Dammit! No! No! No!" I pounded the grey couch. "It must have been that stupid-ass kiss. It ruined everything."

"63!" he shouts.

First my mouth dropped open. Then I shouted, "Yes!" and vaulted to my feet, dancing, waving my arms. "We did it! We did it, Spencer! Oh, my Goddess! OH-MY-GODDESS!" The couch exhaled as I collapsed into the cushions, my feet still kicking in excitement. "What was the Power Ball?" Dany danced around celebrating with us.

Spencer closed the laptop and shoved it under the couch, shaking his head in disgust.

"What? There's no way I missed the Powerball, Spence. That was the easy one. 25."

He only raised his eyebrow and scrunched half his face, apologizing for disappointing me.

"So…what? That kiss changed the future? No big deal. We got FIVE of them, Spencer! That's more money than either of us could ever spend."

And then, he screamed, jumping onto the coffee table. "588 million dollars, Ivy!"

Hopping up with him, I fell into his chest. The snack trash toppled onto the floor when Dany joined us on the table. We jumped down and danced in it, hands clasped until we both fell over laughing onto the cushions.

He couldn't help himself. Spencer threw his arm around my shoulder, pulled me tight against his chest, and kissed my lips soundly like he was sealing a deal. "Don't take this the wrong way, Ivy, but I gotta tell you. At this point, you are the only flower in the field of weeds that is my life. I love you, girl."

We hugged a little longer, euphoria swirling all about our fortune-struck limbs. It wasn't just the buzz of winning. It was bigger than that. We teetered drunk on the power of beating the system. This gift I had…it could be harnessed. "You know what this means, Spencer?"

"That you're a goddess?"

"No…a seer, maybe…but, seriously! It means I can control it…I can engineer seeing stuff and do something about it. Do you realize how much good we can do with this gift? Oh, my Goddess! We're going to need Barry. He'll tell us what to do and who to help. He knows everything."

"Okay, but first, I'm getting a new car…and a better apartment…and I'm going to pay off my school loans." Even after the scholarships, Spencer still had loans. He had to live. My aunt's estate paid my tuition. I bought Spence food whenever I could. He wouldn't let me pay his way, though.

"Slow down, dude! We have to be careful. Our mothers can NEVER know about this money."

The vision of the damage our addict moms could do to themselves with unlimited funds sobered us up for a moment. Spence nodded his agreement. "Talk to Barry before you do anything." I paced around chewing my fingernails. The power and possibilities of being able to feed myself information from the future swirled in my head until it bloated. "Oh, my Goddess!" Dany leaned on my shoulder. "You want a steak, puppy? You're definitely getting a steak!"

The euphoria dulled quickly. Two days later, I hadn't heard an electronic peep from Amr for nearly twenty-four hours, and Friday afternoon, just outside the Pie Pizzeria, I watched him suck face with a skinny blond before sliding into the passenger seat of her navy-blue Toyota.

I'd love to say that knowing it would happen in advance cushioned the blow, that I was expecting it, so it really didn't punch me in the gut or wreak havoc on my neurons and hormones. But that would be a lie. To be more precise, my chest cavity turned to stone while my throat trapped the air for a matter of seconds. A surge of proprietary adrenaline urged me to stalk over and slap Amr's face. My grip tightened on the door of the coffee shop I was exiting. My heart melted into a swamp of memories of kissing on the trails overlooking the city tinted in shades of sunrise sherbet. My fingers trenched through my hair. I bit my lip and brushed the tears from my cheeks as a massive headache began forming behind my right eye. I'd learned to change events, but it wasn't possible to change people and the way they felt. Even if it was, maybe it wasn't ethical.

That's why Friday night, even though the two of us had just recently become multimillionaires, I sat huddled up and miserable with Spencer. I wore a purple sweatshirt, my black layered hair tied up in a messy knot, last Wednesday's lottery numbers folded in a square in my pocket. Hazelnut Lindt ball wrappers, Ben and Jerry's cartons, Oreo crumbs—all the essentials for wiping out the pain of a still tender to the touch loveburn—cluttered the table in front of us. Spencer slurped his chocolate shake and my consciousness slipped away for 7 seconds while my past glimpsed my unhappy present.

# CHAPTER 17

The side pocket of my baggy black pants bulged around a stun gun. I'd stuffed it in there along with my usual pepper spray—just in case the knife drift crashed into reality.

Dread, or low blood sugar, or both trembled my hands. My keys jangled in the lock, and the iron gate rattled open, just wide enough for me to fit through. Only three keys dangled from my chain: one to my house, one to my shop, and one to the cash register. I assumed that if the drift caught up with me at work today, the woman in the scarf would be after the money.

*"What's wrong with you? Didn't you hear me? Just tell me where it is..."* Those words she'd uttered had been mulling around in my head for over a decade.

The woman in the drift, the one wielding the sharp, antique dagger, was talking about the key to the cash register. I was sure of it—as sure as a 7 second drift allowed. Losing the money didn't worry me—Spencer and I didn't worry about money anymore. But the knife—

Sighing, I shoved the gate all the way back behind the display window and secured the chain. Inches of honey-blond roots at the tops of my lavender shoulder-length peeked out at me from my shadowy reflection in the glass. If the knife drift happened today, it would be the first in a long series of ominous events scheduled for this year. Spencer had decreed this the year of lavender shoulder length in honor my graduation and Barry signing complete ownership of my Aunt Grace's bath boutique over to me. He had no idea what kind of mayhem he was triggering—well, it doesn't really work like that.

The stick figure pictures from my elementary days were harder to decipher than my more recent depictions of drifts and

I'm not sure I even understood my hairstyle dating system back then. But the picture definitely showed roots. Sometime during the knife drift, I would turn and glance in the mirror on the shop wall. That much I knew for certain. I recognized the mirror the day I first walked into *Indulgence* and fell in love with my Aunt Grace's profession. What I didn't know was how meticulous my second-grade self was about the length of the roots…*Oh, Goddess! It could happen today—Wednesday, a black shirt day.*

Cinnamon bun bliss wafted along the worn cobblestone walkway of the shopping mall that had once been a bustling trolley station. My empty stomach gurgled. A riot of butter and brown sugar rushed in the open door and mingled with the bouquet of perfumes from my shop.

Flickering fluorescent light assaulted my retina. The center display, stacked with pyramids of garden-colored balls appeared two-dimensional, as if some neurons were failing to fire and only certain senses were getting enough blood flow to come online. My fingertips tingled and my tongue felt swollen.

After logging into the register, I shoved the gate fully open and anchored the glass doors. Mmmm. Baking bread. My stomach rumbled again as I slipped into the back room to gather the supplies for today's creations. Spencer would be here shortly to cover the store front while I whipped up Eve's Apple bath bombs. Our inventory was getting low. People were gearing up for summer and hitting the park running. The Apple Cider Vinegar in Eve's Apple bombs was a great detoxifier; it also helped with muscle ache brought on by physical exertion. As a bonus, it controlled excessive body odor. I didn't usually mention that benefit to the customers, unless they brought it up first.

The huge bags of sodium bicarbonate and sodium chloride thudded onto the wooden counter in the back room. Since we lived in Salt Lake City, to add local flare, I only purchased salts from the lake. Citric acid, apple cider vinegar powder, juniper oil, sage oil, and honey provided some of the therapeutic ingredients that would return the skin to a slightly acidic pH, making it difficult for candida to thrive.

In the hallway, the early birds wandered into *Pottery Barn* and *Whole Foods*, the big brand outfits that drew enough sporadic traffic to sustain the small locals.

A flickering, metallic rainbow emerged into the center of my vision as I peered into the darkness of the shelves beneath the cash register checking our supply of cellophane bags and ribbon. The glimmering circle grew, leaving a void in my vision at its center. A drift was imminent. Whether it was the drift from my past, that I was dreading, or a new one to my future, I had no way of knowing. At least, Spencer would arrive for his shift in time to peel me off the floor.

When I stood up, a petit woman walked through the door. An acute sense of déjà-vu rippled up from my memory. I'd sketched this woman over a decade ago—tousled, black hair tied up in a scarf and a very pointy nose.

A surge of adrenaline made me gasp. Grabbing the edge of the counter, I squinted and adjusted my focus to the left of the pulsing void in the center of my vision.

"Excuse me. I didn't mean to frighten you." She held her purse in front of her like a shield. Timid? Maybe I was wrong. Maybe she was looking for the shop down the hall where they sharpened knives. I'd gotten things all wrong before.

"Oh, no, I'm fine. I'm getting a migraine." My left hand cradled my temples while my right wandered toward the stun gun—just in case. *Where the hell is Spencer?* "How can I help you?"

"I'm looking for Ivy…Ivy Leif." Her accent was strong French. I recognized it from five years with Mme. Gregoire. The woman's hawkish eyes glanced back at the door and took in the scant traffic.

"I'm Ivy. What can I do for you?" Walking into a store where the language was foreign would put anyone on edge. I dusted off a little rusty AP French for her. "*Vous désirez, Madame*?"

Declining my offer to switch languages, she stepped closer. I stepped back. "I'm not sleeping well. My friend told me you had a product called…"

Oh, *Pasithea's Balm.* She's after a relaxation, sleep bomb. The citrus reticulata and origanum majorana combine with lavender to help relax the muscles and calm the mind.

She reached into her purse. Gulping and dropping my hand to my pocket, I hesitated to pull a weapon on an unsuspecting, innocent customer, just in case I had misconstrued the whole thing and she was just rummaging through her purse for the name of a bath bomb she'd written down and happened to pull out a knife she had in there so she could see better. *Doubtful.*

Her fist slipped out of the purse clutching a small dagger. "Where's the amulet?"

"What? Are you looking for the jewelry store?"

The purse, only a prop anyway, plopped to the floor as she grabbed my shirt and pressed the point of her dagger against my skin. "The amulet or blood. Which would you prefer?"

"I don't know what you're talking about. I don't have an amulet." My fingers fumbled blindly for the stun gun.

*Oh Goddess, I'm drifting.* Too late. The scene snapped black and I floated in oblivion while my second-grade consciousness drifted forward into my present to confront the knife—for 7 seconds. *"What's wrong with you? Didn't you hear me? Just tell me where it is..."*

7 Seconds later, I tumbled back into my present with the force of a space shuttle reentering orbit. As the flashing spirals faded into an obscene pounding in my head, my eyes focused on the scene before me. The woman, taking advantage of the blackout between my past exiting and my present resurfacing, throttled an arm around my throat. The knife still in her fist, she dragged me, my head throbbing, toward the door. Above my head, where her long coat flapped open, a gun holster peeked out from her side. She clearly wasn't here to rob or kill me, this was an abduction—the distinction didn't comfort me much.

My hand groped blindly, searching for the stun gun. A shadow appeared in the doorway. My skull thudded onto the cobblestone floor as the woman whirled to face the unsuspecting customer. But it wasn't a customer. Amr walked in tapping his thumbs on his iPhone screen. *What the hell is he doing here*? "Amr!" Plowing through the neuro-muck in my brain, I rolled and whipped out the stun gun. The woman stepped away and I missed her ankle.

She lunged at Amr with the knife. He ducked at the last second, his ambush reflexes fine-tuned by a pack of wild older brothers. "Ivy, get out of here!" His iPhone crashed to the floor as he charged the woman recklessly.

I wasn't going anywhere. Amr was a lover not a fighter, a neuro-science student on summer break. What was he thinking, attacking a knife-wielding stranger? I scrambled to my feet.

The woman sidestepped Amr's attack and grasped his arm, flipping him into the crowded center display case. Definitely a professional. Bath bombs and baskets tumbled and crumbled to the floor with him. Lunging, I swiped at her with my stun gun. She pivoted and blocked, launching the weapon into the mirror behind the wall display. Glass shattered and peppered the cobblestones. "Blood, then." With a single jab, she stabbed the delicate blade into the flesh just below my shoulder. A jolt of pain burned through my chest. I groaned.

Spencer finally strolled into the boutique, oblivious, engrossed in his screen.

The woman couldn't have been counting on this much early foot traffic. She slid the blade, dripping with my blood, from my shoulder. Grinning, she dropped it in a plastic bag and stuffed it in her coat pocket. She plowed right through Spence as she bolted for the door. He crashed against the side of the window case.

Amr scrambled to his feet and chased after her. "Call 911!"

Spencer hauled himself up, open-mouthed, taking in the chaos. His phone dropped to the floor when he saw the blood streaming in a widening stain around my shoulder. Ripping the fabric of my sleeve at the seams, he exposed the wound.

"God, Ivy, I've never seen this much blood..." He retrieved his phone, dialed 911, then hustled into the store room, and came back with a first-aid kit and clean towels.

"Don't worry about me, Spence." I tried to stand but my stomach lurched and I crashed back onto my butt. "Shit! It burns." Spence knelt next to me with a wad of bandages, but I pushed him off. "Go stop Amr. She's too dangerous. She flipped him around like a handful of spaghetti. He's in way over his head."

"This is bad, girl." He pressed the gauze against the free flow of blood.

Grabbing the wad from him, I pushed him toward the door. "You don't get it. I think she was here to kidnap me. She wanted my blood."

Amr's shouts echoed up the hallway.

"I'm fine. Go! Stop Amr." I made a weak effort at standing and got a nasty pang for my efforts.

A deafening crack in the hallway startled us both to our feet. "What the hell was that?" A second crack sent us sprinting and shambling out the door.

"Goddess, those were gun shots, Spence!" Grimacing through the pain, I huffed to catch up as he rounded the corner into the hallway near the restrooms and the emergency exit. At the end of the corridor, the woman shoved the door open, tripping the alarm.

In the middle of the hallway, Amr's body sprawled, a pool of blood dousing the glazed cobblestones beneath his head and chest.

# CHAPTER 18

For three soggy-eyed weeks, Spence and I frequented the ICU waiting room at the university hospital. We held Amr's hand and talked to him—on the off-chance he could hear us. Waiting for him to surface into consciousness, I did some serious existential soul searching. I was anchored to the waiting room, but the vision of a boy drowning from the third marijuana bounce tugged at my moorings. I had the ticket to France and the reservation for the hotel *La Fiancée du Pirate*, but the risks of altering the future loomed heavy on my conscience. I was responsible for Amr lying unconscious in that hospital room. I wondered if I hadn't interfered with Yana and gotten myself on the radar of whoever sent that woman to collect my blood, would Amr still be fighting for his life? But how could I have not tried to save her? Would I have if I'd known this would happen to Amr? Maybe it was all going to happen regardless of what I did.

"You have to go." Spence stopped shoveling hospital fries into his mouth. "You don't have a choice."

"I can't leave Amr. This is my fault."

"This is the fault of the woman that shot him. Amr has me. I'm not going anywhere. You have to go see Barry. Tell him what happened. Tell him about the boy you're supposed to save. You can't just abandon that kid. Barry will know what to do."

"But…" I played with my salad. The black-haired woman was clearly there to kidnap me or steal my blood. If my upcoming trip had only been a vacation, I'd have canceled in a heartbeat. But a little boy's life hung on this trip. How could I ignore the blue-eyed boy's warnings?

"That bitch tried to drag you off, Ivy, and then stabbed you. You can't just sit here waiting for these—what did drift boy call them?—Guild people to come back and finish the job. Go see Barry and go save that kid. You don't have a choice."

Two days before my trip, Amr woke up. The doctors determined his prospects were good—no permanent damage—but he'd need some serious in-patient therapy.

Given our history, he was surprisingly happy to see me. Shaved on one side, bandages wrapped around his head, not even a bullet grazing his skull could douse the charm of Amr's smile. "You know I'd never leave you, Ivy. I'd take a bullet to the head to get you back." He squeezed my hand.

My heart twittered like a brainless bird ignoring the cat crouched in the bushes. "Yeah, until the next cute blonde comes along—or are you into redheads now?"

"But that's what I love about you. You're all of them."

"Let's maybe give the romance a hot minute. You have to walk before you can chase women." I planted a kiss on his forehead and then left the hospital to confer with Barry. My fear of interfering with the trajectories of the future and my compulsion to do something constructive with my oddity were wrestling in my brain. I needed a referee.

I'd already learned that what seemed to be the right thing to do from the myopic lenses of a 7-second drift might easily turn into a disaster—at least for me. Yin Yang. Then again, I was willing to suck up a few bruised ribs again if it meant saving a kid's life.

I felt older, wiser. I figured, before I did anything, I really needed to consult a professional, someone with more life experience than I had.

Dany and I walked the several blocks to visit the only certified adult I knew. My mother didn't count. She'd lost her license. The law offices of Brattweiler and Winn, a restored $19^{th}$-century brick and stone mansion on 100 South in the Avenues, rose up regally from the street. I'd never been to Barry's office before. He usually made house calls.

Bowed beneath the weight of a century of traffic, stone steps invited travelers to the grand entrance at the back of the porch. I attached Dany to one of the columns and approached the imposing double doors. Wolves snarled from the brass knockers. The door squeaked slightly. Unsettling. I never imagined that anything connected with Barry would dare to squeak.

My mouth dropped open. Victorian floral patterns covered the rich walnut paneling of the reception offices. A grand staircase led to a landing, and double doors guarded an office on the second floor.

The receptionist, announced by the clicking of her black pumps on the wooden floors, greeted me.

"I'm here to see Mr. Brattweiler." My finger twisted in a lock of hair until I realized I was displaying my insecurities and dropped my hand.

"Is he expecting you?" She tipped her reading glasses down the bridge of her well-sculpted nose and scrutinized my lavender braid, combat boots, and baggy black pants.

"No, but…I'm sure…well, I'm Ivy Leif. Mr. Brattweiler was a good friend, uh, associate of my great aunt. Grace Sedona…?"

The young woman's eyes widened. Her flawlessly secured ponytail bobbed slightly in astonishment. Suddenly, she seemed to be looking up at me instead of down. Her fingers flitted toward the antique chairs lining the waiting room. "I'll let him know you're here. Can I get you something to drink while you wait?" On a sideboard carved with vines, elegant glass and copper pedestal dispensers offered a variety of fruit and mint-laced waters. The several blocks walk from the hospital in late May had conjured up a fairly decent thirst.

"Yes, thank you. I'll help myself."

She nodded and hustled back to her phone to announce me.

The refreshing mélange of lemon, cucumber, and mint settled the churning in my stomach as I climbed the stairs with my china teacup. The door opened and Barry, smiling broadly, stepped into the hallway. "Ivy! To what do I owe the pleasure?" Although his name screamed Irish, I always imagined that a Russian woman had crept up the family tree somewhere. Wrapping a patriarchal arm around my shoulders, my lawyer ushered me into his office, where we took a seat on the green velvet settee.

The shelves of law volumes surprised me very little. Barry's name was on the law building at the university I attended. The sculptured face carved into the crests of the shelves, however, piqued my interest. The ancient mask of the mythical Green Man gazed down at the deep greens, earthy golds, and autumn reds in the carpets and the furnishings.

"Look, Barry, I…I know I'm not paying you for personal life coaching, but…" I sipped from my teacup.

"Ivy, always remember this. More binds us than financial affairs. Your Aunt Grace and I were not just business partners. If you had no money to be managed, your well-being would still rank as my first priority. I know I didn't show up until the money was there, but there were reasons for that. It was the money and your great aunt's death that put your well-being at risk."

"You know, I don't remember my father. I think my Aunt Grace filled the spot he left empty. I appreciate you stepping in when she moved on." My chest swelled, and though not the most demonstrative of introverts, I couldn't stop myself from snatching a hug from him.

Barry patted my knee. "I know why you're here." Shaking his head, he muttered, "Damn them!"

"Who?"

He didn't say. "Ivy, you should know that hidden forces tug on the strings of your destiny. Your Aunt Grace knew this. She did her best to shelter you, keep you from the vision of the all-seeing eyes." Pensively he rubbed his palms across the tan wool of his suit pants. "The same service she tried to render your mother."

"Wait, why would Aunt Grace need to shelter my mom?"

Barry shifted on the couch and then got up, walked to the bookshelf where the cut crystal decanter of brandy twinkled bronze in the light of the windows. He poured himself a shot, swigged it, poured another, and marched back to the couch without offering me anything stronger than the water I was drinking.

"Your seizures, the psycho-traumatic episodes you have, they're genetic. Your Aunt Grace and her twin, your Grandmother Sabrina, both experienced related phenomena. I believe Sabrina passed away before you had the opportunity to make her acquaintance. Grace had a gift…"

"...for healing?" No shock there. Aunt Grace's garden and bath boutique had whispered that secret truth to me when I was very young.

Barry nodded and exhaled as if he were blowing a memory off the path of his mind. "Your mother, unfortunately, inherited in her DNA an anomaly twisted by mutation that manifested itself as more of a curse."

"Is that your polite way of saying she's an alcoholic? I read a study on that. Some people just have the gene for it. And then, my mom's life hasn't been ideal, has it? She's had me to worry about."

Barry sipped his brandy, savored it, and then set the glass on the wood. The crystal reflected the walnut hues on the surface, and the color of the alcohol deepened. "Be that as it may, your mother, like her mother—and you, as we both know—inherited a sight."

"My mother drifts?" The only visual anomaly I could imagine afflicting my mother was myopia—impaired foresight.

Barry leaned back and closed his eyes as if he were reliving a very unpleasant moment of his life. "No, not exactly. That phenomenon is unique to your DNA. In short, your mother's nightmares are other people's realities."

"What do you mean by that? Like, if she has a nightmare, it happens?"

"Just the opposite. When people within a certain radius experience terror, she lives it with them in her dreams in real time. As you can imagine, the physiological effects, the adrenaline rush, the increased heart rate, all the body's natural reactions to trauma became…dangerous…life-threatening even."

"Alcohol blocks her sight." The connection wasn't hard to make, but the revelation shocked me in a King-Lear-epiphany sort of way. I'd judged my own mom quite harshly. Running my fingers through my hair, I sighed, letting my hands rest on the back of my neck. I wished someone had told me. I was so caught up in my own problems.

"Grace's failure to shield Sabrina only made her more determined to protect you. Losing her sister devastated her." He stood and walked across the room. Reaching beneath his desk, he slid his hand along the undersurface, found what he was looking for, and then, with a click and a rub of wood on wood, a hidden compartment popped out. From the secret drawer, he produced a key and headed for the bookshelves.

"These old Victorian homes have a handy knack for hiding secrets." He slid the ladder along the shelves. Stopping at the third from the window, he climbed to the second shelf from the ceiling. "You're not here to learn about your history, though, are you, Ivy? You've seen the blue-eyed boy, and he wants you to use your powers of future perception to help someone."

"How do you know that? How do you know about *him*?"

"I have my sources."

A wry grin cut his profile as he reached for a book. On the second shelf, a bronze clock dinged the hour: 2 p.m. Barry pulled the two books to the right of the clock from the shelf and lifted a false panel from the side, exposing a hidden safe. With the key, he opened it and extracted what appeared to be an old-fashioned timepiece.

A vibrant green stone set in the middle of the face caught the light and shivered as the pendant swung in his fist. Closing the panel and replacing the camouflage, he descended the ladder and replaced the key.

The timepiece dangled from a bronze chain. "You have a choice to make, Ivy."

# CHAPTER 19

I would have sworn that the stone throbbed and ignited when I touched it. Startled I jumped in my seat.

"Your grandmother's choice cost her her life but produced this amulet."

On closer inspection, the timepiece revealed three separate dials marked in runes. "What does it do?"

"Gives you control over your drifts. Your grandmother would have wanted you to have it. I promised to keep it for you so you could make your choice."

"What choice?" I snorted in response, shaking a fistful of chain his direction. "Why the hell did you let me spend my time experimenting with plants when you could have just handed me this?"

"Because that stone allows you to control the phenomenon, but the side effects are toxic. Have you heard of Mme. Curie?"

I was minoring in French so, of course, I'd heard of her. The stone pulsed unexpectedly. I flung the amulet onto the table and inspected my palm, half expecting to find burn marks.

"Don't be afraid of it. The engineered gem contains chemical properties that interact with the electric impulses in your brain and produce the drifts, but the various metal bands surrounding it block and filter them so that you can control the experience. We're fairly certain you're actually accessing data from parallel universes. The stone only becomes toxic when used too frequently…"

"Wait, Barry, go back. Who is 'we'? Those 'forces' you mentioned, they're not, by chance," I rummaged through my memories to find the names from the drift, "the Guild?"

Barry stood, a bit nonplussed by the revelation that I was vaguely aware of the forces that hovered about me, but recovered quickly. He was, after all, a brilliant lawyer.

"Who are they?"

My attorney retrieved his shot glass from the table and polished it off in one gulp and then returned to the bar for a refill. "The Guild, the Cult, and the Coven Commune are the three hidden societies that have always pulled the strings of civilization from behind the curtain. They are the minds of humanity, the purveyors of perspective. They are the choice you must make, Ivy. You should know that your Aunt Grace and your Grandmother Sabrina were well respected and renowned members of the Coven Commune. Well…until your Grandmother made her alliance…"

"And you, too? You're a member of the Coven Commune?"

"I am associated with all three in a, shall we say, legal capacity."

Before I could respond, or my solicitor could elaborate, a jagged black streak ripped the space between us from ceiling to floor. The air screeched as if a blade were chewing through metal. Thundering wind rattled the windows

"Damn! The amulet, Ivy!" Barry ran for the trinket on the table as the streak shred apart to reveal a hole through which I could just glimpse the weathered grey of stone walls. A leather-shod foot, attached to a black denim-clad human leg, penetrated the center of the rift. The violent rumbling of hurricane winds accompanied the emergence of a man I recognized: curly black slicked-back hair, olive skin—the man driving the Mercedes in my kidnapping drift.

He knew why he was here and went straight for the trinket on the table. For seconds, my mouth gaped open. My familiarity with mind-bending jumps into alternate times allowed me to accept the impossible a little more quickly than the average on-looker. Closer to the goal, I snapped my mouth shut and snatched up the amulet. The Mercedes man was having none of that and, for the second time—or really the first—his bony knuckles hammered my cheek. The impact knocked me sideways, rippling my vision. While I staggered, he grasped my arm, wrested the amulet from my fist, stuffed it in his pocket, and scooped me up over his shoulder, heading back toward the rift.

As he turned, Barry intercepted him head on, tackling us to the floor. My head throbbed, but I had ample experience plowing through massive headaches. While the two men grappled on the carpet between the gash in space and the table, I rummaged in my pocket for my stun gun. Jumping into the fray, I went for the intruder's neck. The charge vibrated through his skin. He convulsed and rolled onto his back. The rift rumbled and trembled. Violent lacerations cracked the gap.

"Shit!" Barry huffed, breathless from the scuffle. "I knew the Cult was making a play to dominate the Guild, I just didn't know that they knew about you."

"The Cult? I thought the Guild was…"

While Barry frisked him for the amulet, the intruder recovered his senses and whipped a gun from his coat.

My hand flew to my mouth as my heart pounded. This was the second time in a very short life time that a gun barrel had invaded my personal space. Barry backed off. The rift groaned, shivered and began to mend itself. The man cast a regretful look my direction before he dove back through the shrinking gap, the amulet still in his pocket.

"Damn!" Barry's fist pounded the floor. His gaze darted about the room, as if assessing the situation before he settled on his plan of action. It was the first time I had ever seen him flustered. "I have to leave, Ivy. Now. We simply can't allow this type of power play. The balance is tenuous as it is."

"What are you talking about, Barry? The Guild, the Cult, the Coven—you can't just leave and not tell me who these people are."

"Time is of the essence, my dear." He walked around his office gathering keys and wallet as if he really were leaving immediately. Last of all he opened a safe piled high with currency. He removed a small stack of colorful notes, split it in half, tucked one stack into his wallet and shoved the other into my palm. "Look, the Coven Commune was content for centuries to exist in the shadow of the Cult. But the Cult has a power lust. It has been at war since the Renaissance and the Age of Reason when a minority of the governing quorum splintered off to pursue a more scientific, capitalist course and created the Guild. Ever since the Industrial Revolution, the influence of the Cult has waned as the Guild gained preeminence. A coup is brewing. The recent political climate has tipped the balance of power among the governing quorums. The Guild is pulling too many of the power strings. The Cult simply won't allow it. We need the stabilizing force of the Coven. But the Coven needs a Crone."

Draping his arm around my shoulders, he ushered me onto the landing. "Go meet this blue-eyed boy. It's inevitable now. You're in the game whether you—or your aunt and I—like it or not, I suppose. It was wishful thinking to believe the Guild's radar didn't blip when you saved Yana and then bought that lottery ticket. If they know about you, it's a sure bet the Cult has caught wind of you as well. We can only hope the boy comes down on your side and tells you what you need to know. Whatever his reasons for visiting your drifts, they're connected with this power play…which is why I have to retrieve the amulet. Without it, you lose the freedom to choose your path." He kissed me on the forehead and rushed down the hall.

# CHAPTER 20

Poolside at *La Fiancée du Pirate* reeked of chlorine, but the view was stunning. The sapphire water shimmered under a barrage of falling sun rays. Straddling the cliffside of the property, the pool gave the impression of plummeting into the ocean horizon. Across the bay, terracotta tiled roofs dotted the leafy landscape of St. Jean Cap-Ferrat. I'd been camped out on a deck chair in my Friday purple one-piece since 5pm, lamenting that none of my Thursday evening visits to the restaurants lining the port had yielded the monumental first, in the flesh, meeting of the blue-eyed boy.

The boy I'd come to save and a tiny, elegant woman—his mother, I assumed—emerged poolside around 6pm. While the woman settled into a lounge chair, the boy bolted to the edge and jumped in. Dropping my Kindle, I grabbed the side of my seat, assuming he couldn't swim. He scurried through the water like an otter. His mother didn't even glance twice in his direction. An air of affluence clung to her as if she disposed of a large amount of wealth as easily as she brushed her teeth: the cut of her Sari, the simple, yet elegant, watch on her arm, the sleek dark hair, nails, and make-up, strictly unostentatious, but very tasteful.

Another young woman, a dyed blonde, soaked in the Jacuzzi with a much older, sweating man, sporting a rug of grizzled hair on his plump chest.

The soon-to-be drowning victim splashed his mother and laughed, his big brown eyes crinkling under a mop of black hair. A tiny smile peeked from the corner of her lips as she sorted through the pages of a magazine. Once or twice, she tossed a red toy into the pool, and he dove to retrieve it. Afraid to take my eyes off of him, guessing his mother had no idea what was going to happen, I watched his play. A smile curled my lips at the antics he employed to get her to watch him. I could relate.

From time to time, the specter of the Mercedes man, who ripped space and could appear out of nowhere, loomed its head above the pool. The sight haunted me. How easy would it be to open a seam, drown an eight-year-old, and disappear back into the rift?

The stun gun in my pool bag seemed like the wrong answer given the water. The pepper spray would work better. Even with weapons and some after-school karate classes that Barry insisted on, thinking of the coming confrontations dumped adrenalin into my veins. My finger twirled a strand of lavender that had escaped the confines of my braid, and I wondered what possessed me to come here. What did I actually hope to be able to do? The pool was only five feet deep. The boy was obviously an accomplished swimmer, and his mother was sitting only steps from the edge. I didn't even know how to swim.

At 6:15, the couple in the Jacuzzi left, padding dark, wet shadows into the black and white checkered stone tiles of the deck. The little boy paddled up to the side of the pool directly in front of me and rested his arms on the ledge. "*Bonjour, Mlle. Je vous connais. Comment vous appelez-vous*?" Nothing could ever be more darling than the sound of small French people speaking French.

"*Tu me connais? Je ne crois pas. Je ne t'ai jamais vu.*" I explained that it was impossible for him to know me because I'd never seen him.

*"Mais, moi, je vous ai vue."*

"*Sagar, ne la dérange pas*," his mother scolded without bothering to look up from her magazine. An Indian accent stilted her French, but Sagar's was indistinguishable. He paid his mother no attention. No surprise there.

"*Je m'appelle, Ivy. Enchantée. Et toi?*"

*"Sagar."*

*"Tu nages bien, mon petit*."

My compliment on his swimming pleased him briefly before he frowned and astonished me by continuing our conversation in English. Perfect English, flawless French, definitely not an average third grader. "Yes, but not well enough. I'm going to drown." His face didn't flinch as mine contorted in surprise. "You can't save me, Ivy. The Gleaner is coming for me. Thank you for trying, though." He glanced back at his mother as I stiffened in my seat, my lips pursed in a question. "Pease, don't tell her. She doesn't know, and I don't want her to. She will be very sad."

"Wait, Sagar!" I hopped off my lounge chair. Keeping my voice low enough to not startle his mother, I approached the side of the pool and knelt above him. "How do you know this?"

"Because I see, Ivy! I don't see what WILL happen like you, but I see all the things that CAN happen. I saw you, too." He flipped a somersault. The current of the water slicked his black hair close to his head as he surfaced. "In my dreams. I see you in the games I play. Do you play video games, Ivy?"

"Not much. I mostly watch my friend Spencer play."

"I play the future in my dreams. Multi-screen—screens up to the sky. I have to play them all to see what can happen. I'm tired, Ivy. I wish I just knew which one was going to happen like you do. Then Papa and I wouldn't have to play and guess and keep trying new games. How many screens do you see when you play the future, Ivy?"

And I thought I was seriously messed up! What would that be like to see multiple possibilities and outcomes from any one moment and have to try to choose which one is most likely to happen? I can't even pick a coffee flavoring without a pro/con list. How would that be to try to choose how to manipulate events so that the best future is the one that happens? How do you even make that call?

My life started to make some cosmic sense. Yana and I had some sort of neuro-psych connection, and I got the heads up to save her. I was pretty sure Sagar and I shared the same kind of bond. That's why I had to save him. "Look, Sagar, I don't—I don't play the games. I don't see all the possible futures. I drift into one future—mine—and I'm really there. Sometimes, there's a boy who comes to my drifts and helps me. He told me to save you. So, that's what I'm going to do." I reached for his hand. "Now c'mon, kidlet, get out of the pool."

He bobbed just beyond my reach. “They’re coming for you, too, like they’re coming for me. They collect us, you know.”

“Who?”

“The Guild. We have fairy blood.”

“Oh geez, kidlet. Fairies aren’t real.” I hated to pop his bubble. I knew only too well what it was to be “special” and wish it was some kind of magical power rather than a notch on the freak-o-meter.

“Faery is the name of the story that grew up to explain our powers. The genes are real. My papa studies genes. He calls ours the Druid Gene. But I like fairy better. I wish I could fly.” He tossed the red toy into the deep end and dove after to intercept it before it reached the bottom.

His head popped back up just beyond my chair. Grabbing the edge, he sloshed the toy onto the deck. “Did you know the Guild hunts kids like us? They turn our gifts into science, and then they turn the science into money. Papa says the Guild loves money! They don’t just want some of it; they want all of it! And then they want some more! What do you think they’ll do with all the money, Ivy?”

“I don’t know. Maybe they’ll buy a rocket and fly into space.”

“To find more money?”

“Probably.”

“If I could fly, I wouldn’t look for money. I’d look for friends.” He sank back into the water and then propelled himself up from the bottom with a rapid slosh. “The Cult steals our gifts, too. They like money, but they steal our power because they’re sad and regular. They want to be special so everyone will look at them and do what they say.” Splashing and sloshing, he swam off to the other side of the pool.

Money and influence. I was in college before I understood they were the twin fangs of our vampire society. I think, at some point, I imagined it was love or some sappy thing like that.

A Sagar-shaped torpedo sped toward my chair. When his head broke the surface, he wiped his face and furrowed his brow. “Since you came here to save me, they’ll be looking for you. I’ve played those games in my dreams.” He frowns into the water. "When they're finished with you, or if you won't play with them, you usually die."

Before I even met Sagar, the responsibility of knowing the future seemed an overwhelming burden. I couldn't fathom how such a small head could wrap itself around so many possibilities. So much chaos. So much fear. How did he even roll out of bed in the morning without second-guessing whether or not it was the right thing to do?

"Who is trying to drown you, Sagar? The Cult or the Guild?" I couldn't decide which of the rival societies was the enemy. Barry hadn't given me an opinion. In my book, the society murdering small boys was definitely the evil one.

He sank beneath the water and then emerged in a flood of bubbles. Wiping his eyes, he pushed his hair back from his face. "The Cult. They have a Gleaner, a Banshee. She's Irish. I'd like to visit Ireland and see the leprechauns. Mummy says she'll take me there next summer. But I know she won't. I looked. The Gleaner is coming to take me." He pointed at the clock. "In ten minutes." He seemed to understand his own death and to accept it with a calm that only a child who had never seen it up close and personal could adopt. Why would anyone kill this child—or any child? "You better go now, Ivy. They already sent the Ripper to steal you and your amulet. You're not safe here."

"Then we have to leave now, Sagar. Let me help you. We should tell your mother, at least…"

"No! It's too risky. No matter what I do, they kill her in every game I've played if we tell her now!"

So, this was the choice he was making. He was going to die to save his mother. "Sagar, you don't have to do this. We have ten minutes. We can run. Come on. Get out of the pool."

I reached for him, but he shook his head and paddled farther beyond my reach. "That game is bad for you, Ivy."

I could have jumped in after him without drowning—maybe—but at that moment, an extraordinarily thin Indian man in a tailored grey suit stepped into the pool area and approached Sagar's mother. "Harita." He bent and spoke in her ear. Bad news, obviously. Her face screwed up, and her mouth dropped open before she hopped up and headed for the door. She stopped abruptly, turned, and pointed at her son. The man in the suit reassured her with a nod and a few hand signals before she bolted into the hotel.

The messenger glared at me for a moment like I was some sort of cockroach in his cabinet. He tapped out a message on his cell, waited for a response, shrugged, stuffed it back in his pocket, straightened his suit jacket, and walked back into the hotel.

"You see? It's starting," Sagar said. "Running away by myself doesn't help. There are too many other players to be certain how it will turn out. I played that game over and over and Mummy dies and the Gleaner still finds me wherever I hide. She'll be here soon. You should go. If she sees you here, it will change your game, too. You don't want to play that game. You almost always lose."

"Everything changes, kidlet. The future is fluid. We can mold it. That's what the boy in my drifts told me. He also told me to save you—no matter what."

"Can you see him when you're awake?" Sagar asked randomly as if this were the moment for scientific inquiry.

"Of course, I can…well, no. I've only seen him during drifts, actually. My conscious mind leaves my present to drift into my future body. But, I'm awake. I never drift in my sleep…at least I think I don't. I haven't actually met the boy yet…in the present."

"And can everyone else see him during your drift?" The boy's tenacious curiosity in the face of impending death reminded me of the Little Prince.

"No. They can walk right through him. Except for once, on the beach, here in Villefranche, I think, a little girl tripped over him. It was like he was really there…and he looked, I don't know, younger, less worried, not so driven…it's hard to explain. Look, I can answer all your questions later." I wiggled the fingers I'd extended across the water, hoping to attract him like a kitten. If he didn't come soon, I would jump in after him. He wasn't old enough, or nearly scared enough, to make life and death decisions for himself.

He drifted farther into the middle of the pool. "Then you can see the Travelers from other games. I see them too—but only when I'm playing." *Wait! I think he's telling me he's seen the blue-eyed boy.* I wouldn't have left him behind before, but at those words, my resolve doubled down. "You should leave now. I played the game where you take me with you. We end up in a whole new level, and you die in every game I played. I wish I knew what really happens and didn't have to guess anymore. This level is hard. The best way for everyone to reach the next level of this game is for the Gleaner to take me now. All the other ways have too many choices and too many dead ends."

"There's no way I'm going to stand here and let you drown…"

"It's not like that. It only looks like that. She'll take me to the in-between. I'll miss my mummy." His brow clouds. "If you get in the way, Ivy, Game Over for you—no matter how we play. It's best for everyone if I just go with her now."

The inner chords of my deepest, ingrained fears vibrated. What frightened me most in life was the possibility of changing what should be. And yet, I had just begun to question the whole concept of "should be." Who was deciding what "should be" and why should I go along with them blindly? The water drowned Sagar's optimistic smile as he turned and dived toward the opposite side.

Philosophy aside, there was no way I was going to walk away and leave a child to die. Hefting my pool bag, I grabbed a towel from the black metal shelves and hustled around the shallow end of the pool. The waterfall at the deep end fell from a narrow ledge. When Sagar reached the other side, he wiped the chlorinated water from his eyes. I rounded the corner of the pool as he climbed out. "You should leave and make sure someone sees you—alone."

"I told you. I came here to help you. I'm not leaving you. Even if I have to…" I had only covered half the space between the end of the pool and the boy when a gut-wrenching screech announced a sudden flash of darkness. A torrential wind engulfed the pool room. My stomach lurched. My head throbbed, and pinpricks crawled along my arm up to my shoulder. For a second, I thought the chlorine smell had triggered a drift. Then I realized the black and white tiles on the floor had all faded to greyscale. I was still in the present, but this was definitely not the same plane I'd been on two seconds before. The water was purple. My arms and legs glowed red. The boy's orange-tinged body dripped with lavender drops.

"Sagar! C'mon! Please, we have to get out of here!" The din of the howling wind drowned my desperate plea. The boy turned, hypnotized to the source of the screeching. Near the back of the pool stood a young woman. Strands of soaked and stringy red hair dangled about her contorted, pale face like seaweed on a sun-bleached stone. She vomited her wailing into the pool room. Spreading her arms wide, she opened the tattered black shroud she wore as a cloak, inviting Sagar into her morbid embrace.

The boy's arms reached for hers, and the magnetism between them dragged him away from me.

As I ran to intercept him, my hand lunged into my bag. The air in this place crushed against me, stifling and thick, an unseen wall of gelatinous goo. Not even sure if electricity followed the same rules in this space, I grasped the stun gun. One thing I knew, what isn't chemical in humans, is electrical.

The boy was only inches from the Gleaner's skeletal fingers when I charged into her awareness. Her sunken eyes connected with mine. For a moment, the screeching stopped, the echo of it hanging suspended between us. She appeared astonished, completely unprepared for the presence of another being in the reality she'd opened up. In the brief second that her enticing squall ceased, Sagar turned pleading eyes to me.

The Gleaner saw my resolve and focused her gaze on the boy, amplifying her piercing shriek. In the time that it took for the hypnotic wail to recapture Sagar and propel him into the grasp of her boney fingers, I grabbed his glowing orange torso with my left hand and stabbed the crackling stun gun directly into the banshee's forehead. The whole grey room erupted in a shocking bolt of bright blue light. The stun gun superheated in my hand and clattered when I dropped it. The screeching morphed into a keening yowl, and the world snapped shut, whisking the girl away with it.

The boy and I stared at each other, silently, our chests heaving, until he pointed at the glass doors that led from the pool enclosure to the hotel corridors. Harita, gesticulating wildly and angrily at the man in the grey suit, was barreling down the corridor. I breathed a sigh of relief, knowing the moment of the drowning had passed, anxious to pass the boy, living and breathing, into his mother's frantic embrace.

Sagar tugged at my hand. "Everything has changed now, Ivy. Level Complete. We must run. Stay or go, it's Game Over for you, sooner or later. But if I stay now, my mummy dies. We'll just have to wait until the new level loads."

"C'mon! It's Game Over for all of us at some time or another."

Our only option for escape was the waterfall. Sagar's hand tightly in mine, we scampered to the ledge as his mother fumbled with her key card. Followed by the man in the grey suit, who, most certainly, was complicit with the attempt to assassinate her son, Harita barreled through the glass door. "Sagar! Sagar, *mon cher...*"

About five feet below us, the falls ended in a narrow basin in the lower gardens.

"Stop them! Sagar, *mon fils!* Help him…" Harita cried. Her traitorous employee rushed forward.

"We'll go to the house where you're staying." Normally, I would have found it astonishing that the boy knew about the Airbnb I'd rented. From previous experience, I didn't think it would be wise to stay in the same space where I was going to challenge Mistress Fate. After what I'd seen in the last fifteen minutes, I took the small seer at his word. With no time to remove my cover-up, I abandoned my pool bag on the deck and waded in with Sagar.

The markings of the lower level pool indicated it was quite deep. Apparently, the owners had foreseen this possible scene as well, although they had more likely envisioned it with drunken hotel guests playing the major roles.

Harita and her attendant were rapidly closing the narrow gap between us. She was already yelling and crying into her phone. The police would be here soon. Taking a deep breath, I squeezed the boy's hand. It was either this or go down the many paths where assassins murdered his mother and the Gleaner took him anyway. Given the choice myself, regardless of the complicated relationship I had with my own mother, and the illuminating information Barry had revealed about her, I had to agree with the boy that this was the best choice—maybe not for me. But we hadn't met the blue-eyed boy yet. That could reshuffle all the variables. Still, I end up in that chair—. "I don't swim, Sagar. I black out, so I never learned."

"I know. I learned to swim so that I could save you if you decided to play this game. I told you, Ivy. I've seen you in all the games. When your feet touch the bottom, kick off, and I'll guide you to the surface. I swim well." He flashed me a cheeky grin. "I do many things well." We breathed deeply and slid our butts to the edge of the precipice. It wasn't safe to arc far from the waterfall. The pool below was deep but narrow, built more for aesthetics than sport. Gardens stretched away from the basin, and we could escape, assuming I didn't drown. My heart pounded in my ears.

The man in the grey suit dove for us, literally, as we propelled ourselves over the edge. Or, more precisely, I propelled myself. Sagar's hand wrenched free from mine as I plummeted. The fall was interminable, plenty long enough to tilt my head back and see the struggle between the boy and the grey-suited man. "Sagar!" I shouted, using up all the air in my lungs that I should have been saving for the plunge. *Oh, shit!* I felt a bit like a five-year-old whose life jacket has been ripped off in the fall from the speedboat.

Randomly, I thought how ironic it was that I had come here to save Sagar from drowning, and now, most likely, I would be the one to drown instead. What bugged me most was that I hadn't saved him at all. He was back in the hands of the man I had watched betray him.

My feet crashed through the surface of the narrow pool. Water invaded my nose and mouth, choking me as I sank. The pool was deeper than I expected. The moment my toe scraped the cement bottom, I pushed myself up, heart and hope pounding.

Halfway up, my momentum died against the pounding crush of the descending wall of water—along with my breath. I was empty and spluttering, my head felt like it would explode. The translucent ceiling churned, inaccessible, just out of reach. The purple cover-up I wore over my suit bloated and floated in the rivaling currents, obscuring my vision and hampering my motion. My arms and legs thrashed and my lungs insisted I suck in. Two feet had never looked so far. Why had I never seen this?

I didn't have any breath to hold to float to the surface and definitely not enough to sink back to the bottom and try pushing off again. Oh, Goddess! What was I thinking? My lungs burned. Flecks of black streaked across my vision. Strange how I would never actually meet the boy that had brought me here to die.

An enormous splash troubled the water behind me. Sagar's hand wrapped itself around mine, and the upward momentum crashed me through the surface. Only inches away from the edge, he deposited my palm firmly on the cement lip and scrambled out as I choked out the water and gulped the air. "Hurry! Naheed is right behind you!" Blood trickled down Sagar's cheek. Judging from the crimson cloud orbiting the water about Naheed, the two of them had collided in the fall. Sucking air, I heaved my soaking body onto the deck, Naheed's wrist broke the water line and grabbed my ankle.

Harita screamed from the edge above. *"Arrête-la! Arrête-la!"*

I'd dropped my stun gun on the upper deck, but my community karate came with me. I absolutely could not let Naheed pull me back into the water. Drowning me would be child's play. My free foot flew on its own and found a likely target in Naheed's large and crooked nose. The cartilage bruised my heel as it cracked and blood spurted from the man's nostrils. Freed, I scrambled away.

"The police are coming." Sagar dragged me down a stone path that led to the edge of the property. "We have to hide at your other house, but we only have a few days before they find us again. We need to find your friend. He might help."

"You've seen him in this new level?" Small stones poked and stabbed at our bare feet.

"Yes." Drops of water from Sagar's soaked swimsuit and my drooping cover-up pelted the path as we approached a fence with a service gate.

"And then what? What happens when we find him?" The gate swung shut after us. French sirens blared in the distance.

The sound struck me with the force of what had just happened. I had actually altered the future—again. In another reality, this boy drowned, and now, instead of drowning, he'd been kidnapped—by me. Déjà-vu of another sort haunted me.

"I don't know." His big eyes stared up at me. The wise oracle had exited the premises leaving only the naïve boy in his place. I was going to have to be the adult now. I'd been the adult at my home since I was old enough to climb on the kitchen counter and make coffee.

"Then let's hope I find that boy before the police find us." I grabbed his hand and headed for the winding, one-way streets and a circuitous route back to my Airbnb.

# CHAPTER 21

Although I'd made him a little bed on the sofa in the living area, halfway through the night, Sagar sneaked into the big bed with me.

"Ivy, are you awake?"

My dreams tumbled through the drama of the day and I was only half crashed. "Yeah, Sagar." Assuming he was missing his mom, I brushed my hand across his feverish little forehead. "Are you okay?"

"Yes. I was dreaming."

"Try to sleep. We'll figure this out in the morning, kidlet."

Silence nestled around us, and I thought he might have drifted off until the covers rumpled up with his twisting as he scooched closer. "Ivy?"

"Yeah, kidlet?"

"Thank you for not letting the Gleaner take me. It was the best play for the level for me to go with her, but I didn't want to. I wanted to stay with my papa."

For a moment, the pressure gripping my chest dissolved in pinpricks of empathy. Whatever else happened, I'd created a bond between me and the little boy snuggled against me. Perhaps that was the moment when the meaning of life shifted for me. The humane leap-frogged past the pre-destined.

My 7 seconds showed me brief images of what would be, but the picture lacked the substance of person-to-person connections. We will all certainly die, one way or the other, sooner or later, but the connections we make, those bear the meaning of the minutes in between. I couldn't let my own survival reign as supreme overlord anymore. I was no longer a disciple of fate; I had become a sister of humanity.

Sagar was in a little ball under my arm when I woke up to the sound of cars zipping past the window and slipped out to buy breakfast.

He devoured his *pain au chocolat.* Despite the wizened soul, veteran of countless lives, that masqueraded about in his slight body, the boy inside could not escape indulging. He stared at me, chewing softly, while I sipped a *café au noisette* from the bakery on the corner across the street—okay, so yes, I was also indulging in a crème brûlée *for breakfast.* Seriously! Food of the gods! Don't judge me. I'd just saved another child's life—sort of—and thought I'd reward myself.

"Can I have some money?" Sagar stretched his palm across the table.

"Sure. I have lots of money." I still had a decent pile from the wad of bills Barry stuffed in my fist before he left. My purse was hanging on the back of my chair. Digging out my wallet, I handed him several. "But Sagar, you can't go out, kidlet. We have to stay hidden until I meet the boy from my drifts."

"You're wrong, Ivy." My eyebrows popped up. I'd been called many things during my aberrational life, but "wrong" was not one of them. "I don't need to hide. You do." He pointed to an article in the copy of *Nice-Matin*, sitting on the table. It reported the abduction of Sagar Singh, son of a prominent—and obviously quite wealthy—neurologist. The article informed the public of a substantial reward for information on the whereabouts of a young American woman named Ivy Leif with lavender, shoulder-length hair.

"Oh, shit!" The *crème brûlée* curdled in my stomach. My college education hadn't prepared me to deal with this type of problem-solving. "I'm pretty sure I'm the only girl with purple hair in the entire village." Suddenly the pile of bills on the table gained more significance. I picked it up and counted them. I'd been using my credit card mostly, saving the cash for emergencies. This situation probably qualified. "Okay, I used my credit card at the hotel. That's where they got my name. I'm sure they remembered the guest with the purple hair. This means I can't use the card anywhere or they'll track us down."

All the consequences of my choice to rescue Sagar—I'm not sure I could call it that, seeing that he was the one who dragged my butt out of the pool—converged. My plane ticket, my passport, I couldn't use either of them without alerting the authorities. And then, worst of all, "If I can't go to the restaurants on the beach, I'll never meet the boy. He's our only hope. I've already called my lawyer's office. Barry's not expected back until next week and his assistant has no idea how to contact him."

Sagar scooped up the money. "Don't worry, Ivy. Your hair will help us. Lots of Americans come here. If the police are looking for purple hair, we'll change yours."

"You're right! No one probably noticed anything else about me, and I'd be willing to bet Naheed arranged for the hotel cameras at the pool to malfunction before the Gleaner showed up."

Changing my hair color was the obvious answer. And yet…I bit my lip. What impact would that have on my notebooks full of drawings, my diary of the future? Possibly, they were all obsolete, now that the future had altered course. But if not, I hated to lose that sense of control. Then again, maybe the future had already taken into account this sequence of events? "Sagar, what about the boy in my drifts? He sent me to save you…I'm not sure how that works. But, I think I was supposed to meet him, I mean really, in the flesh, on this trip. Now that I've changed things, I may never meet him. I may have erased him from my future." I felt a migraine coming on and rubbed my temples.

"Then you'll play a new game, one you created." He dabbed at the crumbs on his plate. "I did not sleep well last night."

"I'm so sorry, kidlet. Were you cold? I'm sure I can find another blanket. I noticed the traffic noise outside the bedroom window was really loud."

The boy pushed away from the breakfast table. I went to my room, pulled on a yellow Saturday shirt and white shorts, and then picked out the smallest t-shirt I owned, and brought it back to him. "No, I wasn't cold; the new level scared me. In the best games, you still meet the boy, but in some of the scary ones, he is there, too. His player is a wild card."

Not good news. It's hard to tell in 7 seconds, but I had always assumed that the boy who haunted my drifts was a guide. I'd never bothered to ask myself to what destination. "So, do you think I should still try to meet him?" Stuffing the bills in the pocket of his swimsuit, Sagar lifted his arms and I dropped my smallest t-shirt over his head. It hung off his slim shoulders and dangled almost to the hem of his suit. As soon as it was safe for me to leave the apartment, I'd have to outfit him. He looked like a miniature vagrant.

"I can't choose your game, Ivy. I don't see enough details. You're the only one who knows what's actually going to happen. Even if I win a game, I can't make sure that's the one we'll all play. Only you know which future we're heading for. You have to pick your own players and your team. Every level you win changes the next one that loads. You have to choose your own endgame, Ivy."

"Yes, but what about the other players that change our game? We can't control their play."

"Multi-player can be easier or harder. If the other players on your team have the same endgame, and you play off of each other's moves, it's easier to beat the level."

"But what if they aren't even trying to get to the same endgame you are, and they make moves that make it impossible for you to win?"

The door moaned and resisted but opened reluctantly. "That's why the future is a game. You never know exactly what game you'll be playing. What color do you want?"

"Oh no, I never make any of the choices for my hair. That has to be random or I'll know what's coming for me, but I won't know when. You choose."

From the window, I watched him look both ways before he crossed the street. In front of the store marked with the large green cross that announced it was a pharmacy, he tripped on the curb. He'd seen so much in his few years, it was hard to remember he was only primary school age. I twisted a lock of lavender around my finger and wished I'd at least had a smaller pair of flip-flops to loan him.

# CHAPTER 22

While Sagar bought hair color, I tried again to reach Barry. Bits and pieces of solid future from drifts had always anchored me. Now that their existence was threatened, I felt unmoored. Barry was the only buoy in sight.

My call went to voicemail. Outside, a siren wailed. Grabbing my bag, I prepared to run to the roof and take the fire escape in the back of the building should the police find me sooner than Sagar's dreams had foreseen. We'd settled on an emergency *rendezvous* in an alley that dated back to the Renaissance, *Rue Obscure,* in case we had to separate.

My hand shook on the doorknob as the tone of the siren rose from the right. When the urgent wailing receded to the left, my bag plopped to the floor by the door. This life was far too intense for an artistic biologist. How the hell did I get here? I flopped onto the couch.

When he came in, Sagar pulled a box of hair color from the bag. "We'll have to cut it, too. This game has too many levels. I couldn't play enough of them. I don't know where we're going."

"Sometimes I wonder what good it does to see the future. I think it would be better to see the past. It's much more reliable. It doesn't change."

"But, knowing the past can't change the future. Papa says money and power are in knowing the future. Mummy says the Guild pays Papa lots of money to study the Druids. Maybe Papa can help you control your power. He taught me to play the games. The Cult wants Papa to work for them."

"So, you're a pawn in their game? They've threatened you to recruit your father? That's horrible! What is the Cult? If it's as old as you say it is, it doesn't mean what it means now—some sinister, religion that brainwashes its followers. It probably means just the way of worship—like the cult of Dionysus or something."

"The Cult is like the Guild, but they like religion more than science." He pulled up a chair near the kitchen sink. "Do you want a mirror?"

"No thanks, kidlet. Better not to know some things before there's nothing you can do about them." As a matter of principle, I never made any of the choices that went into my hairstyle. Since I'd already seen the future drift, it would ruin my whole dating system if I meddled. That's why Spencer never got to look in my book. I fetched my substitute stylist a brush from the bathroom—Spencer wasn't going to like this.

"I bought the foam." The package crinkled as he set the ingredients on the counter and began brushing through my hair. "You have to be careful, Ivy. Your gift is more valuable than mine. Mine has too many choices. It's not reliable. When Papa sent me away from the Guild in Marseille, he told me that M. Aycelin, the new Bishop, needs a seer to make the Cult great again."

"What does he mean by *great again*?"

"I think it means *mean*. Mummy is reading me the hunchback story. Have you read it?"

"Has any French student NOT read The Hunchback of Notre Dame—or at least seen the movie?"

"Papa says I have to read as many history books as I can because the past will show me how to choose a better future. But Mummy likes a story better."

"Your papa sounds like a very smart man, Sagar. And your mom sounds very nice."

"Mummy says I'm like Papa." He grins.

"Yeah, well, no one likes a know-it-all—believe me I know. But I think you're like your mom, too."

"Papa says the Cult was great during the hunchback story. Like Frollo. But Frollo is mean to Quasimoto and Esmerelda. Do you think being great makes you mean, Ivy?

"They say power corrupts and total power corrupts totally. Maybe they don't start out mean, but having power makes them mean."

"I'm glad Papa sent me away. I met M. Aycelin once. He looks like a hawk—like he wants to carry me off and eat me. He made me think of Frollo."

"So, this M. Aycelin wants to make the Cult *great* again? Brutal!" It was unclear whether I was referring to the history of the Inquisition or the way Sagar tugged the brush through my tangles. I was actually thinking of my day trip to Carcassonne. In the citadel, a small torture museum lured tourists with its display of macabre tools. The walled city had been a seat of the Inquisition.

"Yes, especially for the children of the Druid Gene like you and me. In the old days, the Coven protected us. That's when we were fairies!" His pleased grin flashed in front of my face and then melted dramatically into a pout. "But then, the Christians came, and the Cult sent the Coven away." His storytelling passion ramped up considerably. The comb dropped, and he planted his palms on my shoulders to hiss in my ear. "They *hunted* us, Ivy! They burned us at the stake! And sometimes," he grabbed the bottle of dye and shook it in front of me, "they squeezed all the power out of us until we died!" A blob squirted from the top into his hand. He smeared it cold against my scalp. My nose scrunched against the acrid ammonia.

I shivered, not from the cool as much as from the prospect of falling into the Cult's hands. My future strapped to a chair and dying haunted me. I didn't have the heart to tell him about it. He had enough possibilities to haunt him without knowing what I knew for a relative certainty. Sagar's hands moved along the lines he'd carved in my scalp. "So, who is—what was his name—M. Aycelin?"

"Papa says he has a donjon at the Palais in Narbonne. Papa also says—but only when he thinks I'm not listening—that he's kidnapping Druids again. He fixed up the donjon to use it for research to steal their gifts. That's why he wants Papa to work for him instead of the Guild." He stacked the hair on top of my head. The last of the foam splatted into his palm and he smeared it through the pile. "It says we have to wait 20 minutes."

Sagar played video games—real ones—until I was ready for the rinse cycle. "Sagar, if I told the boy—what did you call him? a Traveler?—if I told him things in the future that brought him into my drifts, don't you think I actually need to meet him now in order to not erase what's already happened?"

"Yes." Sagar rinsed away the dye and then wrapped my hair in a towel.

"Have you seen the possibility of me meeting him—before the police come, I mean?" Because so many of my life choices, my personality, my attitudes, had grown from the seconds-long interactions with the blue-eyed boy, I felt he played an integral part in my life. What would I be if I never actually met him? "Should I keep going down to the restaurants on the shoreline to meet him? Is it safe? What's the best choice?" After rubbing my hair briskly, I threw off the towel and sat in the chair.

Taking advice from an eight-year-old ranked right up there on the fringe scale with letting him cut my hair. But, then again, Sagar's gift lent him the wisdom gleaned from multiple realities lived and learned from. What he lacked in years and certainty, he made up for in lives played.

"I don't know, Ivy. In some of our best games—and some of your worst—the Traveler who sent you to save me, helps us. There are too many choices and too many players that I haven't seen now."

I sighed. There was a certain comfort in the reliability of my drifts. If I saw it, it was going to happen—unless I did something to change it. And I only saw one vector, so it was easier to train my mind to retain most of the relevant details—even if there were only 7 seconds worth of them. "You'll need scissors." A brief rifling through the kitchen drawers produced a decently sharp pair. "Are you up for this?"

He nodded. "Are you sure you don't want to do it yourself?"

Not that fringe moves had disappeared from my everyday life, but still, I had at least learned to minimize them. Setting an eight-year-old loose on my hair with scissors was definitely a step backward. "Nope, the most important thing is to never influence the choice and keep it totally random. My hair color puts a kind of time stamp on my drifts…"

He brushed through my damp hair, collected a wad, and began snipping. "That's very clever, Ivy. But—I think Papa could help you find a better way."

"It works well enough." I avoided looking at the clippings that tumbled to the kitchen floor. "During a drift that happened when my hair was lavender shoulder-length, I told the Traveler the number 521. He found me dying during another drift and told me to tell him that number. Will that drift where I told him the number never happen now that we've changed my hair? Or have I just altered some of the minor details of it? Do you think other drifts calculated in the probability that you would change my hair?" The metal chill of scissors brushed against my neck. "Did your father ever try to shape the future, Sagar, based on your games?"

He snipped a couple more handfuls before he responded. "Yes. But it's hard. We don't know which one is most probable, and it's really hard to control all of the players' moves. Sometimes, I play a game that helps us level up, and we try to remember all the parts so we can get all the players to make the right moves for that game to happen." More clipping, more clumps falling. "You only see one game. It must be the most probable. Did you learn about probabilities in math?"

"Oh, Goddess! Please don't constipate my brain with probabilities."

"Hmm. You don't like math, Ivy? I love math! Papa says I'm good at it." He stood in front of me and combed my bangs forward. "The trajectory of your present has probably changed since that drift."

I closed my eyes.

The scissors snipped just above my cheekbone. "What about infinite universe theories? Did you learn about those?" His breath whispered past my nose as he combed through a second batch.

"Did you?"

"Papa and I study many things, especially things that can help me choose which games to play."

"Of course, you do. Do you ever get to play—just for fun?"

"Not very often. There's too much to learn. Sometimes, there are only a few games, but other times, there are so many that I don't even play the one that happens before it happens." The scissors snipped again and another strand fell. My head was beginning to feel noticeably lighter. "Papa says we exist on an infinite number of planes—like in an infinite number of games—and that every game that I see happens somewhere. Maybe, when you drift forward, you get to see the most probable game."

"So, small details—or even a large one—could vary. I wonder if the drift itself could be totally erased."

"Possible. Not probable." He set the scissors on the sink, wiped the hair from his hands, and then pulled the brush through the strands one more time. "Too many of the variables have already come together to make that probability. The game will probably detour and then get back to where it was." He used his fingers as vectors to illustrate the concept for me.

"The Traveler, he's one of us, right? A Druid?"

"Mmhmm. Travelers don't really play the game. Most of them are more like ghosts. The future can't be played in the past. That's why the Guild doesn't care much about Travelers."

"But since I can interact with the blue-eyed boy in my drifts, he could bring me messages from myself in the future. He could be like…a sort of…envoy between my future, my present, and my past."

"If you trust him, he'd be a great player for your team."

"But I only see him during my drifts." Suddenly the value of my notebook increased immeasurably. "I could send him back with a message to any of the drift moments recorded in my sketchpad!"

The moment of truth had arrived. Rifling my fingers through my new 'do, I went in search of the blow dryer while Sagar grabbed the broom from the closet. "But, Sagar, what if the two of us, in changing the future where you drowned, erased all the drifts in my notebook that haven't happened yet?"

"The drifts still took place. Maybe they'll just be dreams of possibilities now like all the games I play but never actually live."

"The question is, has the blue-eyed boy dreamt those dreams as well?"

A jetted tub, a shower, and a sink formed the bathroom loft above the bedroom. I stood in front of the mirror to see how Sagar's choices had altered *my* future.

Staring back at me, from rounded, coffee brown eyes, was a rather pale-skinned, auburn *redhead—chin-length, with long bangs.* Leaning my elbows on the porcelain rim of the sink, I covered my mouth. The choices that had brought me here had accelerated the arrival of the year of catastrophes. If any of my drifts still held force, this was the year the Mercedes man kidnapped me and the year I died strapped to an operating chair. As far as I could tell, we'd essentially deleted the drifts of me meeting the blue-eyed boy and kissing Amr in the year of shoulder-length lavender.

# CHAPTER 23

Sagar was shuffling through the video games in a basket by the television when I woke up, ready to face my first day as a redhead.

"Which game are you looking for?" The allure of a coffee from the café down the street had coaxed me out of bed. An empty purple bowl in the sink told me Sagar had already taken care of himself.

He looked a bit guilty, and I imagined that his genius father doled out the screen time with a miserly hand. "Sometimes, I like to play *The Last of Us*." He hurried to justify his delinquency. "Not for the game. I like the story."

"Actually, so do I. That's the only one I play with my friend, Spencer. You remind me of a much smaller metaphysical version of him." I gathered up my purse and keys from the kitchen table. His shoulders relaxed a little when he realized I wouldn't be busting his balls for wasting valuable instructional time. "Promise me you won't go out?"

He popped a game in the console and nodded without looking at me. "Unless I have to."

"Oh, that's reassuring." I turned the doorknob and looked back suspiciously. "*Are* you going to have to?"

Total immersion in the game. No response. "At least, you remember where we'll meet if we get separated, right?"

Nod.

I caught a bus to Nice. Sagar was right. No one gave me a second glance. The hunt was on for an American girl with lavender hair. The abandoned newspaper on the seat next to me provided broader camouflage than my sunglasses and short red hair. I positioned it strategically so that my newly reddened locks would discourage a closer look at my face. Sagar's disappearance, accompanied by a fuzzy picture of me in profile, probably from the hotel cameras, had only caught a bottom corner of the second page. The family was offering rewards for any leads to the American girl who was a person of interest in the case.

A photo of the Vatican and the announcement of an upcoming visit of a delegation of cardinals to the Carcassonne-Narbonne diocese dominated the front page. Special services had been scheduled at the Cathédrale de St. Just et Saint Pasteur in Narbonne. Following the death of the Archbishop of Montpellier, an influential member of the College of Cardinals, speculation ran high that the Bishop of Carcassonne and Narbonne, Gilles Aycelin, might ascend to the vacant position. However, the opposition speculated that the highly controversial Tweets issuing from the Bishop had prompted the distinguished visit and most likely announced a papal attempt to privately quell the rising spirit of unrest that had spilled beyond the diocese's borders. The Bishop's most recent less than 140-character sermon admonished the faithful to seek "forgers of the future, not purveyors of the past."

Hefting my bag on my shoulder, I got off in one of the commercial areas of Nice. Heavily armed, uniformed *gendarmes* strolled the streets but seemed concentrated at the nearby train station. My pulse racing, I forced myself to smile and nod at the imposing twenty-something toting an automatic something or other. He tilted his head to scrutinize me as I passed.

Testing my freedom to walk in public before I risked looking for the Traveler was one of my goals. But Sagar also needed clothes that would not attract attention, and I needed another stun gun. It had already proved quite handy against the Cult's odd collection of what Sagar called Druids. The scientific side of my brain rebelled against the magical term, but the artistic side embraced it. With a troubled chill, I sighed and followed my phone to a local *armurerie*.

The shop owner seemed quite pleased that he didn't have to whip out his spotty English, and we negotiated the transaction fairly easily. Having successfully completed the risky part of the mission, I set off in search of clothing stores. Happening upon an electronics shop, I picked up a copy of *The Last of Us* for Sagar before ducking into a *Monoprix*. A couple pairs of shorts and t-shirts would do the trick, and I grabbed some sandals. If I hadn't passed the sock and underwear aisle, I would have totally not foreseen those items. All in all, the success of the day stilled my quaking heart and trembling hands. To reward myself and give Sagar a little guiltless game time, I found a cozy sidewalk café in a sleepy alley far enough from the train station to not be crawling with police patrols.

Scanning my texts for news from Spencer about Amr, I waited for my salad laced with warm goat's cheese and Kalamata olives. The waiter had just set the plate in front of me when the world around me warped into greyscale.

The metal café chair across from me scraped across the paving stones. A cold, pale, soggy hand fell on mine. The only being who still appeared in normal colors was the strikingly pale, sopping wet, red-head connected to the hand that refused to relinquish mine which now glowed red. A shiver slithered up my arm. "Do you mind if I join you?" Her accent was faintly Irish as if she hadn't been home for a while.

"You? Oh, my Goddess! You're the bitch, that...Gleaner, that tried to drown Sagar!" Yanking my hand from beneath her poisonous touch, I jumped to my feet, practically knocking over the rickety, metal chair. "Listen, you stay away from him. What kind of people are you that you would murder an eight-year-old boy?" I glanced around for the waiter, anybody, but they all seemed to have receded into slow motion.

Unruffled by my reaction, her hair floating about her as if she were immersed in the ashen liquid of this realm, she invited me to sit with a gentle wave. "I've been rude. Let me introduce myself. Gwen." She held out a hand that I didn't take. "I'm here about the boy."

My gasp at the sudden skip in my chest was inaudible. Of course, to me, "the boy" had always been the unnamed accomplice of my drifts. Moments like these flaunted in front of my consciousness just how attached to him I was. I truly felt that my destiny was a series of events leading to him. I leaned across the table and practically whispered. "You know him?"

"Of course, I know him. Why do you think I came to take him from the pool?" I'd forgotten that another boy had entered the stage in this scene. Her chiming laughter caused the heads about us to turn in an eerily slow and painful arc. I must have looked to them like some crazy girl talking with the voices in her head. Gwen stifled her giggle. "You understand so little. Sagar is only a tiny cog that turns a wheel in a much more complex machine. The hand that guides the machine adjusts such minor parts routinely."

"How can you have so little respect for life? One person might be insignificant in the tapestry of the universe, but every one of us counts our handful of threads as precious."

"The will of the Hand is the will of the Word. The Word is the great Weaver. The threads curve and bend, come and go, at His pleasure."

For the first time in my short, oddly punctuated life, I had come face to face with the incomprehensible mentality that spawned the dehumanization of millions of people during the Holocaust. "You're a monster, Gleaner." Shaken, I stood to leave, my appetite squelched.

Reaching across the table, she grabbed my wrist again. "No more than Death is a monster. Sit down!" The sudden hardening of her voice stalled my exit. "You're interfering with forces so vast you cannot possibly comprehend the consequences of your blind actions." Jerking my arm from her grasp, I sat rigid, glaring. On the edge of the seat, I fought back the urge to slap her. Only a vague hope that perhaps she might enlighten me restrained me. Barry had only opened a small peephole into the world to which she was referring. I wanted a better glimpse inside.

"The tides have turned, Ivy. The Guild has grown fat and reaches its grubby hands beyond its own borders. Don't you see how those that serve the Guild have overrun your own government? They seek nothing more than to line the coffers of the merchant barons they serve and to eradicate all opposition." I couldn't fault her there. The cabinet was now a gathering of generals and businessmen rather than a satisfying, sometimes ineffectual, mix of statesmen of many perspectives. "To fill the voids of their limitless coffers, they will harvest our gifts, suck the life from the marrow of our Druid blood, and then cast us aside as worthless dross."

"At least they're not killing children to suit their ends."

"Don't fool yourself, Ivy. You have not been traveling the world of the societies for as long as I have. The Guild knows you now. They will come for you…"

My face betrayed me. I couldn't help thinking of the woman in the scarf who tried to drag me off.

"…they already have, haven't they? They will suck your power dry." The Gleaner's face changed. For a moment, her eyes pleaded. Her sincerity gave me pause—but only for a second.

"I won't argue with you. I know very little. But what I do know is that the only people I've ever trusted served the Coven." My Aunt Grace was a quietly charming woman and nothing if not gentle. The thought of her leveraging the life of a small boy to serve her own ends contradicted every memory I had of her. She gave; she didn't take. If her choice had been the Coven, it would be mine too.

A small white car topped with a line of flashing grey lights rounded the corner and rolled, as if through a smog of gelatinous grey, down the street toward our seats on the sidewalk. I held my breath but could do nothing to stop the adrenaline-fueled rampage in my blood. The streets were narrow, the opportunities for escape practically non-existent. I wondered if, in our current plane, the Gleaner could flag them down and thrust me into a future that most likely involved barred cells and interrogation rooms.

Noticing my shoulders stiffen, Gwen turned to watch the tortoise-like progress of the patrol car. Her eyes narrowed. The corner of her lip curled. Suddenly, I was nothing more than a frail bird perched on the open door to the metal cage that dangled from her hand. As the police officers passed, oblivious to my identity, she smiled and reached across the table to touch my fingers with the tips of hers. I shivered at the chill that rippled up my arm.

"You see, I am not your enemy. I do not seek to destroy you but to bring you into the true fold. You and I, Ivy, we have godly gifts. We could be sisters in the Word. The Word loves us. He will set us free. His faith moves the Hand that guides us to the New Earth. Very little stands in our way now. The Word will unite our strength, and the world will once again subdue its desires for riches and submit to the will of the Word. It will shun the avarice of the Guild and return to the paths of holiness."

Her soft words rang hollow in my mind. Even though the danger had passed, she hadn't hesitated to profit from it. When Barry first told me of the societies, he had offered me the freedom to choose. He didn't use the fear and anxiety of the moment to influence my choice in his favor. The Coven was not a force that coerced and bent others to its will. The Cult, evidently, was. "I'm not likely to cast my allegiance and the exploitation of my psycho-abnormalities to a culture that finds murdering children an acceptable solution to the world's problems."

"Then you are foolish. Have you never heard of Abraham and his son Isaac?" Of course, I had. I hadn't spent the first 10 years of my life attending weekly Sunday School to learn nothing. What I had learned, however, may not have been what they had set out to teach. Against the grey surrounding us, Gwen's eyes sparkled as she spoke. "It is precisely the devotion and obedience to the Word which the Cult commands that gives it the power to oppose the Guild's avarice. The Coven is only a weak coalition of independents." She folded her fingers almost in prayer. "The Word calls for you, Ivy. Join us." Her eyes and voice pleaded so tenderly that I wondered whether this was a studied act for recruiting or if she truly believed the nonsense she was spouting.

"Who is this 'Word'? That's a little pretentious, don't you think, claiming to speak for God?"

She grimaced and covered her ears. "I will hear no more of your blasphemy." Clearly, a fanatic. "The Word is the mouthpiece of God to the children of the Druid. His servant, the Hand, guides our steps toward the New Earth while the Guild herds us toward the oblivion of gluttony. The merchant barons will drive us to the very cliffs of war, and then all humanity will plunge, like frenzied lemmings, into the abyss. We must strip them of their weapons and compel their agents to serve the light. We're going to take Sagar, Ivy. The Word has decreed it and the Hand will make it so. Don't interfere."

"Oh, but I will interfere. I will never bow to an order which embraces the killing of a child to manipulate his father into doing their bidding. What sort of 'New Earth' would that be? Your *Word*, whoever he is, is a fraud. He's exploiting you…"

Gwen slammed her fist on the metal table and looked to the side as if frightened of whom she might see in the void of the street. More calmly, she slicked back the sopping red strands that had strayed into her vision. "We're going to take the boy. Don't get in my way again."

"Be assured. I will get in your way because we can see you coming." Feeling not nearly as sure of myself as I sounded and hoping to hide the vague trembling of my fingers, I stood and reached under the table to gather my purchases. Pulling a 10 Euro bill from the wallet in my pocket, I tucked it beneath the nearly full glass of purple water.

As I turned my back on her and headed for the train station, her voice followed me. "Don't forget, Ivy. It's not just Sagar I can find. Any child who carries the blood of the Druid and walks the grey realm, I can find. I am a Gleaner, and I will do the bidding of the Word."

I didn't glance back when the world shifted suddenly into technicolor and resumed its normal speed. I didn't want her to think that her threats on my life had shaken my resolve to thwart the Cult. But, in truth, for a moment, I wished I'd never set in motion this train wreck of events. But now that I was on the track, I could see no destination where I abandoned Sagar to the intrigues of either of these rival factions.

# CHAPTER 24

Exiting the seaside bus stop in Villefranche, I cut through *Rue Obscure*, an alley that transported pedestrians into the Renaissance. A sloping path led up worn and warped stone steps to the ancient town laundry fountain. The crumbling cement basin, stained blue, reminded passersby of a time when the more mundane activities of life, now left to machines, dictated the center of society. My hypersensitive nose still picked up a faint reek of lye.

Villefranche wound up from sea level to the cliffs of the coastline in a series of switchbacks. By the time I had hiked the stairs from the laundry to the street, reached the center of town, and then climbed the stairway up to our rental, my lungs were pumping at a decent pace. Part of that may have been residual indignation at Gwen's threats aggravated by my fear for Sagar. My missed lunch, probably mingled with the smell of lye and the chemical reactions of overexertion and worry, was threatening to revenge itself in a drift.

The words Gwen had thrown at my back stewed in my subconscious. She could "find" the Druids. Although the police might need a few days before they finally traced my whereabouts, the Gleaner had her own means of hunting Sagar down. Sagar and I needed to find the blue-eyed boy of my drifts—and soon. We had to leave the apartment right away but, without knowing the details of how Gwen's sight worked, it was impossible to formulate a plan to hide from it.

The large sky-blue door creaked mournfully every time I bothered the hinges. The apartment building had clearly been a single home at one time. A grand staircase spiraled up above the black and white tiles to the apartments carved out of the upper floors.

Clinging to the wrought iron railing, an elderly resident from the apartment above hobbled down the stairway that led to the mailboxes below. We exchanged nods. My key rattled in the century-old lock before the tumblers consented, reluctantly, to slide.

A roaring rush greeted me as the door groaned open. The sound struck a chord of familiarity. From the doorway, I could only see the small, make-shift dining area carved from the hallway and the far end of the family room. I dropped my packages and rushed around the corner into the open space of the family room and kitchen.

In the center of the room, a rift like the one I had seen in Barry's office gaped open. "Sagar!"

"Where is he?" Mercedes man shouted over the roaring wind. His accent was Italian. No surprise there. He had the thin build, attention to fashion detail, and shoes. But his features were Arabic.

My second thought was that the new stun gun I'd just bought was still in a box in the plastic bag I'd dropped by the door. I turned to run, knowing why Sagar had refused to promise to stay inside that morning. My hope was he was long gone.

Mercedes man was across the small apartment in seconds. My hand was tugging on the reluctant doorknob when he slung his arm around my neck and dragged me back to the living room. "I don't know where he is!" That was, for the most part, true. My best guess was that he had headed straight for *Rue Obscure* where we had planned to meet should we get separated. "He was supposed to be here. I told him not to go out."

Yanking on my neck, he hissed in my ear. "He's hiding. The Gleaner saw him here. Call him! Make him come out."

"Sagar!" I rasped. The Rifter loosened his grip on my neck to allow me more air. "Sagar! If you're still here, run! Get out now!" Profiting from the leeway, I dropped my chin, stepped into the crook of his elbow, and then swung my right fist back into his groin—exactly the way my self-defense teacher showed us.

Grunting, my attacker doubled over and I jabbed my elbow up into his face. My target was his nose, but my technique proved a bit rough, and I smacked his left cheek instead. Apparently, he relied too heavily on the element of surprise. He was built more to model the latest fashion than to brawl in the streets. He lost his grip, and I scrambled for the door. The lilac rug covering the slick wood floor in front of the dining table folded and bunched beneath my feet. I stumbled.

Groaning, the Rifter hauled himself after me as I caught my balance. He sprang and tackled me to the floor. My head rapped the edge of a metal dining chair between the living room and the entry as we toppled over. The world expanded, shivered, and then bloated into an airy vision. Another chair fell over the top of the Mercedes man. As he extracted himself, I powered through the throbbing in my temples, pulled my foot free, and slammed it in his face.

A stream of blood trickled down my cheek as I scrambled up and to the door, scooping my bags on the way.

"Join the Cult or die!" the Rifter bellowed. "Give us the boy!"

"I'd rather die." It was the right thing to say, but I didn't really understand the consequences until I yanked at the doorknob and the thundering crack of gunfire accompanied the shattering of the wood on the doorframe. *O, my Goddess! He's shooting at me! I just don't learn. I am a fool.*

Yanking the door open, I fled, pulling it shut behind me. In the front entryway, I hesitated while the Rifter wrestled with the knob inside my apartment. The exterior door required a good shove. The air outside was clear and the intermittent zoom of cars from the street below replaced the roaring torrent echoing in the building. My feet hit the stairs running.

An archway marked the entrance from the street into the alley stairwell. I grabbed the pillar to steady myself as I turned onto the foot-wide sidewalk. Another shot rang out from above, and the plaster just above my head exploded and sprayed dust into my red hair.

Rather than heading directly for the *rendezvous* point Sagar and I had settled on, I sped down the street away from it. If the Rifter followed me, I didn't want to lead him to the boy. After a few blocks, in front of the second bakery and across from the bar, I realized he wasn't following me. That was when I first wondered if the Rifter experienced some type of negative consequences from not returning through the hole he'd torn. At Barry's office, he seemed highly reluctant to let it close on him. Perhaps he experienced time and space restraints.

I kept walking a few more blocks, not seeing anyone, but unable to shake the feeling that I was being followed. Once or twice, I glanced back, positive I felt the presence of someone just behind me. Just to be safe, I stopped in a café and ordered a coffee to stave off the tell-tale signs of the drift I felt coming on. If I'd known it was my last chance to eat for the day, I wouldn't have abandoned my salad in Nice.

The man behind the counter wore thick-rimmed glasses, and his nose was straight out of a French caricature. The large chef's knife he was using to chop whatever was hidden behind the counter flashed intermittently in the sun streaming in from the upper row of windows. The chopping halted abruptly when I spoke. The stocky, barrel-chested hulk nodded, wiped the knife on his comically diminutive white apron, and squinted down at me. A drying trace of blood had trickled from my temple to my chin. Without a word, the man took a smooth, cloth napkin, dampened it in the bar tap, and handed it to me.

"*Euh…il y a un W.C.?*" My real reason for coming into the café was to unpack my stun gun in private. The barista jerked his head toward a small hallway on the left. The hour was odd, so the café was empty except for a mature couple speaking German at a table near the window. They paid no attention as I walked by, dabbing at the dried blood and wincing. The wound was a little swollen and tender.

The W.C. was nothing more than a closet at the bottom of a narrow stairwell. The door rubbed against the frame as I tugged. Once it had cleared the jam, it flew open so fast that the residual force unbalanced me.

"*Salut*, Ivy."

# CHAPTER 25

My hand flew to my chest as I jumped and caught my breath. When I spotted Sagar huddled in a little ball next to the sink, I exhaled noisily. "Goddess, kidlet, you scared me! What are you doing here?" The ludicrousness of the question occurred to both of us at the same time. Of course, he was here because he'd already seen the possibilities of what could happen and had chosen this as the most likely. What if he'd been wrong?

Looking both ways first, unable to shake the feeling I'd been followed, I stepped into the closet and closed the door behind me. "I brought you some clothes." The contents of the bag tumbled to the floor and, as he slipped them on, I unboxed my stun gun. Once he'd finished dressing, I nodded, quite pleased with the final product. The sandals with back straps were a good choice, considering there was a good chance we'd be running—often.

Sagar stood on his tiptoes to try and see himself in the mirror, but only the collar of the shirt appeared along the bottom edge. He jumped a little to try and see more.

"Here, kidlet." Grinning at this contradiction of small boy and old wise man that had wormed its way into my heart, I wrapped my arms around his waist and lifted him to stand on the ledge of the sink. His eyes popped open and then his smile lit the somber little closet as he admired his new western look.

"I like them, Ivy!" Pivoting he jumped into my arms. I have to say that, when Sagar threw his arms around my neck and laid his head on my shoulder, he stopped being a responsibility, a pawn in a power struggle, or a wonder of nature, and for a few seconds, he was a little boy full of affection who needed hugs. My arms tightened around his waist.

When he'd had his fill, he leaned back and grinned. "I love you, Ivy. Thank you for saving me, even though it wasn't the best game for you. I didn't really want to go with Gwen." His smile faded into concern. "The Cult is your enemy now, you know?"

I nodded. "So, you know Gwen?"

He nodded.

"She crashed my table when I stopped for lunch. I think it was just a diversion. The man who rips holes in the air came to the apartment. Do you know him too?"

The boy cinched the buckles on his sandals a bit tighter. "Yes, I know him. I saw him, too, in my games last night. His name is Sayid." That piece of information was a relief. Now I didn't have to call him the Rifter or Mercedes Man anymore—although, I was a bit partial to Mercedes Man. "My father knows them all. That's his job. He tracks them and studies their psycho-genetic anomalies. The Guild hopes to engineer these gifts."

"So…your father, does he know me, too? Has he been tracking me?"

"Yes." Bored with our conversation, or avoiding more of it, Sagar cracked the door open and peeked out. "We have to go. Now. It's bad but not as bad as when we wait. You might need your stun gun."

*Shit.* Rarely is it better to know impending drama in advance. For me, disaster is more of a destination trip than an enjoy-the-journey affair. Good luck never needs advanced notice.

At the top of the stairs, the waiter nodded toward one of the tables. "Le café, Mademoiselle."

I grimaced apologetically at Sagar and walked toward the cup, wondering if he had foreseen the coffee break. I really needed a shot of caffeine before the toxic mixture of adrenaline and acid rumbling around in my empty stomach erupted into a drift. The boy followed as if all were going according to plan. Without sitting down, I sipped as ravenously as the temperature allowed. Sagar tugged on my shirt. "C'mon!" He grabbed my hand and pulled me away. "We should go now. It might already be too late."

Coffee sloshed onto the floor as Sagar dragged me to the door. Gulping down one more swig, I dug out five euros and dropped them with the cup on a table.

"C'mon, Ivy! Run!" We ran up the thin sidewalk. At the corner, we risked the oncoming traffic to cross the street. It was no coincidence that a police car rolled up as we jumped onto the curb. The older man who lived upstairs from my apartment would most certainly have reported the shots fired there less than a quarter of an hour ago.

The city was looking for an American girl who had abducted a small Indian boy, so, despite my new hairstyle, we were bound to grab the attention of the officer. In an attempt to avoid suspicion, I reigned Sagar into a stroll but to no avail. The siren wailed through the narrow street, and we sprinted away.

"This way!" Our only hope was to reach the winding cobblestone pedestrian streets that wandered through the old city and down to the beach. There might be enough people there in the late afternoon that we could simply blend in or hide.

The sudden silence of the siren told me the policeman must have veered into the parking lot at the top of the hill to follow us on foot. I heard the muffled "*Arrêtez*!" as the faint smell of lye accosted my nose. We rushed past the city laundry and down the stone steps.

At the bottom of the street, the post office lay behind a breakfast café. The street that descended into the pedestrian district ran past the post. "C'mon, Sagar." We ducked behind a yellow mail truck and waited to see which direction the police officer would pursue.

"He's already called for help," Sagar informed me.

"Let's just see which way he goes, and then we'll go the other."

The policeman disappeared up the road past the café.

Sagar's hand snuggly in mine, I trailed him toward the parking lot and the steps to the old city. We had reached the cobblestone street at the bottom when a whistle from the top alerted us that the policeman had doubled back and found our trail. "*Arrêtez*!"

# CHAPTER 26

Sagar and I twisted and turned through the alleys and old stone shops. The crooked cobblestone tripped us up every few yards. Past *Rue Obscure*, we ducked into what must have been an old tunnel for water deliveries before the sea receded. Boxes, crates, and refuse from the restaurant that now inhabited this spot camouflaged the entrance. A smudged and scrawny half-dozen homeless wanderers fished through the garbage for scraps.

Our breath rushed through our noses as we crouched in the narrow archway. I practically felt Sagar's heart pumping at my shoulder. I'd been arrested once before, and the thought that I might end up at the police station again had crossed my mind while I sat in Ms. Miller's office with Amr and the brownies. But kidnapping is a serious crime, and this time, I had no way to contact Barry.

A boy, hair rumpled and matted, face emaciated, stopped sorting through the refuse to watch us with hawkish eyes. His free hand clung to the boney fingers of a man that could only be his father. The man stood still, his vacant eyes fixed on the sign above the restaurant's back entrance. The father had clearly suffered some brain trauma. A dent curved the side of his skull. The boy wouldn't stop staring at us and I wondered if he was desperate enough to try to sell us out to the policeman for something to eat.

My imagination ran rampant, trying to create a picture of what it would be like to be thrown into a French prison. As far as the police knew, I kidnapped Sagar. I imagined that, to save him, they wouldn't hesitate to shoot me. I hadn't prepared for this turn of events at all. When I imagined my daring rescue, I simply jumped in, pulled the drowning boy from the abyss, and then simply resumed my search for the blue-eyed boy.

Idiot. I should have known that one circumstance couldn't change independently. The pond would always ripple.

My heart sputtered and then briefly stopped before stampeding forward double-time at the sound of footsteps approaching rapidly. The steps stopped at the arch that led into the alley where we were hiding. We huddled behind trash and scavengers. The policeman asked if anyone had seen a red-headed girl and a small Indian boy. I gripped my stun gun. Goddess! What was the sentence for assaulting an officer?

"*Non, je n'ai rien vu.*" Always the same answer, the person had seen nothing. Scooting forward, I risked a peek through the cracks between the boxes and crates. The boy watched the officer who accosted a woman in a tattered and stained blue t-shirt and a skirt made from a tied-up long coat. The street urchin scratched his chin and then turned to meet my eyes, a frown creasing his brow. He glanced up at his father's lifeless stare.

The officer stepped up and shoved the boy's dad. The man tipped but didn't respond. The officer snorted in disgust. "*Eh, le gamin! T'as vu une rousse avec un p'tit garçon?*" My heart stopped while the boy's crinkled eyes glowered up at the policeman. He said nothing and ducked his head back into the refuse box. Sighing, the officer looked both directions and then trotted down the alley that ran parallel to the shoreline.

Sagar and I emerged from our hole in the wall. As I passed the boy, I dug in my pocket for the bills left over from my shopping outing and stuffed them into his grime-crusted hand. His mouth dropped open in confusion. I glanced up at his father. "*Désolée et merci.*" Squeezing Sagar's hand, I tiptoed out of the alley, wishing I could save more than one kid at a time.

We turned right at the archway and emerged onto the coast road. I scanned our options, looking for cover and the most population. To the right, the street turned sharply into the switchbacks that led up to the village square. Before crossing to mingle with the tourists heading to the beach, I caught sight of a silver Mercedes as it rounded the corner. The driver was unmistakably Sayid.

"Sagar!" I jerked his hand and retreated into the tourist shop behind us. Pretending to browse the variety of t-shirts, bags, and sweatshirts stamped Côte d'Azur, I watched out the window, waiting for the car to pass. Instead, Sayid parked in an open spot at the far point of the crescent beach. Once out of the car, he hustled toward the shop where we were hiding. I glanced in the other direction up the street. The policeman was searching the restaurants and boutiques, making his way toward the shop from that direction.

The symptoms of a drift threatened to gum up my thinking. My vision stuttered, and my fingers tingled. Rubbing my temples, I scouted the possibilities for escape. The café on the corner across the street to our left offered seaside seating. The waiters crossed the road routinely, carrying wine and cheese plates to tourists willing to pay for the luxury.

Almost directly across the street from us, where a shoreline hotel cut off the strip of seaside seating, a short docking pier jetted out from the shore into the bay. A small white and blue sailboat glistened and bobbed under the gentle pounding of the Mediterranean sun. A young man in his early twenties was attaching the boat to the cleats on the docking pier.

Normally, time swirled in skewed lines through my life. In that second, her vast undulations righted themselves and stood at attention. The blue-eyed boy who had been guiding my drifts for two decades stood and stared, unseeing, right into my eyes. I'd have known him anywhere. The sun, no doubt, obscured his view into the shop, but I, from the inside, devoured every detail of his face.

Nearly entranced by this casually random meeting with my destiny, I reached for Sagar and wandered, practically spellbound, toward the door. He trotted obediently behind.

"It's him, Sagar. The boy from my drifts is on that boat." I pointed out the window.

Sagar squinted and bit his lip. "Are you certain you want to meet him, Ivy?"

*Why would he ask me that*? I should have stopped for a moment to consider the question, but the enormity of touching such a key piece of my future drew me like gravity.

A saleswoman brushed aside the crush of indignant customers between the cash register and the door. Reading glasses dangled around her mature neck as she approached in automated, marionette movements. “Join us or die! Give us the boy!” she cried. Scissors poised in her fist, the woman’s coated eyes met mine.

“Run, Ivy. It’s a Jumper. They can jump into anyone.”

Ducking, I shoved Sagar toward the crowd of confused and protesting customers near the door. “Go!” I shouted. The saleswoman, clearly possessed, stabbed at my head as I ducked and dodged, digging for the stun gun in my pocket. Most of the customers cried out and mobbed the exit, alarmed. A couple of crew-cut guys stayed behind, alert, looking as if they wanted to play the hero.

As I pulled out my stun gun, the woman grabbed me by the hair and dragged me past hanging shirts. They clattered off their hangers and crumpled to the floor as I grabbed at them. A rack toppled over between us. My short hair ripped from her grasp. As I scrambled to my feet, stun gun flailing, she turned and stabbed again. “Join us or die!”

Shouting, the two hovering tourists jumped in. One guy slapped my wrist and dislodged the stun gun. It clattered across the stone floor, and he went after it. The other guy grabbed the chain around the saleswoman’s neck just in time to deflect her blow. The point of the shears glanced off my arm and penetrated a stack of pink t-shirts with a dull thud. The lesion near my shoulder sprouted blood drops.

Sagar was trapped behind the alarmed horde fleeing the scuffle. The shopkeeper grappled with the good Samaritan. From the floor, I swept my right leg into hers and toppled her over into the tourist. As they fell, a blue mist abandoned her body to the crash. Sagar and I wasted no time sifting out the door with the other shoppers who flagged down the policeman and frantically pointed toward the shop.

Hesitating only a moment to let a car pass, I glanced right and locked eyes with Sayid. His hand moved to the inside of his jacket. Grabbing Sagar, I sprinted across the street.

Our sandals clomped against the weathered and chipped pier. The boy glanced up, straddling the boat and the dock. His eyes met mine. “Can I help you?” The accent was slightly French but flaunted a significant amount of American exposure.

“Of course, you can. You’re the reason I’m here. You told me to come and save him.” I nodded at Sagar. “Now you have to help us.”

Instinctively, he recoiled from the absurdity of my claim. His eyes narrowed as he studied Sagar’s face. “I know this boy. You’re the girl that kidnapped him.”

I glanced over my shoulder, Sayid was heading for the dock. My drift boy glanced between us, summing up the situation.

“I don’t have much time. I didn’t kidnap him. He *wanted* to come with me.” I glanced back again. “Please.” I pushed Sagar toward him. Sayid’s foot hit the dock. The young man reached for Sagar and lifted him into the boat. “Hurry! Please! They’re trying to kill him.” The boat bobbed and a strip of water gaped open between the starboard and the wood. I held out my arm, looking for the steadying balance of the blue-eyed boy’s hand before braving the widening gap.

“No, mademoiselle, you are mistaken. We’re not trying to kill the boy. We’re trying to kill you, but I suppose we won’t have to, now that you have been so obliging as to bring him to us.”

My shock bound me open-mouthed. Sayid closed the gap between us. The last thing I saw was the descending butt of his gun.

# CHAPTER 27

Apparently, meddling with the present had not changed some bits of my future. My eyes struggled to open and a headache pounded, not as much in the usual spot behind my right eye, but at the back of my skull. The light pouring in from the window directly in front of my face repelled my eyes. To open them, I had to block it with my hands. My fingers wandered around my skull to investigate the source of the throbbing and found sticky, drying blood. The motion of the car rushing past small French shops matched the flowing flood of memories as they rolled back into my consciousness and I gasped. At least now I knew why the hell I got into the car with a man carrying a gun who was going to backhand me. I wondered how long I'd been out.

"This is your own fault." The Mercedes man, Sayid, looked disdainfully down upon my suffering. "You kick against the pricks. The Word pronounces the will of God, and the Hand carries it out. We must all bend our will to the will of the Word. Only then can we be found worthy."

"Worthy of what?" Righting myself in the stiff leather seats of the Mercedes required a fair amount of effort and groaning. "Your god is not my god. Your god is a tyrant."

"There is only one God. He is merciful and seeks only the happiness of His children."

"Is that why he orders the murder of innocent boys?" My stomach growled against the churning acid, irritated by the motion of the vehicle. The tips of my fingers and the right side of my mouth began to tingle.

"The wickedness and disobedience of the fathers must be visited upon the children."

"Yeah, well, I guess I was wrong then. Your god isn't just a tyrant, he's also a murderous son of a bitch." My eyelid twitched. In the center of my vision, a small opaque prism formed. When I closed my eyes, colors danced inside the growing prism. It was coming. Not even a blow to the head would change the course of this wild, tumultuous river that ran through my consciousness. "The goddess I serve isn't a psychopath."

"You only serve yourself. Your vision is narrow."

"Believe me, I see a whole lot more than you know. Besides, you don't know anything about me or whom I serve." I glanced at the console between the seats and then the profile of my chauffeur. A nasty red welt burned on Sayid's cheek. "Compassion is my goddess."

Sayid's cell phone played out some religious tune I vaguely recognized. He reached into his pocket. "This is Sayid." He listened. "I will wait for His Holiness." On hold, he finished our conversation. "To prepare the field for planting, the stones must be dug up, and the withered, fruitless trees uprooted. You will see that the Word's compassion for all sometimes requires the sacrifice of the unyielding. You will see, Seer, or you…"

I was gone before he finished.

*Second 1: Running, frantic, hand locked in the grip of an accomplice. Stumbling. Dark uneven slate stone. Pews in tight rows. Ornate altars. Ancient faded tapestries camouflage the soot-stained walls in red. A church. A large one. Torrential wind.*

*Second 2: Hand belongs to the boy, the Traveler. I have learned better than to follow his lead. Halting abruptly, I yank my hand from his. "Oh, my God! Not now, Ivy. Not now."*

*Second 3: He seizes my hand, and I struggle against the touch of the snake that bit me, shoving him away.*

*Second 4: "We have to run. Trust me."*

*Second 5: "Trust you?"*

*Second 6: "You're trying to help me. I'll show you…"*

*Second 7: A shot from behind explodes in the already pox-marked stone of the pillar, three inches from my head.*

And then I was back in the Mercedes. Disorientation rocked me. When Mercedes Man slapped me, I was supposed to be passed out while my AP Chem self dropped in for a visit. Instead, I flashed forward. The blow to the head on the dock must have aggravated my drifts.

The side of my face stung and throbbed. My fingers gently explored a welt welling up next to my eye. The visor, a hole where the mirror should be, was down. Sayid was readjusting his rearview mirror. We'd be at the destination in five minutes—unless my meddling had altered that part of the drift as well.

The yellow stone towers of the *Palais des Archevêques* loomed above the cobblestoned city square. Behind them, the smoky, grey spires of the *Cathédrale de St. Just et St. Pasteur* poked at the sky. Beneath the palace, the mouth of an underground garage swallowed up the Mercedes. The metal door clanged shut behind us, swallowing the car in shadow.

"Where are we going?"

"Where the Word has commanded."

Reliving visions of myself dying strapped to a medical chair, I glanced at the door handle. I thought I could outrun Sayid. He had a gun, but a couple of metal exit doors and an elevator broke up the cement wall. We pulled up to a stairway. The parking garage was new. It was small and offered few hiding spots, definitely not a commercial venture.

Before Sayid killed the engine, I grabbed the door handle and pulled. Nothing happened. I slapped my palm against the window.

Sayid scoffed and shook his head. "The foolishness of the unyielding." He slid out of the car but stopped to chastise me, "If you will not bend your will to the Word's, you must be compelled." Flicking the door shut behind him, he strutted around to the trunk, which popped open at a beep from his key remote, blocking the rear window. I scrambled over the console into the driver's seat, yanked on the handle, and jumped out as it opened.

The nearest exit marked with a picture of stairs beckoned me. I sprinted past the only other car in the garage.

"*Merde! Salope!*" The words pinged and echoed about the walls.

Shoving my weight against the bar handle, I rammed the door. Locked. *Merde!* The slow and steady slap of Sayid's designer leather soles against the cement floor stalked me. He wasn't even running. He shook his head at my incorrigible refusal to go along quietly as he doused a white cloth from a bottle he'd retrieved from the trunk.

The bottle and the cloth unnerved me. That he felt no compulsion to even stop me from reaching the door killed my hope. The adrenaline doubled, and I dashed, heart pounding, to the elevator kitty-corner to the exit. No buttons. Keycard only. *Merde!*

I swung my body around, ready to fight back. My face met the cloth doused in chloroform. As I struggled to rip his palm from my nose and mouth, a wet heavy blanket shrouded my consciousness. My knees buckled and the cold cement of the floor met my face.

*A firework display of the future erupts in slow motion in the blackness. For a fraction of a second, I'm standing at an altar in a dusty grey cathedral, pulling a gun from my pocket. Space tugs at my consciousness and I find myself running, hand in hand with Amr on a sidewalk downtown. The image slants into static. The boy from my drifts throws himself in front of my chest as the crack of a gun shatters the scene. Flowing red robes, strangers, surgical lights, cloudless blue skies, eddies lapping at the shore. Amr. Sagar, draped in an orange robe, reaches for me. My lips press passionately upon the lips of the boy who has just betrayed me. Visions parade across the darkness in a soupy cascade of images. The mouth of the boy pronounces the number 521, and I plunge into still darkness.*

# CHAPTER 28

French words penetrated the seal of oblivion.

"*Ivy, réveille-toi, mademoiselle.*" The accent was vaguely Indian, the hand gently prodding my shoulder, a rich, deep brown.

"*Imbécile!*" Cold anger in a French voice railed at Sayid's cowering grey silhouette in the corner. My head strained to put a face to it.

A splash of red coalesced into an ample robe topped with a collar of white. From the collar protruded a rounded, olive-hued head, outlined in a fringe of non-descript brown hair. The tall man looked to be in his sixties, maybe late. His stark cheekbones spoke an austere self-denial and his hook nose—protruding from sharp, beady eyes—a hawk-like business acumen. The etched lines between his brows and around his mouth appeared to have been sculpted by years of suspicious disdain for the grasping hordes surrounding him.

In its muddled state, my mind had trouble interpreting the scenery and the language at the same time. Apparently, the man in the red robe was berating Sayid for his careless use of an anesthetic on one of "God's vessels." Even in my impaired condition, a shudder rattled my spine at the term that so objectified my existence. The worst human atrocities all began with the objectification of another being. The robed man's concern for me sprouted from a sense of proprietorship over my psychotic phenomenon rather than from a fear of violating my human rights.

Although Sayid stood in a corner of the room, head bowed in humble subjugation, his Italian suit struck a stark contrast to the aged, yellow stone of the walls. At intervals, rusted chains bolted into the blocks hung as decorations. Presumably, I was in a renovated section of the donjon inside the Palace of the Archbishop. Yet, as the fog faded from my brain and the room came into focus, the modern medical furnishings surrounding the antique wooden bed startled me.

Just as I was thinking *Shit! I'm in a hospital bed in the year of short, red hair, long bangs,* the Indian man, who wore a white doctor's jacket and seemed to be monitoring the machinery, turned to reassure the man in the red robe.

"Cardinal Aycelin, the young woman appears to be recovering…"

The sensor patches and wires attached to my head, as well as the IV in my arm, hampered my sudden bolt to flee the bed. Although barefoot, I was still wearing my capris and t-shirt and had every intention of fighting my way out of the room. Throwing back the white blankets and sitting up as the doctor moved to crush my rebellion, I focused on the man in red, who seemed to be in charge, and demanded, "Where's the little boy? What did you do with Sagar?"

Sayid stepped abruptly forward and slapped my cheek with the force of all the suppressed anger he'd stored during his chastisement. "You must speak with reverence to the Hand of the Word."

Shocked and nauseated from my sudden upward jolt and the slap, I covered my mouth as the world spun and black crept into the edges of my vision. The chaotic, anesthetic-induced drifting had taken a sharp toll on my brain functions.

The doctor pushed Sayid firmly back to the wall and then fetched a kidney-shaped plastic bowl into which I promptly vomited the last churned bits of my breakfast: two sips of coffee diluted in a fair amount of stomach acid.

Turning to Cardinal Aycelin, the doctor nodded toward the monitor tracking my neural impulses. "The young lady has suffered substantial neurological trauma. She must rest undisturbed before any further steps can be taken."

*Steps? What steps?*

He strolled to a tray neatly lined with medical paraphernalia and selected a syringe and a small bottle of liquid. Flicking the tube he had just filled, he educated the other two men in the room. "These subjects are highly susceptible to any form of medication. Even the most commonly used pharmaceuticals often result in catastrophic alteration or weakening of the asset's abilities."

Subject. Asset. Even the doctor, whom I, at first, thought might be caring and kind, saw me as no more than a medical curiosity, a rare specimen to be handled with care. Wielding the syringe, he approached the IV and I tugged at the white cotton blanket to free my arms and legs. "No, get away from me! Please…" My lungs couldn't quite round up enough air to produce the words. This was new. My normal drifts had never affected my pulmonary system.

"Don't worry, Mlle Leif." The doctor took possession of the valve on the IV tube. "For this particular anesthetic—unlike the one so carelessly administered earlier," he cast an icy stare at Sayid, "—testing has produced peaceful repose in 98% of subjects experiencing your psychological phenomenon with virtually no side effects. The recovery is almost instantaneous. Only assets who manifest more kinetic capabilities seem to suffer any negative response to the drug."

*Oh, Goddess! Testing?* A tremor rattled through the nausea and intense headache. I grasped his arm and held it at bay as he tried to insert the needle into the receptor on the IV tube.

Speaking was still a chore. The words and the ideas seemed muddled and the sounds coming from my mouth didn't quite match with the pictures in my head. The air in my lungs ran dry, forcing me to pause and suck up more. The after-effects of the cinematic drifting lingered much longer than those of a natural drift. Frustrated with my impotence, I yanked my arm and kicked over the IV stand. I had to get out, not just for me but for Sagar. I'd handed him over to these ruthless cultists. The rebound effect rocked my guts. I pressed one hand against the throbbing in my head while holding my stomach with the other. In my delirium, the words in my head spilled out my mouth as if speaking his name might rally my resolve. "Sagar! I have to…" I gasped, desperately.

Sayid stepped in, smashing his palm against my face to force my head to the pillow and then clamping down my arm while the doctor righted the metal stand and readjusted the tubing. My struggles came to nothing as a cool stream flowed in my veins. Then the burn set in and my hand felt as if it were on fire and finally as if a burning weight were crushing the muscles. My face scrunched up in pain and a moan escaped my lungs. “Goddess, that hurts!”

“The pain lasts only seconds. Rest.” A soothing hand on my forehead, the doctor leaned over my body. I curled around the lightning burn spreading through my hand. He whispered into my ear. “Do not worry about Sagar. I am his father, Aarav Singh. Thank…”

The doctor was right. I didn’t even register the onset of the darkness.

# CHAPTER 29

One minute I was asleep, the next awake—no nausea, no head pounding, no spinning. Whatever the drug was, or whatever the inhumane methods used to develop it, it certainly delivered sleep with no side effects. Only Dr. Singh's last chilling words lingered in my memory. The Cult had Sagar's father.

The rolling tray displaying a neat array of syringes and scalpels had disappeared. Two small closets occupied the wall adjacent to the bed: a WC and a bathroom with a free-standing tub and a sink. A roll-away stainless-steel cabinet lined the opposite wall. In the corner near the door stood a high-backed wooden chair from the same period as the bed. Everything medical seemed designed for mobility. Tiny bulbs embedded in the foot of the walls cast sickly streams of light across the stone floor. Without them, the room would have been a dark cell with no windows. The arched door itself fit the period of the Inquisition: thick, knotty wood, reinforced with sturdy, iron hinges that extended decoratively across the wooden slats in a fleur-de-lis and spearhead pattern. The handles matched the nostalgic rings and chains dangling from the wall.

Throwing off the blanket, I ripped the IV tape off my hand. The queasy shrinking of my stomach as I slowly extracted the needle reminded me I hadn't eaten for a while. A ball of blood welled up. Rummaging in the cabinet, I found cotton balls and tape and bandaged up the hole.

Hunger rumbled in my stomach, heralding another drift. Since I had no memory of this place, at least no conscious memory, I assumed it would be outgoing—but at this point, who knew? All the rules had changed. Before I found a safe place to black out, I tried the door. Not that I imagined it would be unlocked, just that it would be ridiculously stupid if it *were* open and I didn't bother to try it. Now that they had Sagar and his father, I had to be superfluous. That could be good—or really bad. The metal grated and shifted as I turned the knob, but the door refused to budge.

Sighing, I ran my fingers through my hair and wandered back to sit cross-legged on the bed. Sagar was with his father, but he was the hostage Cardinal Aycelin was using to keep Dr. Singh in line. All I had ever wanted was to keep Sagar safe until I could return him to his parents, alive and well. He was alive, but I wasn't sure if he was well.

If I was completely honest with myself, though, I was not just anxious for his safety, I felt a sense of loss. I'd been an only child all my life. In the short amount of time I'd spent with Sagar, I'd grown attached. Perhaps some of that was due to the bond of Druid blood we shared, but mostly it was that he'd found an empty little pothole in my heart and curled up inside it. Frankly, I missed the feel of his miniature hand in mine—not to mention the conversations with a kindred spirit who walked in my world. I'd never really experienced that before. Now that I had, I knew what I'd been missing.

My fingers began to tingle to the gurgling in my stomach. Sensation buzzed slowly out of my lips. Before I could decide what to do about Sagar, my priority, I supposed, was getting out of this *donjon* and in touch with Barry. The kidnapping situation needed cleaning up—a task way above my pay grade—and I had no idea how to begin extracting Sagar from the intrigues of the Cult and Guild without help. I didn't even know where they were keeping him.

Steps in the corridor outside prompted me to take cover behind the door, an amateur move, but hey, I was working with what was available to me. Since the massive door opened inward, it offered the best substitute for a weapon. I missed my stun gun.

The footsteps stopped outside. My heart pounded in time with a growing throbbing in my head. A key rattled in the lock. The sun-starved stone chilled my back and my bare feet, but my palms felt clammy. The locks gave way with a grumpy clank. I perched on my toes, ready to slam the bulky door back in the face of my unwary guest.

The door swung open, admitting a draft of cool, dank air. In the narrow gap between the lit floor and the bottom of the door, the shadow of one foot crossed the threshold and then a second. Breathing deeply, I sprang, shoving my weight against the sturdy planks. The door flew back with a nasty thud, a groan, the clanging of metal on stone, and the shattering of pottery. Broadsided by the weight of the door, the visitor plowed backward into the frame.

Without wasting a second, I pulled the door open again and tugged on the shirt of the shadowed figure, dragging him into the room. He slipped on smattered food and fell to his knees as I fled. The stone hallway was empty and a vaguely lit opening at the end beckoned me. I hadn't even passed the next doorway down when the spinning prisms in my vision turned to shooting lights and the world went black.

*Second 1: Small, cement and stone structure. Warped and weathered beams crisscross the ceiling. Ticking and chiming. Antique clocks disassembled on the workbench. Warped stairway leads to upper floor, old clocks, and light.*

*Second 2: "Ivy, you're drifting, right? This is the first time I've done this."*

*Second 3: The Traveler again! "You snake!" I shove him away. My arms go right through and I stumble.*

*Second 4: "I'm sorry. I didn't know then what I know now. Please..."*

*Second 5: "...you have to trust me. The cell is monitored." He reaches out a hand.*

*Second 6: I don't take it. "Never again."*

*Second 7: "521, in my dreams..."*

The ceiling spun when I opened my eyes. The blood bludgeoned its way through the constricted vessels in my head. My stomach churned. The stone was cold against my cheek. A lump throbbed and grew on the back of my head where I must have hit the wall or the floor when I fell. Anonymous arms wedged themselves beneath my neck and knees, and suddenly, the ceiling moved closer. The jostling of being carried ignited the acids in my empty stomach until they spewed from my mouth onto my porter's chest.

Passing through the door to the cell that I'd just gone to a lot of trouble to vacate, my ride serpentined around the spilled food and broken pottery on the floor and deposited me, less than gently, onto the bed.

The Traveler stood in front of me, blood trickling from his nostril and a bruise threatening on his cheek. An acrid blotch of stomach fluid stained his shirt. He wiped the smear of blood with the back of his hand. "Well, that was fun. What should we do now?" Okay, it was funny and, in a rough sort of charming way, enough to make me want to laugh in the moment—almost.

My present had collided with my future before, but this was the first time that I'd come face to face with such a stark incongruity between what I had imagined based on my 7 seconds and the reality. My initial reaction at seeing the Traveler's face in the flesh was to crawl off the bed and, the moment the symptoms of my drift receded, top off his glass of pain with a sharp knee to his balls. My hate ran deeper than the betrayal of the day—it was the betrayal of a lifetime of confidence.

And yet, a minute earlier, in the drift in the hallway, I'd seen him apologizing, warning me, pleading with me to understand his ignorance and give him a chance. The boy that I knew so well begged me to forgive the stranger that wore his face. Impossible. I was a fool sometimes, but not this time.

Then again, the boy in my drift just told me himself that this was the first time he had traveled back in time to meet me in the future before it ever happened. As far as I knew, this was part of the plan. This was where it began.

My brain spun, even though the effects of the drift had mostly evaporated.

The world was winding down to a halt. "How about Hide and Seek? You're it." I slid off the bed to stare in his face. His eyes, I knew them so well—I'd seen my future in them so many times. It was hard to keep the rage burning. The memories of what might have been, or still might be, dispersed the heat of the fury like a cool breeze.

He smirked and I saw the boy I hated again. "It's not a prison."

"No, you're right." My glance traveled to the chains on the wall. "The last time I checked, it was a donjon."

"You're free to go." He stepped aside, opening a straight path to the door, and ushered me through with mock gallantry.

"Just like that? No strings attached? Back to the beach?"

He shrugged. "Might be a little tough getting there, seeing as you have no money, no shoes, and no friends to call. But, yeah, you're free to go."

Eyes narrowed suspiciously, I shoved past him, bumping his shoulder—well, really his bicep—he was a head taller.

He didn't flinch, turn around, or make a move to stop me. "But you won't want to, not when you know what's at stake."

I stopped and spun around just as he'd intended. "You really are a bastard, aren't you? It's Sagar, isn't it?" Not only had I hand-delivered that sweet little boy to the Cult, but, by falling into their grasp myself, I'd given them another opportunity to leverage his life to meet their ends.

"No. But Sagar is the reason I know that you'll stay. I have no idea why you helped him. But the fact that you did, without any ulterior motives, says something about your sense of compassion…even though you have the story all wrong. Sagar's father defected to the Cult. He can't stomach the new leadership of the Guild. The High Council of the Guild threatened his son. *They* sent the Gleaner."

"You mean Gwen? Oh, well, now you're just lying. The death bitch dropped in on my lunch threatening to kill me as well as Sagar if I didn't join 'the Word'. He flinched at the word "bitch," but seemed determined not to let me unnerve him. "How long have I been here, anyway?"

"A couple days."

"This 'Word,' he's your boss, right? Is that why he sent you here? To recruit me?"

"No, he sent me to bring your breakfast…" He waved at the coffee, croissants, and fruit splattered on the floor. Picking up the tray, he started blotting coffee with the napkin. "…and ask for your help. Gwen is trying to escape the Guild, too. You have no idea the risk she took to speak with you. She would never hurt Sagar. Her plan was to appear to have taken him, but then deliver him back to us and his father when we got her out. The Guild's high chancellor suggested sending a Reaper to kill him. She talked him out of it. Ivy, you could help us get Gwen, and others like her, out of the Guild."

According to Sagar and Barry, the Cult was no better than the Guild. Why would I risk retaliation by helping the Gleaner—or anyone—jump from one boiling pot to the other?

The smell of the coffee was actually getting to me. Given my failed escape attempt, I slightly regretted my preemptive assault. Strolling across the room, I picked up a croissant, brushed it off, and tore off a bite. I'd eaten worse. "What's a Reaper?"

"*La Mort. La Faucheuse.* In English, you call her the Grim Reaper. A Gleaner is much less dangerous. Her victims only fall into a coma. Her embrace traps them in the realm in-between, but she can always guide them back. With the Reaper, there is no return trip. Her victims are done in this reality."

I began gathering up the bits of coffee cup strewn across the stones. "Then why was Sagar frightened of her? He told me *the Cult* was sending a Gleaner to kill him and he didn't want to go with her."

Shrugging, he joined me. "How should I know? The kid is the only one who sees enough of the possibilities to make choices. Maybe he doesn't understand the difference between the in-between and death. What surprises me more is that he knew about Gwen's allegiance to the Word, although I guess it shouldn't—he sees multiple possibilities of the future. Only the Word, the Hand, and I know about her plan to defect. If Sagar knows, perhaps the Guild suspects. If they do, they'll kill her, as easily as they killed my mother…and your grandmother."

"Wait! What do you know about my grandmother? Who are you, anyway?"

"Me?" He stood, wiping his hands on his pants, and extended one hand. "Joshua Morgana. *Enchanté.*" I rolled my eyes, and yet I was infinitely glad to have reached, at last, the momentous occasion of finally learning his name. The circumstances were far less romantic than I had imagined, though, and I wasn't ready to shake hands. "Everyone calls me Josh. I'm nobody really."

"That's not totally true. You're a Traveler, Josh. You can visit the past."

He stopped, an orange quarter in mid-air. "How do you know that?"

"Sagar told me. Well, he guessed. He didn't actually know you, but his father, apparently, has the means of identifying and tracking Druids and he knew of your kind. Travelers, he called them. Does the Guild know I can see the future?"

"Yes. They infiltrate and maintain databases of all patients with neurological disorders. That's how they identify and track most of us."

Suddenly, I felt so undressed. "How do they do that? That type of medical information is protected." Most of the ruined breakfast was now stacked on the tray. I handed it to him and took a seat on the tall back chair.

My naïveté amused him. "That is the power of the Guild and how they found your grandmother. She was a legend in the Guild when they initiated me. She was a mentor to my mother even though your grandmother was a Traveler like me, only to the future."

"I call it 'drifting'."

"Our anomalies are not the same. Your present ends up in a physical manifestation of your future. Your grandmother's consciousness floated there, invisible. My mother was a seer, but not like you or your grandmother. She would see into the future of whomever she was touching. When she died, I traveled to the past to find out what happened. Thanks to the Word, I was able to defect from the Guild when I saw who murdered her. But the problem with Travelers is that the past is set. There was nothing I could do to stop her death and no one I could tell. No one can see or hear me when I travel to the past, not even other vessels."

That word! Vessel. How could he use that word to define us? I'd been alone for so long that considering myself part of an 'us' struck me oddly.

I brushed off the annoyance because what I desperately needed to know was if the Cult had sent him to infiltrate my drifts as part of an elaborate plan to bring about their coup, or if I was the one that actually sent him to relay messages from the future. I laughed, trying to sound disarming. It was okay but wouldn't have landed me a lead role. "You're invisible in the past. That's a little creepy. Have you ever spied on me?"

"I wouldn't say it was creepy. Your grandmother did the same, only into the future. Why would I have spied on you? I didn't even know you existed until the Word sent me to help Sayid rescue Sagar from you. I'm still trying to figure out why you just handed him to me. You said *I* told you to save him. Were you having some kind of neurological episode connected with your abilities?"

"No." Being the daughter of an alcoholic mother—not to mention a girl that had seizures that weren't really seizures—I'd had my share of practice with bold-faced lies, but this one posed some motivational challenges. "I was under a lot of stress. I mistook you for someone else." I twisted a short lock of red hair on my index finger and my stomach growled, attacking the morsel of croissant.

"Convenient for me." An annoyingly attractive grin curled the side of his lips. "How about we try this again? I'll fill the tray back up with a new breakfast, and you promise two things: not to leave yet—at least not until I've had a chance to talk you out of it—and not to kick the door in my face." The spot on his cheek had started to bruise. He tilted his head inquisitively, but only got an eye roll and a half nod in response. Apparently, that was enough. He turned to leave through the open door but stopped before he passed into the corridor. "Hey, Ivy? um…uh…" This was a side I had never seen but reminded me of the Josh I knew from the drift in which I was dying. He was vulnerable and pessimistically hopeful, a repentant hero. *Damn him*! "Have you ever seen me? You know, in the future?"

I didn't skip a beat. Living with my mother had modified lying from the art of acting to a survival strategy. Besides, in the future, Josh had pretty much warned me not to give anything away in this room. "I'm not like you. I can't wander about where I please. My present consciousness drifts into a consciousness of my future self. And this is the first time we've met." It was only a partial lie. The best lies are mostly truth.

He shrugged and nodded. "So, you've never seen me—in your future?" The wistful glance he let slip only churned up the ambivalence I was feeling.

Goddess, I wanted to trust him! I'd always imagined the two of us were meant to be together—somehow—such a perfect match to our skills. This was the curse of my existence, to crush on boys who were ideal matches for me, all except for one insurmountable roadblock.

The value of linking up with someone who could travel into my drifts in the past and guide my choices for the future was dazzling, but only if I could trust that person implicitly. Otherwise, the formula was a catalyst for catastrophe. "I make it a policy never to tell anyone about their future. Sometimes, for the sake of free-will, it's better not to know what's coming, don't you think?"

"Maybe. Then again, sometimes, it would be nice to know what's coming so you can make better choices." He stepped in the corridor.

"Wait, Josh!" Biting my thumbnail, I crossed the room to look him in the eye. "If only a few of the Cult know that Gwen plans to defect, and you are one of them, along with the Word and the Hand, does that make you…one of the leaders of the society?"

"No." He snorted as if the idea were too absurd to even imagine. "It makes me her twin."

# CHAPTER 30

It was a fair amount to digest. Not the breakfast—I was still waiting for that—the information that Josh—it was good to finally know his name—had just passed to me.

Although I was only an amateur at intrigue, I truly believed that I was the one who had sent him into my past to bring me here. If the Cult had sent him, and he was playing me, I was pretty confident I could smell it. My history with Amr had made me wary of the players and shown me the backstage view of all their moves.

The question was: why did I send him?

If he truly wanted me to help his sister, maybe I was destined to agree, for some compelling reason—although the fact that she was his twin was already tipping my hand. In that case, I may have sent him back to guide my steps toward the Cult, knowing that my instincts would repel me from it.

Since I'd thrown my lot in with Sagar, my memories of past drifts had transformed somehow. They presented themselves like dreams that seemed so real while I slept, but when I awoke were difficult to separate from reality. They lingered, occupying a less than tangible corner of my consciousness. I needed to make sense of the drift I'd just had. And then there was that number—521. My drift on the beach in Villefranche now floated in the realm of dreams remembered. Maybe I had never given that number to Josh when I met him there for the first time—in the flesh. Maybe now it was just a dream to him. I needed to make that a priority. But not here.

Looking around the room, I wondered where the cameras and bugs were. In that most recent drift, Josh warned me about talking in the cells. Perhaps I would put to the test his assurance that I was not a prisoner here.

The door was still a crack open when he came back, this time with breakfast for two. I met him on the threshold and he flinched defensively. Couldn't say I blamed him.

"So, you'll be joining me?

"Well, yes," he actually colored up a bit, "*ça va*?"

"Yeah, it's okay, but I consider it shameless to prey on my hunger to convert me."

"Just fulfilling my Christian mandate to feed the hungry." He grinned. He didn't strike me as the fanatically orthodox follower that his sister was.

"Right. So…since I'm not a prisoner, and this palace has some lovely gardens, how about you and I find a quiet little corner for breakfast? I need some fresh air."

His instinctive glance toward the ceiling told me the Josh of my drift was correct. In that case, even if the Josh in front of me was operating with the Cult, the Josh of my drift was not. Encouraging. Maybe.

Balancing the tray on one hand, he dug in his jeans and checked the time on his cell phone. "The gardens don't open to the public for another couple of hours…they might even be closed to prepare for the visit of the church dignitaries." He shrugged. "I don't see why we couldn't have a picnic."

He led me through the corridors and down the stairs of the donjon. We wound through the palace until we exited the building through a large, medieval double doorway into a gothic arched cloister that surrounded the gardens of the palace's inner courtyard. In the center, a large tree—a Yuca of sorts, or at least of the same family—sprouted from the round intersection of four symmetrical, gravel walks. The garden consisted of mostly grass. From the corridor beyond the door, a gardener, an immense man about double my size, lumbered into the cloister pushing an ancient, rust-splattered cart. An assortment of tools clattered together as he passed: clippers, spades, shovels, and rakes.

"Bonjour, Jérôme." Josh exchanged nods with the man.

Wielding pruning shears, the gardener began to manicure into perfect rectangles the hedges that lined the walks on the opposite end of the garden.

Josh and I took a seat on a stone step in a sun-drenched corner and I fairly dove into the food. When the empty gnawing in my gut had finally subsided, I took a sip of coffee. The warm roast aroma was not the only one I was savoring. For the first time in my life, I think I experienced the power of pheromones. I mean it had to be something chemical. Smells had always triggered my drifts, played a defining role in them even. It had to be the warm, musky smell of Josh that drew me to him, despite the disillusioning shock of our first, in the flesh, meeting.

"I like a girl who can eat." My mouth dropped open. Seriously? Just as I was warming up to him? It wasn't enough that he had betrayed my trust and kidnapped me, he was also going to body-shame me? "No, really. Frankly, I despise all these skinny French girls that nibble at their food like mice. Look at you, you're strong and healthy. You have curves." He nodded appreciatively until he realized he'd gotten a little too personal.

A tiny tilt may have played at the corner of my lips. Rather than show it, though, I plucked a grape from one of his clusters and popped it defiantly into my mouth. Better to keep him on the defensive. "Look, Josh, despite the fact that you're on the wrong team, you seem like a fairly decent guy—you have great taste in breakfast foods, by the way. But I have to tell you, I can't see any reason why I would want either one of us to take on the Guild in order to transfer your twin to the tyranny of the Cult."

"That's because you have no idea how evil the Guild has become. Look!" He pulled his cell phone out. "Don't ask how I got this video. It's from an installation in Marseille that belongs to the Guild. It operates under some phony genetic research front called *Génétique*." Inside, they really control and study the holy vessels."

"I wish you wouldn't call us that. We're people. Call us people. At least Sagar calls us Druids."

"The Cult prefers to call us, God's Holy Vessels. It's less pagan and outdated."

Leaning forward, I poked an accusing finger at his chest. "Less human, you mean. Empathy won't allow humans to inflict pain and suffering on another human being. First, the oppressors call us *vessels*, or *subjects* or *assets* to objectify us. Then, they can use and abuse us for profit. Take this place." I pointed at a small sign just behind us which directed tourists to the donjon museum. "You've seen the chains on the walls. Have you seen the torture devices they developed for witches? The Rack, the Iron Chair, the Pear of Anguish, masks designed to gouge out the eyes, chairs that mangled the vagina, weights that crushed their bones, rats that gnawed their way through the body to escape confinement. Horrifying and vicious. Dr. Singh told Sagar that these 'witches' were, in all likelihood, really only Druids who refused to cooperate with the Cult. The Cult had its day of power with the Inquisition. I think we know where that leads."

"But that's the past, Ivy. You have no idea, the wars, the genocide, the abuse of the poor. The Guild is responsible for most of the destruction on the planet. It's only the loose alliance and truce with the Cult that has curbed its avarice. But the Guild has abandoned peace. They're making a play for total control. The Guild has broken from the leaders of the religions and smashed all façades of decency."

"How is that any different from the Cult when they had power?"

"It's no different. That's why it's crucial that we maintain the balance." Shaking his head, he returned his attention to his phone, pulled up a video, and pressed play.

The setting was a vast laboratory space, all glass, white, and blue with silver metal accents. The camera arrived at a white door and focused through the small observation window in it to document what was happening inside. The main feature of the room was a rectangular pool surrounded by monitors and tubing. Suspended from tubes, a girl floated, submerged just below the waterline. Her long, red hair fanned and swayed like so much seaweed around her face. Gwen. I glanced at Josh and could read the anguish there. No wonder he wanted to rescue his sister.

The beeping heart monitor slowed and then stalled into a steady alarm as the girl flat-lined, setting off a flurry of motion around the pool. The lab assistants, in waterproof blue scrubs, waded into the shallow water that reached their waists, hoisted Gwen, pale, limp, and drenched, and lay her dripping on the deck. They rapidly tore away tubes and injected something into her veins. One of them shouted "Clear!" and jump-started her heart. The whole process was a well-orchestrated and practiced procedure.

Gwen opened her eyes and gasped, convulsing back to life. As soon as the heart monitor registered a normalized rhythm, the assistants began reattaching tubes.

"No. Please!" She could barely breathe. The words were hardly audible, but the camera zoomed in and the tears and anguish on her face rang clear. She looked skeletal, exactly as she looked when she had summoned her in-between world of grey into the colorful world of the sidewalk café. "Let me rest. Please! Just for a day or two. Please!"

Another injection silenced her pleas and she was floating again within a minute.

"This is a daily occurrence, Ivy. She is not living. They keep her suspended in this state perpetually. They will exploit her gift until she refuses to come back."

My fingers covered my mouth and then, as the tears began to slip from my eyes, moved to cover his arm. "I'm so sorry." And now I knew why I changed my mind and joined Josh.

"Sometimes, she finds me. The Word can contact her in her realm, but he is only a visitor and sees only her. He has preached salvation to her, promised to free her. You can understand why she is a devout disciple. The Guild high chancellor visits her as well to command the bidding of the Council. He has threatened to send a Reaper for me if she doesn't obey."

How could people treat a fellow human like this? To them, Gwen was not a person, she was a "subject," an "asset." "Why would they do this to her?"

"Partly because maintaining her in this suspended state," he choked a little on the word, "allows them to control and induce her phenomenon. Otherwise, the events are random. And then…" He turned away for a second and cleared his throat, "partly to punish me for leaving."

My heart cracked. By itself, the suffering of his sister would have convinced me, but the tortured look on Josh's face tugged at time-layered chords that went straight to my heart. I couldn't fly halfway across the country to save a small boy from drowning and walk away from this young woman suffering the atrocities of the Guild's abuse. "You were right. I didn't understand. I'll help you get her out of there."

"Oh, you don't know the worst of it."

He flipped his finger across the screen and tapped a new video. This time, a large machine, an operating bed, and other various monitors filled the room he showed me. The video exploded in shouting. Shots rang out in the background and the picture became a stream of flying images before the camera apparently crashed to the floor and the lens cracked. "What is this, Josh? What do they do with that machine?"

"It was designed to 'harness' the power of the ves…the Druids. From what we know, the Guild doctors induce the psycho-phenomenon. Then, the machine electronically and chemically codes and replicates the process. For it to function," he stopped and put a hand on mine to steady me, "they have to withdraw all the brain fluid and bone marrow from the 'host'."

The nightmarish drift of my death flooded my memories. "Josh…"

"What?" Our eyes met, like they had so many times before, only now something deep and substantial passed between them.

"Remember this number: 521."

He looked at me as if I'd just revealed the darkest secrets of his nightmares. "What does that mean?"

"Just say it!" My eyes teared up at this nightmare of my future realized. I leaned forward so that my tear-glazed eyes were only inches from his face.

Puzzled, he dutifully repeated the number. "521. What does it mean?"

"I can see the future, remember? Trust me. This is just a bit of foresight."

"521. But you don't know what it's supposed to mean? Is it a date? An address? An amount? What?"

"No…no…I don't know." I covered my face with my hands and dragged my fingers through my red hair. "Josh, I lied to you. I have seen you before in my future. I was in that facility." I stabbed my finger at the cell phone he was still holding. "I was strapped to a chair. When you came in and saw that I was drifting, you made me memorize that number. You told me to tell you that number when I met you or you wouldn't find me in time and I would die." I stared out into the courtyard, unseeing, as if, perhaps, my future might play itself out in the empty air.

"That explains a lot. I've been haunted by that number...something from a dream, I think. You see, Ivy? This is part of the plan. We belong together." He watched the gardener clipping away at the hedge for a couple of silent seconds. "The good news is, if you saw us there, we manage to get in."

"Well, yeah, but…"

Josh moved the tray to the side and scooted next to me. My head clunked back against the stone pillar of the cloister. He slid his arm around my shoulders and squeezed, the way Spencer always did when my drifts looked bad. "I told you, Ivy. If enough of us join together, the Cult will have the power to end this abuse."

When I'd seen the glimpse into my future that showed me dying strapped to a chair, very few of the surrounding implications had surfaced through the 7 seconds. My motivation from that point had been simply to avoid going there. Now that my field of vision was broader, my personal tragedy had mushroomed into a community atrocity. I might have to walk straight into my own trauma in order to stop the suffering and exploitation of those around me. Sniffing, I straightened my shoulders. "Of course, I'll help you. But I'm not sure what I can do."

# CHAPTER 31

"Shall we take a stroll?"

The gardener had moved on to trimming up the bushes in our corner of the courtyard.

"Yeah, I could use the exercise."

The cloister was meant for strolling. Josh ushered me back through one of the arches into its shade. He whispered confidentially in my ear. "Actually, I'm not sure it's the best idea for anyone to overhear us. I wasn't lying when I said the Word has spoken to Gwen about extracting her and he agreed that I should use that angle to gain your trust…"

"Wait! Stop..." My index finger thumped his chest. "This has all been an act?"

"No. It's all true. You saw the video. You have to admit, though, it worked."

I shook my head, snorted, and moved on. On principle, I didn't appreciate having my altruism manipulated, but he was right. My petty peeves meant nothing in the face of Gwen's torture.

"There's a hitch. Being able to contact Gwen gives the Cult invaluable insider information into the Guild's plans. With the delegates from the College of Cardinals arriving, I'm not sure the Word would be happy to know we're tampering with his plans and using them to get Gwen out sooner, rather than later. The Guild engineered the election of a humanist, progressive Pope with deep ties to the Cult in exchange for concessions that allowed them to stack the College of Cardinals and branches of the Curia with Archbishops closely tied to the Guild. The balance of power that has reigned for decades has tilted dangerously. The Guild has to be restrained." He looked both ways before whispering close to my ear, “The Cult is planning to remove a key cardinal in order to replace him with one of their own.”

Josh pulled out his cell phone, tapped at the screen, and then flashed me the image of an elderly man dressed in unmistakable red robes. “This man is the most influential man in the Vatican at the moment. He pulls the strings according to the dictates of the Guild. He has to be replaced with one of ours.” He pocketed the phone. “The Word has ordered his removal.”

The irony here staggered me. “His ‘removal’? And you’re okay with that? That’s exactly my point. The Cult is no better than the Guild.”

An awkward silence stood between us as I fumed. We passed a corridor that looked as if it led to an exit and then a double door entrance into the palace. “Look, I hope that, one day, you’ll come to your senses and realize that, at the core, both the Cult and the Guild are evil and manipulative. Until then, I’m nothing special, but I’m willing to chip in my two cents worth to help you get your sister out—even though she did try to drown Sagar and threatened to find me and kill me and I don’t think the Cult is a very good influence on her.”

“I told you, she doesn’t kill people. It’s the in-between, not death. I don’t care about the politics, but I do care about my sister. I need your help if I’m going to use the Word’s plan to extract her. Seers like you and Sagar are rare. Those who can see the future can mold it.”

“You should care about the politics. I’m not saying I’m in for the duration, but I’ll help you get your sister out—however I can.”

“Thank you.” He wrapped his arm around my shoulder and squeezed. The oxytocin wave that rippled into my toes mortified me. “At some point, Ivy, you’re going to see that we have to stand up to the Guild. It’s spinning out of control. You can see it everywhere. The corporations aren’t just pulling the strings from the shadows anymore, they’ve blatantly grabbed power. The Guild is all about money. To fill their coffers, the merchant barons will lay waste to the planet, drive the middle class into poverty, and abandon the sick and the defenseless. Nationalism has ignited in the populist grass again. There will be war, Ivy. War is big business. We need to restore the balance before that happens. The Cult is the only entity with the potential to stand against the Guild."

"My great aunt and my grandmother were members of the Coven. How is the Coven involved in all of this?"

"That's just it. They're not. The Coven is a loose coalition of very talented Druids, with very liberal philosophies. Sure, they're egalitarian humanists, they champion justice and kindness, they don't seek personal fortune or power, but they're a bunch of liberals. They don't like authority. It's very difficult to mobilize a group like that into acting as an efficient whole. We need action."

Listening to Josh's words fired a whole array of neurons and triggered old familiar paths of trust. My whole life I'd followed his advice, curbed my will to his 7 seconds of counsel. I'd molded him into the figure of a caring best friend, maybe more. Reality collided with the myth in my head and created an intolerable ambivalence in my mind. Force of habit and perception pushed me toward him; experience dragged me away.

"I don't have enough facts to argue that point. Right now, we both agree something has to be done about your sister and this machine. I'm new to the whole plotting and sabotage thing, so you'll have to tell me what you want. You probably don't know this, but in real life, I own a bath boutique. The only actual skills I have are in bio-chem. If you need any bath products with medically targeted properties, I'm your girl." We'd made a full circle of the cloister and started on a second lap.

Across the courtyard, a young man with close-cropped, fuzzy black hair watered the greenery growing on the window ledge outside his room. "Remind me to introduce you to Eli." Josh pointed up. The colorful, geometric designs on the young man's loose-fitting tunic rippled in the breeze. "He's a Shifter, our resident botanist. *Ivoirien.*" The sudden insertion of a French term into our English conversation confused me briefly. At first, it made no sense, and then I realized the word meant he was from the Ivory Coast. "His abilities allow him to alter some chemical structures at the molecular level."

"That could be handy."

"Especially, when you're really hot…or cold for that matter. We got caught in a storm in the Himalayas once, miles from any civilization. We'd have died, no doubt about it. But all Eli has to do is touch your skin to speed up the molecules, *et voilà*, you're warm for the night."

"Gives new meaning to cuddling up for warmth."

"Yeah, he can speed up the growth process of plants, as well. He works with our Healer. Needless to say, she loves him...but not quite as much as Daiyu does."

A woman with a heart-shaped face appeared on the same level but on the balcony adjacent to Eli's. Her tight-fitting, geometrically patterned apparel complimented the clean-cut sheen of her dark, straight hair. Every strand seemed in place and I brushed back my own wavy, unruly wisps, suddenly self-conscious about how long it had been since the last time I ran a comb through my hair.

Daiyu waved. The Ivoirian's eyes lit up as he nodded back, his hands occupied with the watering pot. The romantic tension that flew between them was nearly visible. I imagined that living here together, bound by the same struggles associated with our neurological anomalies, fostered a deep kinship that would translate so easily from friendship to love, the same way that the connection grew so quickly between Sagar and me. "How many of us…you know, Druids…live here? Is she one of us?" I had to admit, the commune feeling in this peaceful garden was attractive. But then, that's how Cults operate—preying on fringe dwellers like me.

"Daiyu's a Reader. She reads Chi, the energy around people. To her, it's visible—and tangible. She's sort of a fortune teller that way. She knows what's coming for you." She strolled over to Eli and whispered in his ear. He grinned, his white teeth a sunny contrast to the dusky tones of his skin. He finished his watering and the two of them, fingers tangled together, wandered back into the building. Josh and I exchanged glances. He shrugged, a comical smile curving his lips. "We spend a lot of time working together…closely."

"I can see that."

He cleared his throat. "Asher is a Reader as well, but he needs cards and something that belongs to the person. He's a Gypsy of sorts. Half Hebrew. Very…unique. You've met Sayid, Syrian and Italian. He's a little intense on the obedience side, but…he's actually pretty loyal and friendly—once you get to know him." Scrunching up his forehead, he counted on his fingers as the entities crossed his mind. "There are around, uh, two dozen of us vessels…"

That word again! I nudged him with my elbow. He frowned, rubbing the spot on his arm but altered his diction.

"…disciples…living here with a small variety of skills. Maybe about 50 of us are spread across the globe. In Marseille alone, the Guild has over 100 operatives with a much broader variety of abilities AND the resources to develop and control them. They have an American and an Asian facility as well."

"So, what can WE do? Frankly, I have trouble using my abilities to run my own life. It's only 7 seconds, Josh, and, until a couple months ago, the events occurred pretty randomly. What about you?"

He snorted and rolled his eyes. "My abilities are the past—literally. The past is solid. It can't be changed. There's no worth to exploit."

"No, but at least we can learn from it. We know where it leads when the Cult has unrestrained dominance."

"We also know where it leads when the Guild pulls the strings of the government. Did you know that the same company that's been clogging our arteries for years provided the funds to establish the American Heart Association?" The snipping of the clippers working its way toward us filled the silence of the gap between us.

I folded my arms across my chest. "So here we are again. An impasse. Let's just stick to the problem at hand. What can you actually do?"

"I can visit the past. The Guild found that useful for a while. From time to time, the Council sent me to gather information for blackmailing government and corporate officials or to steal patent information. But that's obsolete now. Your gifts are the future, Ivy." He grinned disarmingly.

"Puns? Oh, my Goddess. Really?" His smile was infectious. "Don't underestimate yourself, boy. There's power in the past. You just have to know where to look." He was skeptical and that gave me confidence that he didn't know how influential he could be when the two of us combined our gifts. "Can you control the events, like when and where you travel?"

"Yeah. That's one of the benefits of having belonged to the Guild…" My grandmother's amulet popped into my mind. Even the blessings of the Guild were curses in disguise. "…although I'd give it up in a heartbeat to free Gwen."

"Were you close?"

"When we were young, they murdered our mother and split us up. I came here and she stayed in Scotland. We stayed in touch the best way we could. Once I learned to pinpoint my visits, I would drop in on her past. She couldn't see me, but we were together. She found me in the grey world sometimes, but that's pretty risky, especially a long stay. She kept it open too long once and fell into a coma for months. That's why they developed the water system in Marseille. You nearly killed her, you know, when you electrocuted her in the grey world. The door slammed shut, sent her into cardiac arrest, and nearly trapped her there. She was lucky to wake up from the coma."

A morbid silence settled between us. Putting myself in his shoes was difficult. I had no siblings. But if Spencer were trapped like Josh's sister, there was no risk I wouldn't take to free him. "I didn't know." I patted his shoulder. "We'll figure something out. Promise."

# CHAPTER 32

A young woman with thick black hair, a warm bronze complexion, and giggling red lips ushered half a dozen children in a variety of styles and shapes into the courtyard. Josh waved and the tiny horde waved back. "That's Salma. Sweetest girl on the planet. She runs the orphanage school. That's a gift in itself. Not my skill set."

Empathetic grimace. Sagar and Yana were my only two references in the world of childcare. Not sure I could call either one a success. I hadn't really saved Sagar. I'd ended up delivering him right into the hands of the people that were trying to kill him. I'd spared Yana from a bullet, but my technique—or lack of it—made it impossible for me to ever show my face in her neighborhood again. By the time I sneaked in to check up on her, the family had moved. "Orphans? That's sad. Where do they come from?"

"All over. Most of them are refugees we've rescued from the Guild. Looks like it's recess."

Salma beckoned to me. "Ivy! Come here!" My eyes went wide, astonished that she knew me and even more wary of wild children. Josh gave me a little shove and I wandered over to meet the family while he disappeared into the tower with the tray. Salma gathered all the children into a little circle around me. "Children, Ivy is new. Remember when you were new? Can you all say 'hello'?"

A volley of *hello*s and *bonjour*s nearly knocked me over. I giggled until one creature crept up behind me and slid her small gloved hand into my palm. My eyes fell on dark curly hair, and big brown eyes. My heart skipped a beat, and for a second, I couldn't breathe. "Yana? Oh, my Goddess! Yana! What are you doing here?" She was a couple years older now, around nine or ten, but tiny for her age. Her face was still the same. I would never forget that little face or the touch of her fingers. Shocked that she remembered me, I snatched her up into my arms and hugged her.

Right after I'd changed her future, Josh appeared in a drift and told me the Guild would go after her, and here she was in the heart of the Cult. More lies? "How did you get here, Yana?" I turned to Salma. "Why is she here? Where's her family?" I tried to remain a reasonably calm human being, but I had too much baggage with the Cult to suddenly assume the best. Abducting small children seemed a frequent pastime for them. "Yana, where's your brother?"

She frowned, shaking her head, eyes drooping. She popped a pinkie into her mouth and sucked at it rhythmically. I turned on Salma. "Where's her family?"

"I'm sorry, Ivy. I…I don't know. I only care for the children until they're old enough to…"

"…to exploit?" Damn! I actually said that. Salma looked at me like I might be toxic and should have a "keep away from children" sign posted on my chest.

"No. To take care of themselves." Josh reappeared from the cloister.

I rounded on him, a better vent for my repressed suspicions. Anger brewed inside. How could I have been gullible enough to let him take me in with this whole big happy family shit? The Cult was a Cult. "Is that what you call it? Because I call it kidnapping." I was actually impressed at how I'd whittled what felt like a tooth full of venom down to a sharp bite.

"Look, Ivy, I know you've had a rough go with the Cult, but we are not the bad guys. I pulled Yana out of a small Guild facility in Idaho about a month ago." Josh reached his arms for the child who spilled gleefully into them. Apparently, she trusted him, even if I obviously didn't, yet. But this was the same little girl that crawled into the driver's seat of a running SUV and locked the door. She was minuscule for her age and obviously suffered from some serious PTSD.

"Yana, where's your mom?" I brushed the curls back from her eyes. She stared at me vacantly and popped her pinkie in her mouth again, sucking hypnotically at the fingertip of her glove.

Salma cuddled her out of Josh's arms. He nudged me away, whispering, "A Guild bounty hunter kidnapped her from ballet lessons a year ago. He got the whole family deported so they couldn't even start an investigation. The Guild has connections everywhere. Don't you think we checked before we brought her here? We're still trying to locate the family. Gods, Ivy, we only house orphans—children and teens that *want* to be here or have nowhere else to go."

The revelation that the Guild kidnapped Yana and deported her family unsettles me. All this time, I imagined I'd kept her safe, living out the life that was nearly stolen from her. If I'd known, I'd have done something. Inwardly I cursed this useless gift of mine. Why couldn't I see that moment with Yana? Why couldn't I see the Guilder that deported her family—or where her family was for that matter? My anger, with nowhere else to go, lashed out at Josh. "Well, how am I supposed to know that? I didn't really get the choice of whether to come here or not, did I?"

"I know. I'm sorry about that." His exasperation that I couldn't let go of the past seeped through his apology. He didn't know that I was angry with myself, with the idiot that turned the dials of fate. "You'll probably never be able to trust me, I get it. All I'm asking is that you count on my gratitude. Nothing means more to me than getting my sister out."

If only he knew how much I wanted to be able to trust him, how much I'd already trusted him. "I can give you that much."

"Ivy!" Yana slipped out of the game that Salma had organized and wandered back to me. We'd shared something between us. I wondered what else her touch did besides read the thoughts in my head. She slipped her hand in mine and tugged. Erasing all the conflict on my face to put on a mask of jubilant reunion, I leaned down to hear her secret. "I love Josh." She favored him with a shy smile and batted her absurdly long eyelashes. "Do you love him, too?" she whispered loud enough for both of us to hear.

Josh swung his arm around my shoulder and squeezed. "Of course, she does! Who doesn't love Josh?" He kissed Yana on the top of her head, twisted her around, and scooted her back to the game. She giggled, happy to find a bubble of harmony in her world of chaos. Josh met my raised eyebrow with a shrug. A tinge of red faded from his smoldering cheeks. His face lit up. "Ivy, can you control your drifts?"

"That's a good question." Of course, Josh stumbled onto the only subject on the planet that could squelch my anger. I snatched at the diversion. I was feeling so neurotic—more than usual. The Josh-of-my-past and Josh-of-my-future dissonance played havoc with my emotions. My mask of suspicion with the stranger slipped when that stranger wore the face of the angel from my youth. My resolve to mistrust him kept dissolving. I checked the hallways before I whispered my somewhat shady secret ingredient. "I've been experimenting with marijuana."

His eyebrows arched and he nodded appreciatively. "No way. Does it work?"

With a babbling group chuckle, the children scattered like marbles across the grass. A tourist couple with two teenagers wandered into the courtyard from the corridor we'd just passed. The mom asked me to snap a picture. Josh stood by as the family jostled about and eventually situated themselves so that the gardener wouldn't end up in the background of their potential Christmas photo.

When the masterpiece was done, the father, mistaking us for another couple of tourists, asked if Josh and I would like a photo of the two of us. We exchanged awkward glances and refused.

"But you're such a cute couple! You shouldn't miss this opportunity. A selfie is never quite as good as a photo taken by a stranger. I'm an amateur photographer, you know." The mother held out her hand for Josh's phone. Reluctantly, he handed it over. For a couple minutes, she waved us left, lower, and then closer together. To satisfy her taste for the ultimate photo op, Josh finally swung his arm around my shoulder and squeezed. The woman gasped with glee and finally snapped the photo. Returning the phone triumphantly to Josh, she herded her family across the garden.

Another eccentric looking young man, trailing a glittering gold cape, emerged from the cloister near the gardening cart. His arm around my waist, Josh pushed us a few steps into a more secluded corner. We wouldn't be able to continue our *tête à tête* much longer. Visitor hours had begun.

Excited to discuss my progress with someone who knew what it was like to long for control, I stopped and turned my back to the garden in order to look him in the face. "Yes, it works…sort of!"

A slow smile curved his mouth, and he rubbed his chin pensively until his eyes gleamed with a look of mischief. "Good, because I think I have a plan," he announced, looking up. As his eyes reached mine, his face contorted into alarm and he shoved me to the ground.

# CHAPTER 33

My cheek, the same one that already had a nice welt from Sayid's backhand, scraped the pavement at the same time as my palms. "What the hell?" I looked up to see Josh grappling with the gardener.

"She must die!" Jérôme cried as the two of them struggled for control of the garden shears. I recognized the glazed-over eyes and robotic rasp of the vocal cords.

Grabbing for a grip on the wooden handles, I joined the fray. "It's a Jumper, Josh!" The gardener was no spindly shopkeeper. A bulky laborer used to heavy outdoor work, he knocked me off his arm. The fabric of his sleeve ripped away as I stumbled back.

Taking advantage of the distraction, Josh wrenched the sheers from Jérôme's grasp and tossed them. They clattered against the stone wall and he pivoted to land a punch on the gardener's jaw. The possessed man's head twisted with the impact but seemed to feel no pain. Josh wound up for another blow. The big man caught his fist.

Scrambling to my feet, I crouched to sweep Jérôme's legs and give Josh a chance. "Watch out!" Daiyu jumped from the second-floor archway, directly above us, and knocked me over just in time. A missile flew by and clattered against the stones of the cloister. "We have a Pusher, Josh!" Next to the garden cart, stood the young man in the gold coat. He waved his hand and another garden tool flew out of the cart, targeting the huddle of children. Erupting in frightened screams, they scattered. Salma scrambled frantically after them.

Yana stood, transfixed and terrified, in the center of the garden beneath the Yuca. I had to get to her.

As I ran, Salma stopped, breathed deeply, as if dismissing the chaos around her, raised one arm, and belted out a single clear note. The other children all froze, then turned and, as if attracted to a magnet, walked hypnotically toward the chime. The flat of a shovel slammed into the Siren's back and she skidded into the boy in front of her. They scuttled back up. Salma groaned and grabbed for his hand. The whole herd disappeared down the corridor. All except for Yana.

Daiyu sprinted past me to confront the launcher. She was not, apparently, an ordinary Chi Reader. The girl had skills. The Pusher launched clippers at me. Daiyu put out her hand and intercepted them in some sort of field before they struck. Grabbing them from thin air, she hurled them back where they came from. A shovel and pickaxe hurtled on a collision course with my chest. I ducked one, but the other gashed my shoulder. Still, Yana stood frozen.

Blood leaked from the laceration and dripped onto my hands as I scooped her up. Pivoting, I ran for the cloister. "Look out!" Daiyu yelled. I ducked, instinctively covering Yana's body. A garden spade flew within centimeters of my scalp, just where my temple was milliseconds before. We skidded into the cloister where I shoved Yana behind a column under the arches.

Despite Josh's agility, the hulking gardener finally landed a crushing blow to his chin. His head jerked and he crashed to the ground. The monolith turned his attention back to me. "She must die!" he rasped, hands reaching for my neck.

I grabbed the shovel and clambered to my feet. Jérôme just kept coming for me. "She must die!"

I swung. The metal collided with his face. Blood spurted from his nose. I cringed, knowing Jérôme was taking the punishment for actions that were not his own. He teetered and kept coming. "She must die!" My second swing cracked against his knees. He wobbled again and kept coming.

Eli sprinted in from the corridor. Josh yanked the shovel from my hand and delivered a nasty blow to the side of Jérôme's head. This one teetered him. Ducking, I charged into his legs and toppled him backward. The big man thudded onto the stones. Eli rushed to the unconscious heap.

Blue mist slithered from the orifices of Jérôme's head and the Shaper gathered them in his hands, whispering. The wisps congealed sluggishly until he had molded them into a rough ball. He walked away, murmuring to keep his captive subdued, while Daiyu and Josh rushed the caped Pusher running short on garden tool ammunition.

He waved his arms in a large arc. The cart itself rose up from the grass and hurdled toward the two of them. Full speed, he sprinted behind it. The wooden box slammed into Daiyu's force field and splintered on the grass. The force of the collision knocked Josh and Daiyu flat on their backs. The Pusher trampled over them. He wasn't coming for them, he was coming for Yana! I cinched my arms around her. He would not have her again—not if I could help it. What was so crucial about Yana's gift that the Guild would come after her? Twice?

The Pusher stopped in front of me. My blood froze in my veins and I caught my breath when I saw the same translucent stone that controlled my grandmother's amulet in his bracelet. Goddess only knew what he could do with it. Josh and Daiyu were just starting to stir on the lawn. The Pusher sneered. "*Amateurs*." His finger flipped a switch. A rushing wind lashed around us. He stretched his arm and focused on Yana. Suddenly, her body became a force of nature. My arms trembled with the strain of holding her back. I yelled against the tension as the force ripped her away and drove her into his arms. The embrace of this nightmare thawed Yana's terror. She screamed loud enough to curdle my blood. The Pusher turned and ran as she wailed. I sprinted after, but his long legs dwarfed my stride.

A handful of other Druids spilled out of the tower. "Yana!" Daiyu yelled, pointing them toward the exit where the Pusher had disappeared. One of them literally flew over my head, down toward the stone wall that enclosed the gardens. Ahead of us, the gate slowly closed. Panting, my shoulder throbbing and stinging, I pushed my legs to go faster.

A sickening thud overhead sent the Flyer careening in an unconscious dive beyond the wall. The door to the outside wouldn't budge. I tugged. "Yana! I'm coming!" Daiyu and the others bottlenecked behind me.

"Move! Move!" A scrawny, pale, red head shoved through the crowd. I wondered what he thought he could do. I could have tossed him over my shoulder without much effort. The Pusher was holding the solid wood and metal door shut with his kinetic force, but the red head walked right through it.

Once he was out, the door swung open, heavy under my pull. I raced into the street, watching as the caped Pusher tossed Yana into the back seat of a red Ferrari. "Oh, Goddess! He's taking her back!" The only thing worse than imagining sweet, innocent Yana in a pool of her own blood in the front seat of an SUV, was the thought of her strapped to a machine in the Guild.

Daiyu and I sprinted to the car. Yana's arms reached for us, fear and pleading writhing on her face. Daiyu's energy field surrounded the two of us and ignored the kinetic power that plastered the rest of the Druids to the tower wall. My hand grazed the trunk as the Ferrari revved into the street, Yana pounding her fists against the back window.

# CHAPTER 34

My knees crumbled beneath me. Yana was gone. I stared, open-mouthed, at the empty street. Daiyu put a hand on my shoulder. I winced. My sleeve was covered in blood. Neither one of us could draw enough air to speak. I wouldn't have known what words to use if I could.

Josh, sucking air, bent over his knees. "We'll get her back, Ivy. We'll get her back." He got a look at the shoulder wound leaking blood down my arm. "C'mon." Ripping off his t-shirt, he wadded it up to staunch the bleeding. The blood throbbed and pounded against the pressure. I winced when he grabbed my whole arm and dragged me back into the palace.

"She's gone! I lost her." The shock doused the pain of my wound. "Why didn't I see this coming?"

"The wound is deep. You're in shock. C'mon." Josh pulled me up and looked me squarely in the eyes. "Ivy, listen to me. We're going to need your help to get Yana back. We're not just going after my sister anymore."

My eyes shifted to Daiyu.

"Daiyu is with us."

The wound throbbed more insistently with less adrenaline to deaden it. I had to focus. Focus on getting Yana back. Focus on helping Josh get his sister back. "I know the Jumper. He…she…was stalking me through *Villefranche* when I brought Sagar to you. It must have followed me here. I thought it was another of yours."

"No. The Jumper is Mila. When she takes her spirit form, half of her ends up in the in-between. Gwen sees her often. Mila works for the Guild. The Cult has never sanctioned Jumpers."

"Of course, not. Every priest loves a good exorcism." The levity did nothing to staunch the growing pain in my shoulder. We didn't take the same door back into the tower. Josh headed up the wing opposite from mine.

With a supportive hand on my back, he guided me along. "The guy throwing garden tools calls himself 'Vlad, the Slav'. His father ran a black-market operation. Rumor has it he traded his only son to the Guild for the rights to sell the Guild's uranium. Of course, the Guild turned around and sent Vlad to assassinate his father."

My head bloated. The loss of blood might trigger a drift. I plowed through the fog. "You know about Yana, right?"

Josh nodded.

"What makes her ability so special that the Guild would risk coming in here to get her back?" The world melted around me and my knees buckled.

Josh grabbed my waist and wrapped my arm around his shoulder. "I wish I knew. The Guild knows something we don't. I don't know all their resources. Both Daiyu and Asher are Readers, but the Guild don't seem as interested in grabbing them."

Daiyu halted at a hallway to our left. "Most likely it's because she's a child and we're grown-ups—too difficult to manage."

My arm pushed against the nausea churning in my stomach. "Goddess, it makes me sick to think of her in a Guild facility."

Daiyu took my hand and squeezed sympathetically. "Don't worry. You're lucky we have Josh with us. He's become something of an extraction legend. I have to talk to Dr. Singh. He'll want to look at that Jumper and we need to know why the Guild wants Yana so desperately. That was a pretty bold move, even for them. I thought we had surveillance."

"What? Like radar?"

"Sort of. The electrical impulses of *Druids*," Josh emphasized the word for my benefit, "are different than those of normal people."

"Hmm. I didn't know. Another notch for me on the fringe-o-meter."

"That's where you're wrong, Ivy. You're not on the fringe of society, you're at its heart." Why the hell did this boy have to be so damn charming and yet so *not* compatible with my worldview?

What really bothered me was that memories of drifts to come still featured him as my accomplice and confidant. I had to be cautious. I had no way of knowing for sure if those drifts were because we would eventually see eye to eye and I would send him to talk with me, or if he had other information that allowed him to manipulate me for the Cult.

Josh and Daiyu exchanged nods and she headed off to find Dr. Singh when we reached a door at the end of the hall.

A tall woman, about our age, answered his knock. Long blonde hair tumbled over her shoulders. Her face radiated pale youth and beauty. Her features defined symmetrical. She floated more than she walked, like a ballerina. Her limbs flowed around her body like branches around a willow tree. She exclaimed at the blood and bruises Jérôme had added to Josh's rough good looks. "*Josh! Qu'est-ce qui s'est passé*? I didn't recognize the accent but guessed it was Scandinavian. The Cult seemed to have gathered a wide selection of twenty-something Druids from all over the world.

At the table, seated in front of a cup of tea, sat Sayid. The set-up was quite cozy and somewhat surprising, but I guess I shouldn't have been astonished that the beauty of this goddess melted even a heart as cold as Sayid's. The stinging throb of my wound distracted me from drawing any conclusions until the mortal deity's eyes fell on me. I was good at capturing events that happened in a flash of fractions of seconds. This girl hated me. She'd never set eyes on me, but she resented my existence, instinctively.

"*Moi, ça va. Tu peux l'aider, Vilja?*" Josh ushered me into the room, explaining that I needed her help. Immediately, she masked the revulsion and mirrored the concern on his face. But I knew what lay beneath the façade of her compassion. Pity, this girl and I could have been friends if a goddess wouldn't mind hanging out with a mortal. Dried bunches of greenery hung from the walls and a myriad of jars neatly stored on racks of shelves displayed an array of botanical specimens. The labels were definitely Scandinavian. In another language, this kitchen could have been mine.

Vilja's eyes grew wide when she saw the gouge. "*La jeune Américaine*? *Viens, viens*! *Entre! Assieds-toi.*" The humane urgency she feigned was so convincing, I almost questioned my snap judgment. But then, I glimpsed her furtive calculations of the effect of her extravagant kindness on Josh and knew I was right. He wasn't as good at reading inside the seconds as I was, or maybe he just had more pressing worries on his mind.

A small stool, tucked beneath a workbench of aged wood, looked as if it might have been an original furnishing of the ancient palace. Vilja ushered me to the seat and then waltzed over to her herbs and selected a few. One of them, I recognized as yarrow, good for stopping bleeding. In a granite mortar, she ground the plants with a pestle and some fluid. As she worked, Josh whispered to Sayid, who left the room, presumably to follow up on the investigation into the intrusion—or not.

Pulling a chair up next to mine, Vilja dabbed the concoction onto my wound. I winced and she grimaced. "*Désolée.*" Setting the mortar on the work table, she met my eyes. "*Attention, ça va piquer un peu.*" Grasping the wound between her palms, she closed her eyes and began to squeeze. As the pressure tightened the wound did more than sting. It seared. The smoldering burn pulled me off the stool, gasping. My body stiffened and a groan slipped out of my throat through clenched teeth. Just when I thought I couldn't stand it anymore and I was going to have to shove her off of me, Vilja let go.

With a soft cloth that she dampened in a small basin of rose water, she wiped the blackened paste from my shoulder. Nothing but a pinkish outline remained of the bloody mess.

"*Oh, mon Dieu*!" My mouth hung open a bit as my fingers gingerly explored the restored skin. "*Merci! C'est incroyable!*" She really was a goddess.

She inclined her head ever so graciously—made me feel like a worm that had crawled up from a rotten tomato.

Josh made the formal introduction. "*Vilja, je te présente, Ivy. Ivy, Vilja.*" Apparently, Vilja spoke no English and since Josh and I spoke no Danish, the conversation continued in French, but it was short. Vilja was a Healer. She'd been with the Word since Josh had engineered her defection. Vilja had studied medicine and been recruited by the Guild, but when she learned of the appalling direction the monolith's medical research was heading, she left.

The predatory longing in her eyes when she looked at Josh made my foot tap involuntarily. Her devotion to the Word only extended from her worship of Josh. It was so obvious, but Josh was clueless.

Other than a slightly hawkish nose perched on well-defined, high cheekbones, Vilja's nearly flawless face and body haunted me as Josh escorted me back to my room. She made me want to skip meals and be a natural blonde. She looked more like a super-model than a physician. Who could resist her? Maybe I misjudged her. Everyone tries to be their ideal image of themselves. I had no right to condemn her for wanting to bury her flaws and cover them in virtue. It was why these gifted souls had gathered together in this palace.

"Vilja has seen the horror that Gwen lives. She'll help us." At the intersection of two corridors, Josh stopped and pointed down the one that led back to my room. "We found you some clean clothes. You can wash up and get changed. I'll come fill you in on the details of what I have in mind when I've talked to Dr. Singh."

"Will you be able to get Yana back?" The terror in the little girl's big brown eyes haunted me. I'd saved her once. I felt responsible for her now. Regardless of the future I'd seen for myself, I would step into the lair of the Guild to make sure she didn't lose her freedom.

"We'll get her back—" Josh's confidence was contagious, "—together."

Only the sickly light of a tiny lamp broke the dimness of the windowless hallway. Somehow, the impression that I had just stepped willingly into a cage still lingered in my mind. "Or I can just leave, right?"

For a millisecond, he looked thwarted by the suggestion that I might leave but recovered and shrugged. Goddess, he was good. "It's up to you. But I really hope you won't." He disappeared down the corridor without looking back to see which way I headed.

Leaving would have been the safe thing to do. Spencer would have told me to get my butt back home. But, I couldn't. More than Yana's life was at stake—her humanity hung in the balance. Who knew how many more like her and Gwen had fallen prey to the Guild's exploitation? Although my drifts had plagued me for most of my life, I harbored hope that they had a purpose. Not just for me. Sure, I'd made Spencer's dreams of wealth a reality, but I craved a purpose for something more lasting, maybe intangible, but impactful on the overall wellbeing of the lives it touched. I secretly hoped this was a place where that could happen. My gut still wanted Josh to play his role in that fantasy, but I still didn't trust him implicitly.

Almost of their own volition, my feet wound back up through the palace to my room, following blindly the path Josh had led me down an hour earlier.

# CHAPTER 35

At the end of the somber hallway, a streak of dull light radiated from a gap between the door to my room and the wall. I didn't recall leaving it ajar. Approaching cautiously, I pushed on the heavy wooden slats. The old door creaked. Fingers appeared in the gap and pulled it open. Finding myself nose to chest with Sayid, I gasped and jumped back. His bruised nose and the cuts on his forehead mirrored the purpling welt on my cheek and the scratches on my face, vivid reminders of our last violent encounters.

"*Merde*! You startled me! What are you doing in my room?" I may have been warming cautiously up to Josh, who hadn't, in fact, tried to kill anyone, at least not that I knew of, and had, after all, simply been returning Sagar to his father. I had a history with him, albeit a history that hadn't yet happened—at least not all of it—and I had enormous sympathy for his quest to release his sister from the Guild's atrocities. Sayid, on the other hand, was a poisonous, prickly plant. He carried a gun, which he didn't hesitate to shoot at me, and backhanded me at will. The air between us ran cool.

"This is not your room. This is the palace of the Archbishop and you are simply a guest of the Hand at the request of the Word who has favored you with his good grace." He bowed submissively to the will of his prophet.

"Okay, fine. But what are you doing in my guestroom?"

"The Hand, who accomplishes the will of the Word, asked me to deliver your belongings." He stepped aside so that I could see my bags, everything I'd left at the apartment, stacked neatly on the bed.

"How did you get these? I heard the police sirens. I thought for sure they would have confiscated all of this once the neighbors reported shots."

"As you see, that is not the case." Surprisingly, he hung his head in an apologetic bow. "Please forgive me for resorting to such extreme tactics. The Hand insisted that the boy be returned to his father *at all costs*. I did not know that you had become a disciple of the Word. It appeared as if you were in league with the merchant barons that sought the boy's death. Accept my deepest apologies for my actions and let there be peace among the disciples of the true Word." He held out a hand.

This was why my entire life I had never had the confidence to rely on the 7-second bits of information about my future that the universe saw fit to divulge. Motivation was everything. Would I, like Sayid, have shot at the enemy attempting to kidnap the boy for the Guild? Probably…I certainly didn't hesitate to stun Gwen…and Sayid for that matter. Not only that, I was pretty sure I had kicked Sayid in the face about as many times as he had backhanded me. I swam to his little island of moral high ground and took the proffered hand up.

"You will be pleased to know that thanks to the Hand, in accordance with the will of the Word, you are no longer sought for the kidnapping of Sagar Singh. His father has explained 'the confusion' and Naheed, his mother's assistant, has been apprehended for his role in an attempted kidnapping. It appears that the man was a soulless mercenary ready to betray his own house for the filthy lucre of the Guild."

A sigh of relief escaped me. It occurred to me that, no longer a fugitive, I could return to my vacation and forget all about the societies, go home and wriggle back into my comfy life as a bio-chem major and the owner of a luxury bath boutique. But the video of Josh's sister and her heart-rending captivity grounded me where I stood. For better or worse, whether or not Josh had engineered this, he was right when he said my compassion would not allow me to leave.

Sayid turned to exit. My revulsion waned, but one thing bothered me. "Sayid!"

He turned back, his hand still on the doorknob.

"Thank you. I'm sorry for…"

"All is forgiven. We are one in the Word."

"Yeah, that too, but…it was you, wasn't it, that ripped the hole into Barry Brattweiler's office?"

His eyebrows rose for a brief moment of surprise before he nodded. Perhaps he hadn't expected that I would remember his face from that encounter. He had, after all, tried to abduct me and had settled for absconding with the amulet.

"Why?"

"The Word requested that we retrieve the amulet."

"But you were going to take me as well."

"At the request of the Word."

"Why?"

"I do not question the Word. I only do his bidding as instructed by the Hand."

"The Hand? You mean Cardinal Aycelin? The man that was here last night with Doctor Singh?"

He nodded. "Excuse me. I have other tasks to attend to in preparation for the arrival of the cardinals." The door closed on him and our hostilities. It seemed, in this society, disciples put aside their differences in order to coexist peacefully and work collaboratively toward their goal. I couldn't deny I found that attractive.

I couldn't say the same for my reflection in the mirror. Two days of running, hiding, and fighting had pretty much trashed my face and hair. Mortification wrung a sigh from my lips. Josh had seen me for the first time in the flesh like this. I shrugged. Why did I care?

With the long European hose in the bath, I showered away the ambiguity I was feeling toward him, letting the stream of water help me focus on the task at hand—freeing Gwen.

When Josh finally knocked again, I couldn't stop myself from checking the mirror before opening the door.

"Wow, you clean up well." He looked for a couple seconds too long, until he met my disapproving eyebrows. "Sorry, it's just that, well, I'm really glad you weren't actually an asset of the Guild."

"So am I." My red bangs fell forward and I flipped them out of my eyes.

"You're actually really pretty…uh, I mean…a pretty decent human being." He was trying so hard. If only he knew just how unawkward this situation needed to be. He was attempting to connect with a relative stranger, but I was finally touching the flesh of a boy I knew and loved. Unfortunately, whenever love and insecurity vie for the same stage, self-doubt will always win the part.

Prudently, I doused the smoldering embers he seemed intent on fanning and retreated into sarcasm. "Thanks for that overwhelming vote of confidence. I'm afraid the best I can do is assure you that, perhaps, you may not be the scum I imagined you to be."

My tone did little to deter him. He stepped up closer, looked me intently in the eye. My finger wandered to a strand of hair and began to twist. His hand brushed mine and a whole array of chemical reactions exploded up my arm and into my chest. Asking and wanting and fearing churned in my veins as he tilted his face toward mine. Goddess, he was practically a stranger. What was I thinking, letting him get this close so fast? And yet, I'd known him my whole life, why wouldn't I finally reach out and let his skin touch mine? My head screamed for the brakes. And then I felt the small corner of folded paper slip from his hand into mine. His lips brushed my cheek as they passed to my ear. "We're performing for the cameras. Play along."

Was I disappointed or relieved? I honestly wouldn't be able to say—but I would tend toward disappointed.

Disengaging myself, I made an excuse and headed for the WC where I looked at the note after scouring the room for other cameras. Videotape in the bath would just be wrong, but these people didn't strike me as having boundaries.

*I know you don't trust us, Ivy, but please play the role of the convert. The Word needs to believe you're with us. The delegation arrives in two days and the plan to remove the Guild-loyal Cardinal di Castoria and replace him with a disciple of the Cult will begin to play out then. We need you to be part of that. It's the only way we'll get access to Gwen—and the Word can't know.*

*I can't tell you how much this means to me…*

Pulling the chain on the tank, I flushed the note down the toilet. Before I opened the door, I breathed deeply and assumed the role of convert.

Josh updated me on the aftermath of the attack. Apparently, the Word was able to contact the part of Mila that stayed with Gwen while the blue essence of her jumped.

"What will happen to her? You said yourself that the church has never accepted Jumpers. They hunt them down and exorcise them."

Josh was taken back, at first, that I'd read the note and come out contrary, but then caught on to what I was doing. He had to convince me. "Things are different now. The mission of the Word is to relieve the Cult of the burden of the past. Today's generations are tired of bowing down to the ideas and decrees of men who couldn't even imagine our world, much less define it. The Word looks to the future. In the New Age, there is a place for Mila in the kingdom. There's a place for everyone." For the sake of the cameras, I hesitated, biting my thumbnail and glancing at the door. "Give us a chance, Ivy. Once you've been here, you'll start to feel that it's right."

"Hmm. It's a lot more welcoming here than I imagined from my drifts. I've only been here a few hours and I feel like I'm part of the 'love club'." Walking over to Josh, I took his hand. A mirthless laugh characterized me as the wandering sheep. "I've spent most of my life as a fuzzball dangling on the fringe of society."

"That's the influence of the Guild. It thrives on the old caste system of wealth and power. You saw how ruthless they are. To the Word, we're all equals. The Cult is the future—like you, Ivy. With your power to see the future, you are the seed for the New Age of the Cult. Help us. Please. The Guild has to be stopped."

I turned away and walked across the room, deep in thought, as if weighing the invitation. In reality, I couldn't see any difference between the Guild and the Cult. One demanded the voluntary surrender of the will and the other forced it. Either way, no one inside was free.

I needed to manufacture a good reason to convert, something sentimental and mushy. "Daiyu doesn't even know me, and she saved my butt out there. And Sayid…well, we've had our…differences." Turning back, I exhibited the marks on my face that tracked my record with the Rifter. "I expected a fight when I found him in here." My face beamed as I sank into the mattress in awed contemplation of the wonder of our encounter. It may have been a tad on the melodramatic side. I shrugged. "Instead, he shook my hand and said we were one in the Word." Channeling my friendship with Spencer, I almost succeeded in squeezing out an actual tear. "I've always been a freak, but here…" I got off the bed and meandered right up to Josh's chest, my fingers latched timidly behind my back "…I don't know what it is…you, Eli, Daiyu, Vilja, even Sayid, you all work together and look after each other. I've been looking for that kind of family my whole life."

Josh slipped his hands through my arms, drawing me close. "Stay with us, Ivy. You'll see. We're family." The script seemed to demand something intimate, a token that would seal the deal. But if his lips touched mine, I was pretty sure the sincerity behind two decades of dreaming would leak through. A few more heartbeats and then there was no turning back. Our mouths wandered so close that gravity closed the gap between them. Kissing him, I wondered why, in all my drifts, I had never seen this, and knew absolutely that, had I ever drifted here, my younger self would not have been able to detect the staged deception of the moment in the fervor of his lips.

"What do you want me to do?" I murmured.

Taking my hand, he led me toward the door. "Walk with me."

# CHAPTER 36

Josh dropped my hand in the courtyard. With a wry grin, that I found just a bit disenchanting, he complimented me on my acting. My smile and shrug were part of the act.

We followed a narrow stone alley that connected the palace to the adjacent *Cathédrale Saint-Just-et-Saint-Pasteur*, named for a couple of schoolboys who were murdered for the faith. The building had housed a place of worship since 313 A.D. In 1268, according to the plaque on the medieval doors, a former Archbishop of Narbonne, Guy de Foulques, after ascending to the position of Pope Clement IV, had decreed the construction of a gothic cathedral on the site.

In the city of Narbonne, the view of the Archbishop's palace and donjon overshadowed the cathedral. We entered from a side door that spilled into the aisle that ran around the nave. In most of the cathedrals I'd visited, the main doors opened in the center of the narthex that led to another set of double doors and, from there, directly into the nave. But this cathedral had never been finished. At the time, it would have required demolishing the city walls.

A deep and foreboding grey smoke—or the congealed screams of agony wrung from the martyrs of the Inquisition—stained the stone of this relic of the Church's eminence. Normally, walking among the arches and pillars of these places of worship connected me to the millions of souls whose feet had crossed, in an endless parade of devotion, the concave troughs of the cobblestone floors. But, here, in this ever-unfinished monument to the abuses of the old church, a cold and clammy blanket of anguish floated on the musty air.

Red, thread-worn tapestries covered the horror etched in the walls of the alcoves. The carved pillars still nursed pox mark gunshots. A plaque displayed on a tomb nestled in the pillars of the crossing bitterly rebuked the damages done to the sacred edifice during the French Revolution. Personally, I imagined the extent of the damage the revolutionaries inflicted must have corresponded directly to the extent of the abuses they had suffered. I had trouble pitying the bones encased in the defaced stone casket. Unlike the other churches I'd toured, where the spirits of saints whispered peace and serenity from their stained-glass perches, in this one, ghosts with gnarled, tortured bodies and grimacing, blind faces bemoaned the agony of their suffering.

"Hey, Ivy, uh," Josh hesitated in front of an altar to St. Anne, "I know we started off badly, but that's just because we didn't have all the info." He dragged his fingers through his hair, obviously intimidated by the malaise of reconciliation. "We can't change the past, but...can we try to forget it?"

"Well, that's probably not going to happen—photographic memory—but I'll agree to let it be water under the bridge."

"I'll take that." His face betrayed disappointment. But he took my hand and led me along the aisle.

Much of the art depicted the suffering of the saints. The tapestries were neglected and tired of telling their stories. "Why'd you bring me here?" The creepy vibes in this church unsettled me. They threatened to trigger a drift—the place smacked of familiarity but I didn't remember ever drawing it. Drawing my drifts always spurred my subconscious to recall more details.

"It's safe to talk in here and they'll think I'm using the tour of the cathedral to expound the virtues of the Cult." He pointed to a painting of a saint whose body was riddled with arrows.

"Very convincing. Where do I sign up?"

As we strolled past the sparsely decorated chapels that lined the outer aisle, Josh unveiled the major points of his plan for breaking Gwen out of the Guild facility in Marseille. By the time we'd made the full circumference, I had the general idea. "So, while Gwen is abducting the cardinal, we'll actually be abducting her. That's the tricky part." He looks around and then leans in. "The Word doesn't know about it so we're on our own."

"She's your sister. You're obviously a crucial recruiter for the Cult. Why don't you insist?"

"Because the Word says everyone needs to sacrifice, and Gwen is so devoted, she made me swear not to push him. She insists he'll free her when the time is right."

"And that doesn't bother you?"

His face fell and he sighed. "I…"

I wasn't up for another philosophical debate. I cut him off. I already knew where he was going. "Well, your plan sounds like suicide. Do you even know if they have armed security? Because I'm thinking they probably do. I don't know a lot about intrigue, but I do know that disaster lurks in the variables. No wonder my drift shows me dying strapped to a chair in the Guild laboratory."

"Sagar has seen us succeed."

"Yes, but for every plan that Sagar sees succeed, there are several alternate futures where things go horribly wrong."

"Okay, I know. It sounds risky, but that's why we need you to induce some drifts. Dr. Singh said the Guild was making some progress with using the chemical properties of thyme to control the neurological anomalies. If you can gather more info about what happens during the rescue, we can alter the basic plan before we go in. Besides, I need someone who, even if something happens to me, won't abandon my twin."

This was the tipping point. Josh looked into my eyes with total confidence and trust. I looked into the eyes I'd known so well and trusted with my future. The whole palace was populated with people whose loyalty he'd earned. How could I say 'no'?

The question was, should I tell him the truth about us? Apparently, I was all in now. Once I'd decided to rescue a small stranger from drowning, I'd started down the road of gambling against the current odds. Besides, if I didn't want the drifts I'd already seen to dwindle into the realm of dreams of possibilities, I was going to have to tell him about his appearances in them. How else would he show up to warn me against medicating, if I never told him he could?

He took my silent reflection as backing out. "The plan might be lame, but…Ivy, I'm desperate. Please! With your gift, if you can focus it…I don't care what happens to me…she's my sister…"

"Okay." His devotion to his sister made me wish for an older brother. In my drifts, that's what he'd been to me as I was growing up. I took the plunge, for better or for worse—yin yang. "Nothing is going to happen to you." I grabbed his fingertips and headed for a wooden pew in the middle of the nave. "I can help you and, of course, I will, but not like you think."

"Please. Just try. Anything you can tell me will make it more likely that we succeed. Sagar already told me this could work. You know, with him, it's a matter of possibilities, but with you it's…"

"That's exactly what it isn't. 7 seconds is nothing. I've spent my whole life misinterpreting the 7-second snapshots I see. If I've learned anything, it's that appearances can be deceiving and I can't plan my life based on them."

"But it's something, at least you're not going in blind. That's all I'm asking. All I can do is go back and see what we did wrong. My gift is useless in this situation."

"That's where you're wrong. The two of us together, that's where our power lies."

Josh grinned, like all over his face, grinned. "I'm really glad you feel that way, too." He exhaled as if he'd just managed to pull out a block buried in the lowest level of a Jenga tower.

Just the way he said it made me think he was reading more into my words than I was saying. My insides smiled as I set him straight. "Uh, what I meant was, your ability to project yourself into the past, it's the key to changing the future. I can't do it without you."

First came a nearly indiscernible wave of awkward embarrassment that confirmed my suspicions he'd misread my meaning. "Yeah, that's fair." Then the cheeky smile and cool nod. "That's what I meant."

Seriously, when he dropped his head, laughing at himself, and then folded his arms, nodding before looking me in the eye again, totally chilled, I had to hold myself back from throwing my arms around him and kissing him. I settled for just dropping my hand on his knee. "No. You don't understand."

"Nope. That part is clear."

"Josh, I can see you when you visit me during a drift."

His eyes and mouth made little round o's of surprise before he looked hunted. "So, like, all those times I visited you yesterday, you remember those?"

"You visited me yesterday? When?" Of course, I wouldn't remember. I could only see him when I was drifting. I hadn't yet told him when I would be drifting so he could show up at just the right moment. This was getting complicated.

"I wanted to know who you were, so I spent a little time visiting your past."

"Stalking me? Since yesterday? How long did you spend doing this?" The shock was impossible to untangle from the indignation at such a violation of my privacy.

"Not long…thirty minutes…maybe an hour. You can see me?" He stood up and began pacing in the aisle, as the possibilities dawned on him. "This is outstanding."

"Oh, my Goddess!" I, on the other hand, was contemplating the hazards.

"You were adorable when you were little, by the way." He pointed to his front teeth. "You had the gap."

"You saw that!"

"And your mom…Ivy, I'm so sorry, but at the same time, you're like a superhero when it comes to looking out for her. What's the deal with this Amr kid, though?"

"Stop! Just stop!"

"Is that how you knew I could travel? You saw me every time I visited you yesterday?"

"No. I didn't see any of those. When I'm not drifting, I'm like everyone else. I can only see you when you travel back to one of my drifts. Sometime…today, obviously…I tell you that I can see you when I'm drifting forward and you're traveling backward. I suppose, after that, you begin showing up in my drifts. You're the one that brought me here. You've been bringing me messages since I was a toddler."

"How is it possible that you see me and no one else can?"

"How would I know? I don't make the laws of physics, I just defy them. Maybe it's because we're both in an altered state at the same time. Maybe not. I don't have data."

Looking stunned and overwhelmed, a little like Spencer when we won the lottery, he wandered back to the bench, sat down, and picked up my hand. "Do you realize what this means, Ivy?"

"It means you're going to have to do some visiting today. The times where I drifted and you visited me are now lost because we've changed things. They've faded into vague dreams rather than memories. It's hard to explain, it's kind of a loop thing, but you have to run a few errands or I'm not sure we'll end up here."

"Okay, but we have to do it now. We're running out of time before the delegates visit. That's our window of opportunity for grabbing Gwen. Where do I need to go? I'm yours to command." He held his arms wide.

"It's not that easy." Having drawn all my drifts, I'd never really bothered to set them all to memory. A few I knew quite well, others not. I needed my notebook. I didn't want to forget one that might prove critical. "I'm going to need Sayid's help." I'm not really sure why the sense of claustrophobia hit me just then, but I really couldn't bear another second of the oppression in the cathedral. "Is there a way out of here?"

"Yeah. Back the way we came." The hand he offered brought warmth and humanity to that chilly palace of demons. With this boy that I had always instinctively trusted, I thought I could approach the future from a new angle. I'd always positioned myself to avoid danger, avoid disturbing the status quo. Maybe that was the wrong way to look at it. Maybe I had the gift so that I could upset the balances and realign them. Why, after all, should the future be left to chance and the random forces of nature? Shouldn't we have some control over destiny? But if free will were to influence and design our paths, whose will should that be? That was the problem that racked me. I just didn't feel like it should be mine. Maybe Josh, and all these others who so worshipped the Word were on the right path. What I had to find out was why the Word's word was so much more divine than anyone else's.

We circled back to the entrance. Josh pulled, but the door resisted. He pulled again, harder, and then jiggled the knob. “I think we’re locked in.”

# CHAPTER 37

"Do you think they lock up for lunch?" The moment that anxiety set in, so did the tingling in my lips and my right arm. I'd never drawn the drift from the pier in Villefranche, but the symptoms of the onset triggered my memory. A sense of dread overwhelmed me. "Josh, I recognize this place, now. I've seen it."

"It's a popular tourist sight."

"No…in a drift, a recent one." We looked around as a girl in a flowing azure skirt emerged into the aisle directly across the nave. "This is going to go badly." Prisms of fractured light twinkled in my vision.

Josh yanked on the door again and then kicked it. I winced a little. I was pretty sure the door was a relic from another age and no one would be happy to see it desecrated.

A sound of rushing wind invaded the dank quiet of the cathedral. As it grew more robust, the fires on the altar candles flickered out. Air swooshed passed our faces, tugging on our clothes and our hair, converging toward the door across the nave. Our eyes were drawn to the direction the air seemed to be rushing, toward the girl who stood head back, arms wide open. The airstream swirled around her and then lifted her slight form about a foot from the ground. Her ample skirt twisted violently, caught in the vortex that was sucking the rest of the air from the cathedral. "Oh, my God! C'mon." Josh grabbed my hand and tugged me up the aisle. We sprinted away toward the choir on the opposite end, pushing against the wind current. As we ran, the air seemed to grow thinner and thinner.

"I can…hardly breathe. What's…going on?" The lack of air fueled the numbness crawling from my hand up my right arm.

A small hole of black invaded the center of the sparkling prisms.

"It's a…Whistler. She controls…movement of air. Vacuum!"

In a smaller room, with the air sucked out, we would have passed out and suffocated in minutes. Yards past the choir, a small corridor veered away to the right. We turned down it and the sound of the rushing gust abated slightly. The air inside seemed a tad thicker. Josh charged the door at the end of the short hallway. Air rushed out when he pulled it open. Behind it, in the center of a small meeting room filled with pews, two men, faces covered in oxygen masks, waited. We overheard the last of their conversation before they saw who we were. "…shoot if you have to, but don't kill the female asset! The high chancellor wants her alive. Any damage can be repaired. The male asset is worthless."

Josh slammed the door and knocked over an antique cabinet to block the passage. We dashed back down the corridor. The howling wind had dwindled to a breeze as the air evacuated toward the girl. The door crashed against the cabinet as we forced our way into the aisle. Hardly able to gather enough oxygen as we ran, we rounded the aisle into the ambulatory and made our way to the opposite end. "Josh, I'm drifting…"

7 Seconds of darkness.

The echo of a gunshot reverberated through my emerging consciousness. Swinging his body around, Josh covered mine as another crack erupted. He jerked, falling into my chest. The wind blustered around us. Movement was a chore. Our pursuers pushed against the current.

"Leave me!" He rolled away, wincing, and pointed toward a crimson curtain at the intersection of the aisle and the ambulatory. "There's an exit…behind that curtain. Go!" A splotch of bluish crimson soaked through his shirt onto my hand.

"I'm not…leaving you."

He groaned and winced as I dragged him. "…leave…me! …make…alone."

"Listen!" Gasping turned to wheezing. "You and I go way…back…not leaving you."

"Gun…pocket." Another shot exploded a glass vase on display just above my head.

"Gun? Goddess…" The air nearly gone, the flapping of the crimson curtain died to a gentle ripple that revealed the light of an exit only yards ahead. Gasping, I extracted a very small pistol from Josh's jeans, turned, and fired. Our masked pursuers took cover in a chapel at the other end of the half-circle. Why would they risk a bullet when they only had to wait for the air to evacuate and then gather up our unconscious bodies?

The wind had died like a fire with no more fuel. Suffocating in the vacuum, the edges of my vision darkening, I dragged Josh through the archway that led to the door. Another bullet followed us, exploding in the stone of the entrance and spraying Josh's head with fine stone dust. Only a yard ahead, a small swinging door rattled and fought against the latch that refused to allow it to relinquish the store of air it hoarded.

Barely able to move, I reached for the metal hook, but couldn't muster enough air to control my muscles. My lungs convulsed. My head spun toward darkness. Josh was out cold. My hand slipped from the latch as I crumbled to the ground. So close! Oh, Goddess, so close!

Another shot smashed the silence as the door flew open and the air from outside rushed in. My mouth sucked in streams of the passing torrent as the fingers of a thin, olive-skinned hand dragged me and Josh's unconscious body into the abundant air of a small outdoor alleyway. Gasping, I looked up. For the first time since I'd known him, I was happy to see Sayid.

"He's…he's shot," I rasped out.

Sucking in oxygen, Josh revived enough for Sayid to haul him up against his shoulder. Choking and spluttering, I followed them down the alley and back to the Archbishop's palace.

# CHAPTER 38

The basement of the donjon had been remodeled into a secured medical facility. Sayid took Josh directly to Dr. Singh. A bullet wound to the shoulder required some surgery and the lack of air had created complications. Vilja didn't have the set-up for that kind of healing. Can't say I wasn't glad.

I sat by the hospital bed waiting for Josh to regain consciousness. It was late in the evening, after dinner, before he stirred and his eyes flitted, struggling to open against the lingering effects of the anesthesia. My hand found his inside the railing. "Hey, Traveler."

For a second, he startled, confusion and anxiety creasing his brow, and then he sighed in relief and struggled to sit up. "Where are we? How did we get out?"

"No. It's okay. Sayid was running an errand for the Hand. He pulled us out of the cathedral." My palm pressing on Josh's good shoulder eased him back onto the pillows.

He stayed put but leaned forward as I plumped his pillow. "He's a pretty decent dude, Sayid. Rough past." Readjusting his position, he relaxed into a chat. "Dad is Syrien. Sold Sayid to the Guild for weapons funding. His mom is Italian with deep ties to the Cult in Vatican City. When she heard that I was freeing the vessels, she convinced me to get him out."

"Hmm. Can't say it was love at first sight. He's a little intense on Word worship. But, I was damn glad to see him in the chapel."

"Yeah, getting him out was worth the effort. We'd have never gotten Vilja if it weren't for him. A Reaper showed up. Didn't realize just how much the chancellor hates me. Guess we wouldn't have gotten Sagar out either without his help."

"Yeah, well, I'm just glad he and I are on the same team now. I was tired of him shooting at me, not to mention that ring he wears leaves a nasty mark." I rubbed the coloring welt near my eye and got up to leave. "Get some rest, boy. I'm going to need you to run a few errands into the past once I get back with my sketch pad."

"Back from where? You're leaving?" His alarm escalated quickly into desperation. "But, Ivy, we don't have time. The delegates are scheduled to arrive..."

"Chill. Sayid agreed to open a rift so I could retrieve my sketch pad. The Hand has enlisted me to help abduct the Secretary into the in-between."

Breathing a sigh of relief, he settled back into his pillows.

Assuming my best Southern belle accent, I leaned up to his ear and whispered, "If I didn't know better, young man, I'd say you'd grown fond of me, and this little plan of yours to abduct one of the world's most influential religious leaders was only a little story y'all invented to keep me here." I grinned coquettishly.

The blood pressure monitor beeped and the cuff around his arm inflated noisily. When he turned his head to respond, I expected that cheeky little grin he had a habit of flashing. Instead, I got a straight-faced stare, charged with sincerity. "Don't leave me, Ivy."

Involuntarily, I caught my breath, then returned the look, ounce for earnest ounce. "I won't…" Slowly I leaned away from the piercing intensity of his gaze and then recollected my senses. "Um…well, uh," my index finger wound a lock of hair nervously, "there are a couple places I need you to travel to in the past…that is…when you're feeling up to it."

"That's no problem. I only need my mind for that. Sitting or lying down works best anyway. When I'm gone, it looks like I've passed out."

"Okay, so, one of the most important visits you made was during my senior year. I drifted in the waiting room of a doctor's office. That's where you first told my five-year-old self that the Guild had me on their radar and that I shouldn't take the medication or the visions would stop and you wouldn't be able to find me in time. The other one is on the plane when you sent me here to save Sagar from drowning. There are a couple others." I handed him a piece of paper. "Here are the times you need to show up and what you told me. These few are easy because I had appointments, plane schedules, clocks, and such."

"Okay. I'll take care of it." He twisted around in the bed, trying to get comfortable, crinkling the blankets and sheets, and giving the distinct impression that he didn't spend much time lying around.

"What about your arm, though? You never showed up broken and in bandages."

"I don't take my physical body with me. I think my travels are some kind of projection of my consciousness."

"And you can control them, just like that? They don't happen to you randomly?"

"They used to. The Guild taught me to control them. Certain hallucinogenic mushrooms induce the phenomenon and minimize the side effects."

"It's marijuana for me…but I already told you that."

"Lucky you." He straightened up a little more in his bed, wincing when he moved the bandaged shoulder. "Vilja will set me up. She always does."

"I'm sure she does. She seems really…helpful. And she *obviously* appreciates what you did for her." The awkward silence screamed with envy. "Is that your new gig? Recruiting for the Word?"

"Like I said, the past is dead. I have to make myself useful somehow. And I wouldn't be sad to see the Guild crash and burn. They won't go easily, though." He reached for my hand. "Ivy, you heard the operatives in the church, right?"

I nodded. "And, by the way, thank you. I think that bullet in the back of your shoulder was meant for me—and, you're not worthless." I squeezed his hand and smiled. "Not to me."

"That's not what I mean, but at least they don't know that you and I, together, can manipulate the future—not yet. Be careful, though. They're ruthless and it worries me that the chancellor wants your gift." It was a little chilling the way he phrased that. As if my gift could be separated from me.

"Don't worry, I'll be fine."

"Don't underestimate their resources and influence…or the depths of inhumanity they will sink to. This is the second time they've tried to kidnap you."

"Third actually."

"I swear, Ivy, I'm not going to let what happened to my sister happen to you." He squeezed my hand. A whole array of memories, dreams, and premonitions sparked at the touch of his fingers.

During the kaleidoscope drift state that Sayid's chloroform had induced, I saw things that didn't actually happen during drifts. At that moment, I was staring at one of them. My mouth was compelled to the yearning on his lips. The gravity of already lived seconds drew us together.

The door opened and I leaned abruptly back to turn and greet Sayid. "Did you want to go now?" he asked, glancing at his watch, obviously sensing the tension in the room.

"Yeah, of course!" Untwisting the hair from my finger, I glanced back at Josh. "I'll see you around, Traveler."

"In your dreams, Drifter."

Exit stage left.

# CHAPTER 39

Sayid closed the door behind us and ushered me to the stairs in silence. His room was not far from mine. The place looked pretty Spartan. I recognized the grey stone on the wall from the other side of the rift he had come through into Barry's office. A rolled-up prayer rug stood in the corner next to a bed, a chair, and a desk. Not period. Just worn and simple wood. An anachronistic silver laptop dated the room.

From beneath his bed, Sayid pulled a simple metal box and then retrieved a key from a drawer in the desk. "You seem to have grown close with Josh." He turned the key in the lock and the lid popped open.

My cheeks flushed a bit, but I brushed off the intimacy of the moment he'd interrupted. "He took a bullet for me." If I was honest with myself, I had to admit that the team ambiance of the Cult sated my hunger for belonging the way the theater group had. But, on a certain level, I felt apart from these people as well. I would never feel devotion to the Word the way that they did. I could, however, get behind their cause of the moment, mostly because it was Josh's cause—that, and human suffering and injustice pushed all my buttons. "I appreciate Josh's loyalty."

"Yes, we all do." He removed a needle and syringe from the box, as well as something that resembled a remote control with buttons, silver plates, and a rounded meter in the center.

"Vilja mentioned, well really gushed, about how he plotted her defection from the Guild. She has nothing but admiration for him." Maybe envy tinged my voice. Sayid glanced up to check the emotion in my face. Suddenly the texture of the grey stones in the wall intrigued me.

As much as I appreciated the oneness here, the devotion to a common cause, I couldn't deny I would rather have found that Josh and I were unique in the world. Everyone's friend is not really anyone's. Without singularity, the value of a friendship dwindles—a single daisy in a voluptuous garden rather than a rare rose blossoming in the desert.

Sayid focused again on his remote. "Josh was instrumental in bringing Eli and Daiyu here as well. Opioids, although ultimately fatal, enhance Daiyu's and Eli's gifts. The Guild made them addicts. Josh not only released them from captivity, but with Vilja's help, he released them from the burden of addiction. She is…a remarkable healer."

"Now I know why they seemed so connected." I was beginning to think maybe Sayid and Vilja were connected. I understood what he meant, though, because Spencer and I had forged a bond through a shared fight. "What was it like for you, Sayid…in the Guild?"

Sayid glanced up from his box and motioned at his startlingly trim form. "I was not always this thin. My ability to maintain and create the rifts is enhanced by hunger." He bowed his head. "To decrease the regeneration period, the Guild fed me only enough to survive, through an IV. I owe my freedom to serve the Word, as well as to feed myself, to Josh."

"I'm so sorry. I'm the same. Hunger triggers my drifts." And now my petty jealousies were just embarrassing. But some of the fault lay in too little information about my future. If I'd had no information, I could have seen it with a much clearer lens as it unfolded. As it was, expectations tainted the reality. I needed to move beyond them. "So how does this work?"

Sayid exhaled, bored at the prospect of explaining. "Most of us owe the control of our holy gifts to the scientific resources of the Guild. Dr. Singh developed this for me. The injection allows me to align my mental projections with the readings on this GPS controller." He injected the serum from the needle into his arm.

"Is that why the Word asked you to retrieve the amulet? Did he plan to experiment with controlling my abilities? Barry, Mr. Brattweiler, wasn't too happy about you taking it away. He would have been a lot unhappier if you'd managed to take me too."

Now Sayid was all sincerity. "We meant you no harm, Ivy, until it appeared you had abducted the boy. We suspected the Guild had used its power and influence to recruit you."

"You mean you thought they bought me?"

"We knew that, with the impending loss of Sagar's abilities, you became a strategic vessel for the Guild. The High Seer of the Guild has recently passed away. Perhaps you have heard of him? Robert Hollister?"

"The name sounds very familiar, like I heard about him on the news recently or something, but didn't pay much attention."

"He was a close advisor to your new American president, who is nothing more than a puppet of the Guild. Now that he is gone, and Dr. Singh has forsaken them as well, taking with him the young vessel, Sagar, the Guild will be anxious to secure your gifts."

His forecast sent a chill up my spine. This part of the story to come, I already knew and wondered if I weren't a little crazy to have followed this path. Josh and Sagar shone like rough diamonds in the coal of that particular future. Now that Josh and I had connected and joined our gifts, perhaps we could still relegate the visions of me dying, strapped to a Guild lab chair into the realm of nightmares as well. In either case, the sketchpad of my drifts was the key to unlocking the value of our collaboration.

"It is not my place to analyze the motives of the Word, but I believe he feared, alone, you were vulnerable to the abuses of the Guild if they held the amulet. He could not take that risk. Now that you have joined us, perhaps Dr. Singh will agree to develop the amulet into a less dangerous tool that will be more useful to you. You, too, could control your drifts the way I control my rifts and Josh his travels."

As amiable as our relationship had become, Sayid was still too much of a Word fundamentalist for me to confide my reservations about jumping all in with the Cult. I still had issues with the Word's world view and strategic methods.

"You'll have to tell me where you live." I'd fallen silent and Sayid glanced up, his fingers poised on the keypad. "Once I've

Googled the location, I can add the coordinates to the controller and open the rift."

"How long do we have once you open it?" I glanced at the screen over his shoulder and caught a glimpse of his desktop photo before the internet window opened. The screen was a photo of Vilja—almost 98% sure of it. The surprise prompted me to look at his face once more to see the very human young man behind the disciple. When he wasn't shooting at me and abducting me, when we were interacting as friends and colleagues, I could actually see the same raw charm in Sayid that had attracted so many girls, myself included, to Amr. Even this far away, my life teeming with churning waters, even now that the blue-eyed boy had become a reality, I couldn't snip the delicate ties that would always attach a small strand of my heart to Amr. It was unsettling. I wondered if, actually hoped, Vilja returned Sayid's hidden sentiment.

"When I was young, the rift would open and close randomly. I could very easily be lost if I stepped through. The tear in the fabric of space lasted but a few seconds. Now, I can maintain the rift for several minutes. Unfortunately, the effort drains the energy which sustains it and I cannot open another window for at least 12 hours. When the Guild found my father, they offered to research my gift and help me establish control of it in exchange for my services."

"And you just went along with the plan to exploit you?"

"I wanted to control the phenomenon. And it was my duty to serve my father, even when his choices were not in my best interest."

To call Sayid out on that account would have made me a hypocrite. I knew what it was to put aside my self-interest for a parent. The sentiments that guided Sayid's choices chimed in harmony with my own. I gave him my address and he typed it into the search field.

"Sayid, how did the Cult know where to find the amulet? Barry kept it pretty well hidden. How did they even know he was taking it out and showing it to me at the precise minute you created the rift?"

"I do not know. I only received the coordinates and the instructions from the Hand to go at once to the location and retrieve the amulet as well as the vessel, if possible."

The objectifying name "vessel" still grated against the grain of my principles. "Didn't you ask the Word why he wanted the amulet, or why he wanted me, when he sent you to steal us?"

"I am only a vessel for the holy gift. I do not question the Word; I only obey his will."

"Have you seen the Word?"

Copying from the computer screen, he adjusted the dials on his remote. "I receive the will of the Word through the Hand." He stopped for a second and thought. "On this particular occasion, I received the instructions from the Hand through Vilja. The hand had pressing business and was unable to deliver the information himself."

My attempt at nonchalance failed epically. "So, you didn't ask her why the Hand wanted it? You trust Vilja?" It was a back-handed inquiry into their relationship status.

His sidelong glance betrayed his hidden sentiments. "We trust each other. In the Cult, all are equal before the Word and equally devoted to his service. I had no reason to question her when she relayed the request."

Apparently, the problem with really good disciples was that they really knew nothing because they asked no questions. The scientific quest for answers about my condition was my *raison d'être*. Questions were my way of life. As much as I appreciated the sense of brotherhood that reigned here, I didn't see myself fitting in for the long term…maybe not even with Josh. Then again, I did have to say, Sayid was really more of a fundamentalist, like Gwen. Josh didn't strike me as a great disciple; like me, he had too much of an internal sense of direction. "Tell me, if you've never met the Word, how do you know you agree with what he says?"

"It is not for me to agree. I am here by his grace—as are you." He bowed slightly and then glanced at his watch. "We must go. To regenerate the psychokinetic energy that I need to play my part in the plan to remove the Guild's cardinal, I must return from this rift by 8:00 p.m. to assure a safe buffer period."

"Okay, let's do this."

# CHAPTER 40

Beneath his palm, a metal sensor on the base of the remote, similar to those that track a heartbeat on exercise equipment, channeled the energy emanating from Sayid's hand. He set his eyebrows and touched a silver button on the side of the remote. It projected a thin, blue beam that shot out for about a yard and then appeared to strike an invisible solid surface. Sayid's eyes cringed in concentration. The beam slowly ripped the air. As the blue-tinged edges of the rift tore apart, a whistling wind surged into the gap. Through the tear, I recognized the piano in my Aunt Grace's sitting room and the portrait of her and my grandmother Sabrina that hung above it.

When the rift was wide enough, Sayid pressed another button, then turned and grabbed my hand. The wind, grown to a howling gale, forced him to shout. "We have only three minutes and then we'll be trapped there for at least 12 hours. That cannot happen."

Nodding, I followed him to the gaping, blue-lipped mouth. He lifted a leg and forced it through. The air at the center of the tear rippled around his body as he passed. When he had lowered his other foot into the sitting room, I took a deep breath and raised my leg. The power of the energy field in the rift surprised me, slapping my foot back with such force that I toppled and nearly dragged Sayid back through. His hand steadied me and, this time, I kicked my foot. The sensation of passing through the rip was like a millisecond blip of all the symptoms related to a drift. My mouth, arm, and hand tingled, my head throbbed, and then the force of Sayid's hand tugging on mine pulled me through to the other side.

In my living room, Sayid steadied my shoulders as prisms of light swirled into my field of vision. I swayed and then stumbled into the blackness of a drift forward.

*Second 1: Ears ring and throb. Head feels ripped down the center. Violent screeching in temples.*

*Second 2: Unfamiliar surroundings. White halls. Numbered metal doors with observation windows. White tile floors. Clock.*

*Second 3: Stumbling. Powering through brain-splitting roar in my head. Peering through the wire-reinforced window of nearest door.*

*Second 4: A pool. Red-headed girl attached to plastic medical tubes floats in it. Gwen.*

*Second 5: Deep breaths. Screeching volts in my ears. Reaching for doorknob. Josh stops me.*

*Second 6: "It's a trap, Ivy. I'm late. We have a..."*

*Second 7: "...traitor. Tell me we can't trust..."*

My eyes refocused as the rushing din replaced the pulsing pain. Sayid stared into my face. "Are you alright, Ivy? You drifted."

The dizziness was unsettling. "I'll be okay. Passing through your energy field triggered all my symptoms." I grabbed his sleeve. "I was in the Guild facility, Sayid. Standing just outside Gwen's door. I have to warn Josh…something about a traitor..." Steadying myself against his chest, I caught my bearings and then stumbled again.

The room was a disastrous mess of overturned furniture as if someone had been searching for something. "Mom?" The mayhem around me echoed alarms into the pounding throb in my brain. Although it was evening in Narbonne, France, it was only early afternoon in Salt Lake. My mother was, in theory, at work.

"We only have three minutes," Sayid reminded me cryptically, taking in the mess. "I must remain within proximity of the rift or it will close."

"I don't understand what's happened here." Down the hall, the chaos in the kitchen and the family room mirrored the disaster in the living room. "Mom!"

"Ivy! Three minutes. We need the notebook."

"But…" He was right. I needed to focus. Gwen's freedom was at stake. The mess here could be cleaned up later. Stepping over books and pillows, I made for the basement. As I descended, the rushing roar of Sayid's rift diminished.

At the bottom of the stairs, the landing turned left into the family room where Spencer and I did most of our hanging out on the infamous grey couch. This room, too, had been ransacked. But, when I saw it, all thoughts of my reason for being there snapped shut.

Beneath the midday light that filtered in from the ground level window, my mother lay on the grey couch, face down, her arm flopped over the edge. My first thought was that she'd taken advantage of my absence to go on a binge. But then, in a flash of neural synapses, I connected the ransacking of our house to her current state. As I rushed to the sofa, horror flooded my veins. In my stomach, the emotional overload swirled with my reaction to Sayid's energy field. An airy bubble formed in my head as I reached the coffee table.

My knees had just hit the carpet in front of my mom's sprawled body when, for the second time in less than two minutes, the hammering pulse screeched in my ears, and the sparkling prisms invaded my sight. I blacked out—for 7 seconds.

Oh, Goddess, No! When I returned, I woke with a wail. This drift was the reason fear gripped my pre-school chest every time I woke to find my mother passed out in a drunken daze on this grey couch. This was the drift I had blocked from my memories, hoping that if I didn't acknowledge it, it would die.

"Mom?" Trembling, I reached my hand for the arm. The hand that had held mine through so many dark nights, down so many long and lonely roads, was cold. The tears of the little girl in me, who had just come from the past and witnessed the tragedy of this moment, had left soggy trails of salt on my cheeks. My eyes were already puffy; my heart was breaking.

I knelt face to face with the nightmare that had haunted most of my childhood. The burden of a vision that no child should be asked to carry: her mother dead on a couch. But now there was something new in that memory. Josh was there. He had his arm around me as I stifled sobs and he whispered desperately in my ear. "*I'm so sorry, Ivy! But, it's a Reaper! Get the notebook and get back through the rift or she'll have you, too. Come back to me!*"

"Ivy, two minutes, and then I leave without you." Sayid's voice drifted down the stairs.

"Oh, Goddess! Oh, Goddess, Mom! I think this is my fault!"

A gut-wrenching yowl announced a sudden flash of darkness followed by a torrential wind. My stomach lurched again. Throbbing racked my brain and pinpricks crawled along my arm up to my shoulder. The room snapped into greyscale and I knew that someone had conjured the in-between.

In the corner of the room, the skeletal figure of a woman wailed hypnotically. It was not Gwen. The hair was black, a stark contrast to the sickly pale of the face. The bony fingers of her outstretched arms compelled me.

"NO!" The scream from my lips answered the yowl of the Reaper. My soul was rending. How could I leave my mother? How could I have let this happen?

It was only the image of Josh beside me in my drift, his warnings and his pleas, that spurred me to fight the urge to crawl up onto the couch and hold my mother's chilled body, to fight against the screaming in my head, to fight against the gale of wind and force myself down the dim hallway. The greyscale crept slowly after me as I went. The Reaper was in no hurry, walking as if through the clinging mud of a swamp. Death is inevitable; she could afford to be inexorably patient.

The door to the right was my lab, and the door to the left, the bathroom. Drawers, papers, and books lay strewn across the floor. Splintered picture frames with cracked glass hung crookedly. Plant specimens, broken glass containers, and other shattered paraphernalia covered the tile floor.

I'd never imagined that I was hiding my notebook from a violent society of ruthless murderers. I was only trying to keep it safe from the prying eyes of Spencer, Amr, and my mom. At the thought of her, I winced and grabbed my forehead, my eyes welling up into tears. Somehow, I imagined that this moment was what insanity felt like, a stark detachment from reality, cluttered with a cacophony of voices.

"One minute, Ivy." Sayid's voice was subdued, inaudible through the convergence of the two rushing winds and only seeping through the small back stairway.

My lab wasn't a modern metal and glass place. It was more of a 19th-century steampunk place. The lower drawer of the antique wooden desk that had belonged to my great aunt hid a smaller drawer beneath it. It was very tricky to access and, unless you knew it was there, impossible to discover. The upper drawer was just slightly thinner than it should have been. The space was perfect for my sketchpad, my only real treasure. I'd never imagined anyone else would want it so badly they'd kill my mother to get it—or maybe that piece was just intimidation and punishment for resisting the Guild. The upper drawer hung open, the contents scattered on the tile floor. Triggering the release of the lower drawer, I extracted the notebook.

The greyscale seeped into the lab in the wake of its windy gusts. I wouldn't be able to go back up the front stairway. Fighting the urge to run back to my mother, to weep over her loss, I fled to the locked door of the back stairwell, wishing I had thought to bring a stun gun. The door, which opened into the room, locked from both sides and required a key, which I hid, granted not very creatively, on the molding above the door on the other side. The spare was in the desk, but the contents of most of the drawers had been thrown out. I was on the floor, frantically sifting through plant samples and glass, when the Reaper appeared in the doorway.

Her billowing rags ushered in rot and decay. My blood churned in despair. She truly was mortality come to swallow me. I thought I had stared death down before, but her overwhelming, frigid finality sunk into my bones. I wanted my mom, and she wasn't there. Tears stung my eyes. Too many neurological attacks at once flustered my thinking. My arm tingled, my lips bubbled into indeterminate blobs. Words no longer formed properly in my head. The presence crawled toward me and slimy greyscale invaded the edge of the rug. No key.

Jumping up, I tugged at the door and pounded. "Sayid! A Reaper! I'm stuck in here!" One cold embrace from the wailing specter and I was as good as dead. If the door had opened outward, I'd have tried kicking it. The hinges were nearly a century old.

The grey crept up my ankles, enveloping me in a sense of anesthetic wonder. Abandoning my struggle against the locked door, I turned, a tiny ballerina, free to pirouette at the opening of a music box. And there she was, right behind me! My mother! Amid a light-drenched beam, arms extended, a serene smile gracing her face. "Come, Ivy. Come hug mommy."

A rush of joy rippled from my re-stitched heart down to my fingers and toes. "Mom! I was so sad. I thought you were dead!" My arms reached for hers and the magnetic bond of love between two people that only had each other, such as they were, drew me to her.

She giggled, carefree and tranquil. "Not dead, Ivy. Here. With you. In this place of peace and stillness. Come! We're done with the sorrow and the worry. Come! Let me hold you in my arms."

It was true. Pink blossoms rained down from the leaves of an enormous tree shading her head. In its branches, a rainbow pallet of birds twittered and coaxed. From the ground around us sprang a multitude of delicately sculpted, verdant greenery. Beyond her welcoming arms, purple hyacinths dotted a rolling field of grass that caressed the azure sky above. And, oh the sunshine! I could almost touch it. I was sure that small droplets of radiant rain would sprinkle my hand if I could just reach a little farther. My fingers stretched. Hers coaxed. It was perfect, all but the annoying, muffled caw from behind my ear. "Ai wee! Ai wee!" Not all the birds in this place sang lovely melodies.

My feet glided forward to the irresistible draw of my mother's fingers. They had held mine through the drama of drift-spotted decades. "Come, Ivy. We've always wanted this. Peace. The two of us floating above the struggles."

"Ai wee! Ai wee!" The insistent cawing gave me pause.

"Ivy, sweetie. Leave it behind." My mother was right. I could ignore the annoying call, let the beam of light envelope me and carry us away.

The tips of my fingers reached hers. A chill slithered up my arm, trailing tiny ice snowflakes on my greying skin. "Mom?"

My breath thickened and the caw of the birds behind congealed into a warning, "Ai wee! Ai vee! Ivy!"

A bolt of lightning flashed diagonally from behind me, striking the tree above my mother's head. The sickening crack split the trunk asunder and a film of grey rushed over the field as Sayid's hand gripped my wrist, yanking it from the outstretched fingers of the Reaper. "Ivy!"

The door behind us hung limply from its hinges. Sayid scooped up the sketchpad that I'd let fall and hauled me up the stairs. His palm was sweaty. "I can't hold the rift much longer!"

We raced down the hallway. My head throbbed, my hand and right arm buzzed numbly. Multi-colored prisms darted through my vision. Sayid kicked his foot through the trembling field. Even as he passed through, the edges shrank, stitching themselves together. The wind seemed to be sucking itself back into the rift.

Sayid tugged at my wrist. I kicked my leg into the field. Halfway through, I blacked out.

*Second 1: Ringing wail in my ears squeezes my brain. Writhing against straps. Head, arms, and legs restrained.*

*Second 2: Gasping through pain screeching in my temples. Hands grip metal chair. Marijuana fumes hang heavy. Blinding fluorescent lights.*

*Second 3: "What is happening now?" Elderly man in red robes.*

*Second 4: Woman in white lab coat. "A forward drift from her past. We..." Suddenly, Josh is at my side, pointing to the upper right corner of the television. 8:46.*

*Second 5: "Once you have established control, Dr. Petrov..." Third person. Grey business suit. Striking blue eyes. Josh whispers over his conversation, "They're going to release you to recover..."*

*Second 6: "...from the effects of multiple drifting."*

*"Now that the influence of the High Seer is no longer an obstacle," the chancellor, responds to the doctor, "Asset 521..."*

*Second 7: "We'll be here soon..."*

# CHAPTER 41

I blasted back into consciousness on the floor of the room I'd just seen in my vision. Presently, it was furnished with a medical bed, the white sheets and blankets tucked in crisply, a television, a chair and side table, and a rolling physician's stool. My drift inside of Sayid's rift must have resulted in some sort of melding of our psycho-phenomena, rerouting the rip to the location of my drift inside the heart of *Génétique,* the genetic research facility of the Guild. Across my mind flitted the image of a WWII parachutist dropped, by some disastrous failure to calculate the effect of the wind, into the heart of enemy territory.

In the first moments of silence, though, the loss of my mother upstaged all the throbbing pain, the anxiety of landing on hostile territory, and the solitude. For several minutes, as the blood tingled back into my hands and lips, I sobbed, my head buried in my hands. In those minutes, it wasn't images of hang-overs and neglect that floated through my memory, it was the countless hours she'd held my hand as we sat in doctors' waiting rooms, the times she'd skipped the meal because there wasn't enough money for two, and the nights I'd crawled into bed with her to escape the monsters in my dreams, oblivious that the monsters in hers were real. Perhaps the loss of love in death stings more acutely when it was underappreciated in life. When the tears had exhausted themselves into a numb acceptance of reality, my mind gravitated to the other ghost that wandered through my memories. Josh.

Josh had appeared to me twice in the last three minutes in this building—well, really in the future. Goddess, it was getting complicated. I could only hope that Sayid had delivered the sketchpad. He must have told Josh that I drifted to the facility that first time at least. How else would Josh have been there? Unless he was coming from farther in the future and I'd sent him. That would be the only reason he'd know I was here now. Perhaps he didn't know.

The mixture of mourning, drifting, and rifting had thoroughly rattled my brain. I sifted through the chaotic images and receding pulsing to find the messages that Josh had left. As I stood at the door to Gwen's room, he'd warned me that it was a trap. What I didn't know was whether or not to make my way there. What time was it? There was a clock on the wall during the drift. I surveyed the room for some type of timepiece. Nothing. Wait! There was something else, something more important—someone we couldn't trust.

Of course, my thoughts ran to Sayid. As grateful as I was for the two times he'd pulled me out of nasty scrapes, I couldn't quite get past our rough and violent beginnings. Did he calculate sending me here? I really had no idea how his abilities worked and what control he had over them. Then again, he was too much of a disciple to defy the Word. At least, he gave that impression. What if that was all it was? An impression. But, I'd seen his eyes—the look of genuine, deep suffering when he told me what it was like to be starved by the Guild. He couldn't possibly still be loyal to them…unless his father…

Unconsciously, I'd begun pacing the room, a finger twirling my hair as I weighed my options. Footsteps in the hallway outside the door cut me off in mid-step. More than one pair of feet was headed my direction.

Josh and the others would not set in motion their plans for another twelve hours. If it was a trap, maybe they wouldn't even come. The best option for me was to hide and hope to stay off the Guild's radar. Knowing the future, however, I resigned myself to the inevitability of them strapping me to a chair. Hiding, running, they were futile. In the end, I would see myself as I was in my drift, strapped to a chair and dying in the year of the short red hair, long bangs. Perhaps it was better to be civil and glean what information I could. Yin Yang. My fingers unwound from my hair.

The bed was too submissive. Shoulders straight, resolve stiffening my back, I settled into the bedside chair as the face of the doctor from my most recent drift scrutinized me from behind the wire-reinforced glass of the observation window through rectangular black glasses perched on her nose, rather than dangling from the chain around her neck.

She nodded, the door opened and one of the scrub-clad orderlies that accompanied her stepped into the room. The man was more of a bouncer than a nurse. All thoughts of escape fled before his bulk. He was here to restrain "the patient." That much was clear. Stepping reverentially to the side of the door, he made way for the doctor. Her modest heels clicked sharply against the pristine white tiles. A second "nurse," not quite as massive as the first, and bearing a black leather tablet, followed her in, and then took up a post on the other side of the door.

Without addressing me, the doctor whipped a Dictaphone from the pocket of her lab coat and read from a clipboard in her hand. "Asset 521 successfully located at coordinates supplied by Asset 478." Although she rattled off flawless English, the woman's accent flagged her as Slavic. "Visual confirmation of the dislocating effect of the spatial displacement field of Asset 463 on the psycho-physical temporal displacement phenomenon of Asset 521."

Temporal displacement phenomenon. Asset 521. That was me. At the very least, my decision to not run had given me the answer to the puzzle of 521. The Guild had assigned me an asset number. But even more concerning, another "asset" had supplied the information that I would be here. Who?

The doctor pocketed the Dictaphone and sneered down at me over her glasses. "You seem to demonstrate a modicum of sense, as you have clearly realized that flight would be futile and have chosen to cooperate without incurring additional physical harm." She gestured at the two attendants. "Let me be plain, then. I am Dr. Petrov. My assignment is to research your psycho-temporal phenomenon. The chancellor of the Guild—I assume by now you know who we are and what we can do—has expressed a keen interest in your abilities. If you choose to cooperate, you may be subject to a rigorous battery of tests, but in the end, we will develop the technological means by which you may control the phenomenon. In return, the Guild asks only that you render us your services until such time as the costs of research and development have been recuperated—as well as the substantial fee for our services."

Now I was sneering. "You want me to pay you to torture me? No, thank you. I think I'm making sufficient progress on my own." I'd already seen myself here, in another twelve or so hours. I knew that the "battery of tests" threatened to be lethal. It may even be that my resistance made it so. But, I simply couldn't bring myself to condone their methods and ideologies by participating willingly. I folded my arms across my chest, not nearly as stiff in my resolve as in the posture of my spine.

Dr. Petrov raised the Dictaphone to her lips once again. "The asset possesses data from research conducted on the phenomenon. This data must be extracted." It was all so antiseptic, the way she referred to her work of abuse and torture as if that somehow cleansed the blood and suffering on her hands. She tucked the recorder into her pocket again and stepped forward. "Given your particular talents, I must assume you have seen that the Guild will ultimately achieve its ends, with or without your cooperation. It would be the most logical choice, and most beneficial to all, for you to comply willingly with our research."

"Logical, maybe, but definitely immoral. I won't help you. You won't make me complicit in a society that condones killing small children to blackmail loyalty from their parents or tortures and abuses fellow humans to wring profit from their gifts. I know how you intentionally addicted Daiyu and Eli to opioids and kept them prisoner to serve your purposes."

"Daiyu and Eli?" She tittered mirthlessly, turning to the smaller of the medical attendants. Stepping forward, he opened the tablet, tapped and scrolled, and then tilted the screen for her to see. "Ah. Assets 469 and 472. Did they also tell you that when we found them, they were outcasts from their communities, living in cardboard and rummaging through the garbage to eke out a miserly existence? Little better than animals. Such ingratitude. The Guild refined their curse into the power to dominate the society that rejected them. They should have been grateful. Instead, they spurned the source of their strength and attempted to defect."

"No. They spurned abuse and captivity."

"We are all captives, 521. But we may choose the cage. It would not be right for the non-compliant few to diminish the luxury of the rest. For an asset whose vision surpasses temporal boundaries, you have a rather myopic view of society."

"My gift *is* myopic. I only see 7 seconds and I only see myself."

"And the Guild will study your episodes and seek to expand your control of both the duration and the frequency of occurrence."

"Thank you very much for the tempting offer, but I believe I prefer to conduct my own research. My methods are less homicidal and sadistic."

Tilting her head, she addressed me as if I were a preschooler too young to understand what she considered a very simple concept. Her tone convinced me that she spurned most of the world's population as her intellectual inferiors. "Are you fond of cake, Asset 521?"

The question was so random that, mystified, I only shrugged and puffed my lips, a habit I'd picked up from the French.

She nodded and sighed dreamily. "I am fond of cake. Moist, rich, chocolate cake that melts on the tongue." For a second, she tasted the description in her mind. "Do you really think that the small crumbs that fall to the floor as the knife carves through the layers diminish, in any way, my enjoyment of a slice? In the picture of society's grand confection, these individual crumbs are insignificant. The cake remains the same, with or without them."

"That's where you're wrong. We're connected. All of us. Every loss, every abuse, every atrocity, ripples through the fabric and diminishes us all."

"No, 521. The Guild is never diminished. But let me appeal to your more practical sentiments. Perhaps you are unaware of the Guild's vast influence and power. The society is generous and lavishes substantial rewards upon its faithful assets. Your grandmother Sabrina knew this."

"My grandmother died because she sold her gifts to the Guild. I won't make her mistake."

"You are selfish, 521. Do you believe that your gifts should serve only you? The Guild would allow you to greatly widen the influence and power that your abilities could control. Imagine the good you could do."

"I'm not sure the Guild and I are on the same page when it comes to the definition of 'good.' The Guild is not my organization of choice when it comes to distributing the benefits of my gift, or anyone else's for that matter. It feeds itself, grinding the rest of us in its gears. But, you're right. I have been selfish because I've been afraid to upset the flow of fate. I'm not anymore. Others *should* benefit from my gift. That's why I came to help Sagar."

"The power and wealth of the planet are wasted upon the rabble. They squander it in self-destruction. Think of your own mother. If she had any imagination her gift might have served the Guild, made you millions. Instead, she wasted her life in drink trying to escape the abilities she'd been given. The enlightened must control the distribution of the gifts."

My train of thought stumbled at the reference to my mother. "The Guild sent the Reaper." I guess I knew this when I first saw her there on the couch. I just didn't want to look it in the face. "You killed my mother?" Truth be told, the face of the Reaper was not truly the guilty party anyway, the face before me, Dr. Petrov, the face of the chancellor from my drift, and the face of the cardinal who served them, these were the faces I needed to search for guilt. But there would be none; of that I was sure. These people deluded themselves with self-righteous justifications.

"Your devotion to your mother, while touching, represses the advancement of your talents. The chancellor deemed it prudent to demonstrate our reach as well as rid you of the obstacle."

My hands flew to my ears and I could no longer maintain my dignified rejection of their cold inhumanity. "Stop calling us that! We are not 'obstacles', 'assets', 'subjects,' and 'vessels.' We are people. We have feelings and hopes and dreams. We are sentient and we have a right to our liberty! We have a right to make the wrong choice as well as the right one and we have the right to decide what that should be."

As I ranted, she glanced at the wall behind me. I knew what was there without looking. Of course, they were watching. There was a surveillance camera. "Well, then, I fear my initial assessment of your sense was inaccurate." She folded her arms and nodded to the hulking attendant.

"Ivan, the bed must be removed and replaced with a medical chair. We'll need to monitor the brain as the drifts occur." She pointed at the flat screen mounted on the wall. "That will serve adequately for our needs. First, however, we will discover the stress triggers so that we can induce the phenomenon."

Ivan nodded and left the room.

"Oscar," she motioned to the shaved, bulk of a man, "secure the patient. Given the impending infiltration of the facility, the testing should begin immediately. To calculate the appropriate response, we must know the target and the venue of the attack in advance."

Oh, Goddess! Josh was right. It was a trap. They knew the Cult was coming.

# CHAPTER 42

The doctor and Oscar marched me down the sanitized hallway in my bra and underwear. Stripping down under the leering gaze of the hulk wasn't a walk in the park, but it was better than submitting myself to the greater indignity of him removing my clothes forcibly.

The cold tile chilled the tender soles of my feet. Dread for the upcoming ordeal chilled the rest of me. Clenching my teeth, I stifled the panic that overwhelmed me as Dr. Petrov explained, "Most assets demonstrate a tendency to display their abilities under certain types of extreme physical distress. Once we have isolated these triggers, we can often replicate the chemical process required to stimulate production of the phenomenon. We'll begin with the ice bath. It has proved successful in inducing an episode in 53% of the 23 genres of assets we have so far catalogued."

The chrome elevator doors at the end of the hall gaped open. We were on the 11th floor of a building with 12. Dr. Petrov's ID key allowed us to descend to the 10th where Oscar pushed me into a room that resembled Gwen's, except that the centerpiece was a small glass coffin structure rather than a pool. No doubt, the designer of the box had intended it to produce the maximum amount of mental anguish. Dr. Petrov removed her ID key card from her lab coat pocket and passed it across the electronic lock. My knees shook a bit as my scantily clad body encountered the frigid temperatures inside the room. "Oscar, prepare the bath."

Oscar lumbered to the casket, unlatched the lid, and adjusted the inner wrist and ankle restraints. My arms instinctively hugged my shivering body. The temperature in the room was only responsible for half of the tremors that resonated from my chest. Along the wall hung a row of thick white terrycloth robes, in a variety of sizes, matched with slippers, neatly laid out on a shelf below. My gaze rested longingly there.

"It would create the illusion of a gesture of humane empathy to offer you the comfort of a robe. That would only allow you to retain your body heat. You don't wish to prolong the time necessary in the bath, do you? By withholding the comfort of such a vain gesture, I am, in truth, showing you a kindness."

She guided me to the bath and the cold metal steps that led to the transparent box. "We are not monsters here, 521. We are scientists."

"So were the Nazis. I doubt anyone would applaud their methods as kindnesses." The anger I felt gave me the resolve to mount the steps without being forced in by the hulk. Perhaps, if I'd had any notion of what I was about to experience, they'd have had to force me in. Lying there as Oscar cinched the straps and Dr. Petrov placed the electrodes on my head and chest, I pitied Gwen and wondered if the bath into which she begged them not to submerge her was ice cold.

"The ice bath often produces the targeted psycho-phenomenon once the body temperature drops below 96°." The doctor's face betrayed not an inkling of human pity. Quite the contrary, an almost anticipatory gleam lit her eyes. My whole body was shivering before the lid was shut. Dr. Petrov glanced at the clock, made a note of the time on her recorder, and then nodded to Oscar. My muscles began to stiffen against the claustrophobia. Oscar flipped the switch.

From the nozzles positioned around the basin, shot ice-cold water that forced a gasp and then a series of rapid breaths from deep in my chest. I had a pretty good idea how long 7 seconds could seem to last in the worst of situations and I was pretty sure by that time, my toes and fingers were tingling numbly. The chattering of my teeth rattled in my head as the freezing water rose around my body. Just as I began to dread that Dr. Petrov's scientific detachment would allow her to drown me, the water level crested around the edges of my face and the jets subsided abruptly into small streams. A steady current of cold water replaced the water my body had warmed. The box amplified the chatter of my teeth and the labored puffs of my breath. The straps didn't even allow me the instinctive comfort of wrapping my arms across my torso.

And then the pain set in. My extremities screamed. In a vain attempt to warm myself with internal chemical reactions, I spouted a stream of heart-felt obscenities. The monitor registered a down-tick in my body temperature. 97°. I tried to stop myself from shivering to allow the cooling process to happen more quickly—anything to end the torture sooner—but had no control.

While my torso convulsed and my fingers and toes burned in the glacial bath, I involuntarily reconsidered my resolve to not cooperate with the Guild and just tell them what I knew. What difference would it make? Even if they succeeded in inducing my drifts, they couldn't force the information they sought from me. The only thing that kept me from screaming out what I knew about the triggers of a warm bath, distinctive smells, flashing fluorescent lights, and the multiplying effects of marijuana was the vision of me dying in the chair Dr. Petrov had ordered the nurse Ivan to prepare. That, and I needed to hold out at least until Gwen was free.

The monitor ticked down. 96°. Sleepiness lulled the pain, the world felt thick and my fingers fumbled in their straps. The expletives that cursed the Guild slurred until I no longer remembered why I was there.

In the blurred vision of hypothermia through glass, I watched Dr. Petrov frown and tap her pen against the clipboard. Short jerks. Ringing in my ears. Minor tremors. And then, an earthquake radiated from my brain and shook my entire body.

The doctor's muffled voice penetrated the glass and warped in the pool of water around my ears. "She's seizing!"

# CHAPTER 43

My head sagged against my chest. A thin line of drool dribbled down my chin to the comfy folds of one of the thick, terry robes from the bath lab. Beneath it, they'd slipped me into a white Spandex jumpsuit with a silver zipper up the front. The hem of the legs constricted around my lower calves so as not to interfere with the straps that bound my ankles to the chair.

"You had an actual seizure," Dr. Petrov explained as I struggled to straighten my neck. My whole body felt exhausted as if I'd run a marathon with no training or been hit by a truck. "A not uncommon occurrence during the initial exploratory testing of a new asset. Fortunately, you were strapped in and unable to do yourself harm."

"You are…a serious…ice bitch," I gasped. The control of my muscles seemed short-circuited.

"We would have allowed you to rest a bit longer, but the chancellor and his guest are anxious for a demonstration of the capabilities of their new asset and they are on a tight schedule." She turned to Ivan who stood at the door. "Bring in Yana."

My heart stopped. He opened the door and stepped into the hall. Yana wandered into the room, sucking on her gloved pinkie finger. Her black hair bounced in curls around her round thick-lashed eyes. She wore pink elbow-length gloves on both hands and a princess gown accessorized with a tiara and glittering plastic dress-up shoes.

"Don't be shy, Yana. Come and say *hello* to 521."

The little girl extended her hand to the doctor and followed her to my chair.

"521, you know Yana. She lives here with us. Yana, can you help me?" The miniature princess nodded, turning her wide-eyed stare to me before stifling a yawn. The passage of time eluded me, but it had to be the wee hours of the morning. "Yana is a Reader." The truth of why the Guild was so desperate to hold Yana struck me like a needle in the eye. Me. They knew in advance that they would have me here. They only wanted her so that they could control and manipulate me. My anomaly was the death warrant of everyone I loved.

Dr. Petrov crouched down to whisper in Yana's ear. She was no more than a tiny songbird trapped in a gilded cage. Pink fairy costumes and a warm bed were no compensation for captivity. The Guild was only interested in exploiting her abilities. Nodding at Dr. Petrov, Yana removed the gloves from her arms and set them on the side table.

The doctor opened a small case labeled 517. She extracted a vial and filled a syringe. When she turned to take Yana's arm, the girl shrank away. A stern look from the doctor convinced her to concede. "Yana is still learning to produce her phenomenon. Isn't that right, Yanska? Pretty soon, you won't need these little shots."

The girl nodded and then winced and shivered as the doctor injected the fluid. "Yana, can you tell us how 521 can use her magic powers? Remember how we had to find what helped you? 521 already knows, and if you can tell us, we won't have to try some of the tests we had to try with you. Wouldn't that be nice for 521?"

Yana nodded, sucking on her pinkie and turning a wide-eyed stare of sympathy on me. There was no way in hell I was going to further burden this child with my pleas. I couldn't put her in a position of openly defying the authority of the monsters who sheltered her.

The injection began to take effect in seconds. Yana's eyes clouded over and Dr. Petrov pushed her to my chair. Mechanically, the child reached up and placed her hands across my cheeks and temples.

"521. Please elaborate upon the catalysts you have found that induce your psychological phenomenon."

Yana's palms snapped tight to my head as Dr. Petrov's prompt initiated an automatic response of images and words in my brain. From the girl's hands emanated not only intense heat but waves that traveled through my skull in throbbing ripples until I felt my head would explode. For a few moments, I clenched my teeth and stiffened against the pain, but the waves screwed tightly the folds of my brain and I cried out. A cerebral earthquake rocked my skull.

"Mary Juana…Flower essant lights…Coffee…Smells…" As I writhed against the waves wreaking havoc in my mind, Yana pronounced her best replication of the words that Dr. Petrov had summoned there with her suggestion.

"That will do nicely, Yana." Dr. Petrov's words brought a sudden, jarring end to the pain. Drops of blood trickling from her nose, eye, and ear, Yana withdrew her hands and collapsed in a flowing, pink heap at my feet. At a nod from the doctor, Ivan scooped her up and removed her from the room.

My ears rang and I couldn't speak for several minutes. Breathing required all my concentration. Whatever its effect on me, though, the episode appeared to be devastating to the small child that produced it. The doctor sniffed away the trauma she had induced and scribbled on the clipboard she held. My mind was only capable of forming one word. *Monster*.

When Ivan returned, Dr. Petrov relayed to him the items that Yana had wrung from my thoughts. She pointed about the room as she spoke. "I'd like to begin in the next thirty minutes."

If the symptoms from Yana reading my thoughts hadn't drained and disoriented me so drastically, I'd have been impressed with how quickly Ivan transformed my room into drift induction central. Clearly, the number 521 that they'd assigned to me indicated that they had some substantial experience in inducing psychotic anomalies. Apparently, as Druids, we all bore some genetic resemblance. That we would respond to similar triggers only made sense. Sayid had, after all, told me that hunger sparked his phenomenon the way it did mine. Daiyu's and Eli's gifts were both sensitive to opioids. It wasn't much of a stretch to imagine the Guild had already identified fluorescent lighting and marijuana as triggers or enhancers for other "assets."

Ivan was just finishing the installation of large, bright fluorescent panels against the stark white walls when the doctor returned with what looked like a humidifier. The machine put off a heavy steam that I immediately recognized as being laced with marijuana oil. She turned on the television that hung in front of the fluorescent lights and tuned it to a news channel.

"Now, 521, you simply tell us what you have seen on the television during your drift. Remember, if you choose to not cooperate, we can always call upon 517 to assist you. Although, I find that each exercise of her psychic abilities requires a longer period of recuperation. It would be better for the child if you were to simply relay the message yourself."

*Monsters.* The word floated through my head, but I had no will to force my lips into movement. A trickle of drool oozed from the corner of my lips.

The anchors on the screen chattered on about the current, socially disturbing tweets of the new U.S. president. My mind, still addled from my encounter with Yana, struggled to sort the words into meaning. Already, the cannabis fumes and the lights had produced a tingling in my right arm that trickled up to my lips. The reading and the rifting had left my brain feeling soft and spongey as if it were full of air holes. I dreaded the side effects of a drift in my current condition. The only consolation was that I knew marijuana deadened them.

"Resistance, 521, would be unwise. We WILL extract the information we desire from your gifts. Your only choice is how much neurological damage you will incur in the process." Even if I'd been able to conjure up a snappy response, forming words had become a challenge for the gods and I was only a mere mortal with a psychotic anomaly. Signaling Ivan, Dr. Petrov followed him out of the room to observe through the window in the door.

My stomach rumbled and the lights bludgeoned my eyes, but within minutes, as marijuana began to infiltrate my brain, the drift symptoms, as well as the side effects from Sayid's rift and Yana's read, relaxed. A warm blanket of tranquility settled over my senses, my eyes flickered and then shut. The drift set in like a dream.

*Second 1: Eyes flicker open. Lying in my bed. "She's coming around." Amr sits by me.*

*Second 2: Struggle to sit up. Trapped in the sheets. Medical light in my eyes. "Ivy, can you hear me?"*

*Second 3: "It's an incoming drift. She's visited this spot in the past."*

*Second 4: Josh, shorter hair than I remember, stands at Amr's side. "The Guild..." the words grate in my throat.*

*Second 5: "521!" Another Josh—or just the essence of him. Longer hair like my present. "We planted a stun inside the defibrillator..."*

*Second 6: "...outside your door." While he whispers, I check the clock and calendar on the dresser. "We'll free you."*

*Second 7: "You scared the hell out of me, Ivy." Amr talks over the instructions coming from Josh at the bottom of the bed. "The roof—get to the roof..."*

My eyes rolled into consciousness as Dr. Petrov pierced my vein with a needle and injected fluid into my arm. "We have observed in other psycho-savants that the chemical properties of thyme restrict the length of the forward projection. We want that to be fairly short. The dose is high." The cool liquid infused my vein. She held up a photo of men robed in cardinal red. "We're looking for these men." In the photo, I recognized the face of the man seated in the front center. I'd already seen him in the drift induced by the rift. The Cult was hoping to abduct him into the in-between. My eyes drooped shut again, the mental suggestion still freshly imprinted on my sub-conscious floated in and out of focus.

*Second 1: Television blares. Strapped to metal chair. Dr. Petrov's face in the observation window.*

*Second 2: Stomach rumbles. Famished. Red ribbon scrolls across the bottom of the screen tuned to CNN.*

*Second 3:* ***Breaking News: Cardinal Marco di Castoria, Secretary of State of the Vatican, falls into coma during visit to genetic research facility.***

*Second 4: "Ivy! We know they know we're coming..."*

*Second 5: "...but they don't know about you and me."*

*Second 6: Right corner of the screen. Small white letters. 9:51. "Cooperate. Tell them we're after the Cardinal. They..."*

*Second 7: "...won't protect Gwen. Vilja, she..."*

This time the drift faded to black and then slowly focused on another scene.

*Second 1: Round dining table. Portrait of Aunt Grace. Home.*

*Second 2: Josh on my right. Drops a napkin over a spill. Stomach gurgles.*

*Second 3: He raises a glass. "To Ivy's future! Long live the new Crone."*

*Second 4: Barry, Daiyu, Eli, Sayid, Sagar, a few faces I don't recognize and...Amr, sitting to my left, raise their glasses.*

*Second 5: Gentle pings erupt around the table as glasses touch in celebration.*

*Second 6: Josh presents his glass to me, his blue eyes smiling, and I touch the rim of mine to his.*

*Second 7: Amr leans close. Axe Fire. He wraps a wisp of my hair on his finger and whispers in my ear, "The year of lavender was only interrupted..."*

When I opened my eyes to the blinding light of the fluorescent panels, Dr. Petrov, leaning over me, clicked the button on her stopwatch.

Dropping it into her lab coat pocket, she raised her Dictaphone to her lips and glanced at her watch. "8:39. 14 seconds. The initial 7-second drift was followed with an injection of thymol to redirect the pursuant drift toward the desired temporal target which was stimulated visually."

After directing Ivan to go and fetch the high chancellor and their distinguished guest, she knelt at the side of my chair.

Dr. Petrov ignored the sweat on my brow and my labored breathing. All my limbs jerked erratically. The marijuana couldn't quite compensate for the strain of the past few hours of psychotic trauma and whatever serum she had pumped into my bloodstream.

"Now, 521, would you like to tell me what you saw, or shall I have Ivan fetch 517?"

# CHAPTER 44

If Josh hadn't appeared in my drift and told me to spill my guts, I would have told Dr. Petrov about the dinner party—or to go to hell. Apparently, though, learning about the impending attack on *Génétique,* through clenched chattering teeth and between labored breaths, convinced her I'd been broken.

Like clockwork, the high chancellor and the cardinal appeared in my room shortly before 8:42. Dr. Petrov, blustering with pride in her efficiency, relayed the information they'd been seeking.

The chancellor, enormously pleased, barked orders to Oscar to heighten security and then scrutinized my situation. "I take it the asset is hostile."

Dr. Petrov shrugged.

"Damn. This psycho-savant would have given me the edge I needed to put Robert in his place years ago. Di Castoria, we absolutely need to crush this little uprising of the Cult. The past has always been their specialty. We can't have this counter-culture of looking to the future and abandoning the dogmas of the past. The Guild is the future. Cardinal Aycelin must be silenced."

"It is not the cardinal, chancellor, but this 'Word' behind him. We know nothing of him. Cardinal Aycelin is our only link. The people, the youth, they flock to the ideas he circulates with his tweets on behalf of the Word."

The chancellor sneered in our direction. "The future is ours now. Why didn't we know anything about her?"

The doctor stepped in. "She seems to have remained off the medical grid until a few years ago when Dr. Singh received her records and was able to begin tracking her."

"Well, evidently, Dr. Petrov, we really have no reason to regret Dr. Singh's defection, do we? I believe you fill the position of head of research quite effectively. Singh was too methodical and plodding for my taste, and his brat too unreliable."

Dr. Petrov raised her pen. "Since our acquisition of Asset 521, we have determined that this psycho-savant is the biological descendant of Sabrina Sedona."

This tidbit of information greatly impressed the chancellor. "THE Sabrina Sedona?"

And then the room went black as I slipped away to make room for the Ivy Leif of twelve hours earlier—for 7 seconds.

I reemerged from my unconsciousness screaming. The residual chemical shit floating in my veins from Sayid's rift, Yana's read, and the multiple drifts induced by the concentrations of fluorescent lights and marijuana finally hit the fan. A trickle seeped from my nose. The doctor wiped the crimson splotch away. A chemical blade sliced through the grey matter in my skull. At any moment, I expected it to rip through my eye socket. My arms and legs stiffened and convulsed in their straps. Sweating and shivering simultaneously, my body worked frantically to eliminate the toxic substances it had secreted in response to the stimuli.

The cardinal looked somewhat distressed at the fuss I was making.

"Handle this, Dr. Petrov." The chancellor's glare rescinded every compliment he had showered on her. "Preserve the asset. Now more than ever, we need this edge." He ushered the confused and concerned clergyman toward the door. "Come this way. We have one more asset with whom you should be acquainted before you leave. I believe the Gleaner might be the key to quietly eliminating the undesirable factions that trouble us..."

The door closed behind them. Dr. Petrov turned to survey my condition. As I gasped against the ripping and tearing in my head, my heart stuttered quickly and then warped into slow motion. Air rasped painfully through my constricted throat. My lungs couldn't quite muster enough energy to expand. Sweat dripped down my face as my limbs trembled and shuddered.

Uncertainty, maybe fear, clouded the characteristic self-satisfaction in the doctor's eyes. She tapped a pen against her clipboard as she observed my struggles to survive. She didn't know what was wrong. She didn't know how to reverse the effects. I didn't care. My will was exhausted. Perhaps I'd find my mother at the end when this was over. There were so many things that I still needed to say to her.

Pivoting on her heel, Dr. Petrov fled the room. My labored breaths and the lugubrious pulse in my veins faded with the clicking of her heels down the sterile white tile of the hallway.

Alone in the room, I waited for the drift I knew was coming. I was dying, strapped to this chair, just like I had seen years earlier. I could have avoided this. The drifts were warnings and I had ignored them. Like my grandmother, I had had the audacity to wager against the decrees of fate and now, like her, I was paying the final bill. My mother and I were dead…but…Sagar was alive…and I couldn't help believe that…somewhere…Mom?

# CHAPTER 45

7 seconds later, my consciousness emerged from the blackness of the drift. I didn't bother to open my eyes. My body was done fighting, this last skirmish with my psychosis had tipped the scales. I'd lost the battle before the war had begun.

An undulant, residual image of Josh floated behind my eyes. He'd just been here, traveling to my last drift, mourning my death. Even the strength to lament the shortness of the drift, my lack of strength for a decent good-bye, escaped me. A tear welled up at the corner of my eye and straggled forlornly down my cheek. I would have liked to have known him better, longer, more presently.

A long, wheezing last breath flowed from my lungs. And then, just outside the door, the pitter-pat of bare feet, small bare feet, slapped rapidly against the tile and pricked at my lethargic ears. The impulse to open my eyes fluttered across my fading consciousness but died unfulfilled.

# CHAPTER 46

The door opened. My lips wheezed out the last of the breath hoarded in my failing lungs. My nose no longer registered the smell of marijuana. My head tipped forward into the strap that restricted it and forced the glow of the fluorescent lights through the blackening curtain of my eyelids.

The padding footsteps stopped at my chair. Small fingers brushed the hair and sweat from my brow. "Wait, Ivy. It's not too late." The words flowed into my ears in muffled slow motion. My brain was shutting down. The impulses necessary to recognize the origin of the sounds had deteriorated. And then a tiny spark of memory ignited a name—Sagar. Sagar? Confusion spurred a last, super-human effort to crack open my eyes and see the little face once more. Somehow, my defiance of the iron fist of fate would all seem worth it if I could see him again.

A small, metal click, the opening of a box, and then his tiny fingers wrapped around my arm, just above the elbow. My body had no resources left for wincing when the point of a needle pierced the skin. The ice-cold liquid scurried into my veins and then bolted for my heart. The sensation was similar to the one I'd had when Sagar dragged me to the surface of the pool. My lungs sucked voraciously at the air they'd been denied and I gasped. The smell of marijuana, the hum of Sagar's breathing, and the white and ice blue of the walls sprang into my consciousness all at once in a vortex of sensation.

As I inhaled them, Sagar undid the straps that bound me.

"What the hell was that?"

"A gift of gratitude from my father for asset 521. He only needed that number to obtain access to Dr. Petrov's notes." He rose up on his tiptoes to whisper in my ear. "Did you know the Cult has a Receiver? They're a new breed, more recent because obviously in ancient times we didn't use electricity much. We have a spy." He grinned broadly, then looked suspiciously around the room before putting a finger to his lips. "Sh. The Guild doesn't know. They don't have one."

"Oh, my Goddess! That was why Josh needed the number 521. Dr. Petrov does all her notes on a Dictaphone."

"Yes, and all the paperwork is on their computers."

In mid euphoria, it dawned on me that Sagar had, for obvious reasons, not been part of the plan. "But what are *you* doing here, Sagar? This is dangerous. How did you even get in?"

"Sayid's door. He's using a machine my father developed for him while he was in the Guild to hold it open. Sayid couldn't stop me. He can't leave the machine or the door will shut and we'll be stuck here."

Sagar was nothing if not hardheaded. I guess if you know the future possibilities, people don't really have a right to tell you what to do. "No, I mean, in this room. How did you get in?"

He giggled, unlocking the last of my straps. "The doors are not locked. Why would the doors be locked when the patients are locked up inside?"

"And Josh let you come?" I slid out of the chair rubbing my wrists and ankles. The convulsions and violent shivering had left purple and pink lesions. I shed the bulky bathrobe in favor of the fitted, less cumbersome white, Spandex jumpsuit beneath. The sight of my bare arms, bruised and bandaged along the veins, shocked me. I didn't realize they'd taken blood samples.

"He did not want to. But I told him he would have to choose between you and Gwen, so he had to let me come."

"Did you dream about this?"

He nodded.

"Is there anything I should know?"

"We're going to make it back—in most of the possibilities."

The sudden extension of my expiration date rippled a shiver of sheer joy down to my toes. Reaching down, I scooped him up in my arms and twirled him about, kissing his cheeks. Not the best idea. My physical strength was restored, but my brain and equilibrium were still catching up. We stumbled, but I caught myself on the chair and set Sagar on his feet. He readjusted the white robes he was wearing and then took my hands in his.

"Most?"

"There are always choices that change the outcomes." An adorable and heart-wrenching sympathy widened his eyes. "I'm sorry your mommy died, Ivy."

I really couldn't go there. Kneeling to his eye level, I reassured him, "I'm sorry, too." My eyes began to sting as I strangled out the words, but I blinked back the welling tears. "You may be the only person I know who understands how I feel." I bit my lip. "Sagar, I think it was my fault…the choices I made…but I…you're alive…and…" my voice betrayed my attempts at courage and broke as I turned away.

Sagar pulled his hand from mine and put his little palms on my cheeks, turning my face so I would have to look him in the eye again. "Your mother did not die because of what you chose to do. She always dies. In every dream, Ivy. My father says everything that can happen, does happen. But here, in the space we occupy, your mother always dies. I know why, but I cannot tell you now."

Sagar's power delved deeper than his visions of the future. The wisdom which sprouted from his gift allowed him to wrap a bandage about the open wound on my heart. A weight lifted from my chest and I seemed to breathe again. Smiling back the tears, I hugged him and kissed his forehead. "You're right, Sagar. C'mon. We have to hurry. Josh planted a stun gun for me."

Grabbing his hand, I piloted us out into the hallway where, sure enough, inside the defibrillator case on the wall was hidden a stun gun, very similar to the one I'd dropped in the café when the Jumper attacked us. Sagar followed along willingly, most likely he'd already played out this scene in his dreams. Peeking into the corridor, I reassured myself that no armed security guards patrolled the hallways. Leaking the Cult's plan to abduct the cardinal had, it seemed, turned the eye of the Guild away from this corner of the facility. “Sagar, where did Sayid open the rift?”

“Downstairs in the pool room with Gwen.”

“Did you come up the stairs?”

He nodded. “The elevator is down there.” He pointed in the direction Dr. Petrov’s heels had receded. “Josh thought the stairs would be safer.”

“Show me.”

Both of us barefoot, we padded down the direction from which I’d heard his footsteps arrive. In the reflection of the observation windows along the corridor, our white robes and Spandex gave us the look of a couple of angels fleeing hell. To me, hell had always been cold and blue like this, not hot and red like the pictures.

At the end of the hall, Sagar pointed toward a metal door marked with a silver plaque displaying a picture of stairs. At the opposite end, the elevator dinged and the doors opened up. Dr. Petrov stepped into the hall as I was shoving Sagar into the stairwell. Whatever subterfuge we’d had the foresight to plan, I may have just thwarted.

“Stop! We’ve already taken steps to secure the cardinal. We know about your plan!”

“Yes!” I shouted back. “But we knew you knew.” The door slammed behind me. Before we were three steps down, a siren blared in electronic monotone, “Security breach. Security breach!”

Panting, Sagar yelled over the siren, “If they secured the cardinal, will Gwen still be able to find him?”

“I don’t know. Is the cardinal a Druid child?”

“I believe he is a Jumper. But he doesn’t practice much. Too old…and the Catholic church frowns upon possession.”

“Then Gwen can find him and open the in-between wherever they’ve secured him. They’re not expecting that. I didn’t tell them that’s what we were planning.” Taking the stairs faster than Sagar’s shorter legs allowed him to, I reached the landing only a step behind him.

As I followed Sagar around the switchback, I learned, a bit too late, that the building did indeed employ armed security guards. A man in the requisite light blue uniform and butch haircut, who looked a little like this was the first time he'd actually been allowed to play guns, tore through the door below us and targeted Sagar. One hand on his gun and the other clutching his gun wrist, he tried, unsuccessfully, to steady his aim.

My stun gun, woefully inadequate for the situation, did, however, serve me well as an impromptu prop. Inhaling deeply, I assumed the role of pursuer. "Oh, thank Goddess! We nearly lost this tricky little guy. Dr. Petrov's got her panties all in a wad." My charged weapon pointed at Sagar, I waved the guard forward with my free hand. "Pass me your handcuffs." Unsure, his gun still trained on the kid, he sidled up the steps, reaching for the handcuffs dangling at his side. "Be careful. Don't touch him," I warned, to increase his suspicion of the boy and deflect his attention from me. "He looks harmless, but he's one of the most powerful little shits I've ever…" When the guard was close enough for me to lunge at him, I slammed the stun gun squarely into his chest. The shock kept him from reacting and I held the charge against his shirt until he convulsed. His gun clattered down the stairs as his head rammed the concrete wall and his body slumped sideways against the railing. Grabbing the cuffs as he fell, I attached him to the metal bar.

Sagar trotted down the stairs and retrieved the firearm. Holding it upside down between his finger and thumb, as if it were infected, he offered it up to me. "My father says I should never play with guns."

Sighing, I searched around for what looked like a safety, found it on the handle, and flicked it. Guns were as much a mystery to me as Sagar. My jumpsuit was ill-equipped for stowing cargo. The belt, perforated with eyelets that the "scientists" here used for Goddess only knows what purpose, offered the only storage option. I tucked the gun in the back.

The door above us opened up and I rushed Sagar to the exit marked ten. Peeking out the door assured me that backup hadn't arrived for our guard. The familiar click of Dr. Petrov's heels descending the concrete steps echoed through the stairwell. Muffling the click of the door as we exited, I tucked Sagar safely behind me and waited for her to emerge into the corridor. Although the injection had produced a physical jumpstart, my mental faculties still lagged. The fluorescent lights above and the thrumming monotonous siren, not to mention the healthy dose of adrenaline my heart was pumping, went straight to my head.

As she threw open the door and charged after us, Dr. Petrov yelled into a walkie-talkie. Russian expletives peppered her diatribes. If I'm honest with myself, I would have to say that the look of shock on her face as the bolt of electricity sizzled the piece of throat between her stiff, white collars was quite satisfying, a pleasant contrast to the sadistic gleam I'd last seen there. When she hit the floor, I requisitioned Sagar's sash to hogtie the monster. A quick rifling through her lab coat pocket produced her ID key card. For lack of any other option in my jumpsuit, I stuffed it down the front.

Seconds later, the doctor recovered consciousness and aimed her expletives at us as we hurried down the hallway. Her impotent cries joined in a cacophonous chorus with the "Security Breach, Security Breach!" moaning overhead.

My right arm began to tingle and my lips numbed. A small flashing prism twinkled in my vision. A drift was coming.

The hallway opened up into something resembling a nurse's station. Sagar spotted the door to Gwen's lab room just beyond and accelerated his little trot. Behind the counter, though, hung a large whiteboard divided into grid squares. The thin middle column contained room numbers from this floor. They all began with 10. The widest column on the end listed meds and procedures. The first column might have been an enigmatic list of three-digit numbers, but the number 517, halfway down the board, told me that I was looking at room assignments for the assets.

"Sagar, wait!" I knew I was about to drift. Josh was going to tell me that stepping into Gwen's lab room was a trap. It was too dangerous for a little boy, no matter how wise. I could send him down to 517's room to free Yana while I stepped into it knowingly. "I need you to help me. There's a girl they're keeping in here. She's a Reader." I glanced up and back, positive I didn't have the time to explain the whole situation. Beyond the elevator, the corridor turned left. The room numbers in the direct vicinity indicated that, most likely,

Yana's room was around the corner. "If they keep exploiting her power to read people, they'll kill her, and they don't care. I need you to run around the hallway there, find her, and bring her back here. Can you do that?"

He hesitated, glancing between Gwen's room, where lay safe passage back to his new home with the Cult and his family, and the end of the hallway.

"What's the matter? Do you know something, Sagar? What have you seen?"

"I can't leave you, Ivy." He tucked his hand into mine.

"I'll be fine. I know what's coming. Please. I can't leave her here. She deserves to be free, not a prisoner to her gifts." I couldn't let Sagar follow me into that room knowing that Josh had already warned me.

His brow wrinkled, but I knew him. He and I were woven from the same thread. He couldn't refuse an act of altruism. He nodded reluctantly, took a few halting steps, and then turned back—just in case I'd changed my mind. I nodded and nudged him on with a little wave of my hand. Turning, he scurried down the hall.

Dr. Petrov was still hurling threats from the end of the corridor. Astonished and vacillating between relief that we had succeeded in diverting their attention and suspicion that no reinforcements had arrived to oppose us because this was part of a trap, I took a few wary steps toward the door to Gwen's room.

The blackness I was expecting invaded my eyes from the edge until my consciousness disappeared to make room for the me of the past who would hear from Josh that this was a trap.

7 seconds later, my hand on the doorknob steadied me when I reemerged into my present.

In a fanfare of metal and shouting, two security guards, wielding guns like the one tucked in my belt, shoved the stairwell door into Dr. Petrov's squirming body. At her livid insistence one stopped to unbind her. The other shouted at me. The door flew open again, this time without hands, smashing into the doctor once more. Vlad the Slav, the garden tool launching Guild asset, strutted through the opening and stepped over the doctor's flailing limbs. As I disappeared into Gwen's lab room, he flexed his arms and growled, showing off a bulky set of thick metal bracelets that matched an electronic crown on his head.

# CHAPTER 47

Inside Gwen's lab room, the familiar rushing gale of Sayid's rift met my ears, but my eyes found Josh. The one from the present. He was in the water helping Vilja unhook Gwen. Halfway down the pool, on the outer wall of the room, a spatial rift outlined in blue rippled the air. Through the rift, I could see Sayid, attached with monitors to a small machine, his hands extended toward the rift, maintaining it. Dr. Singh stood at the machine, gesticulating wildly at him. Sayid remained impassively focused. The doctor peered through the rift. It took very little brainpower to assume Dr. Singh never authorized Sagar's passage into *Génétique.*

Eli and Daiyu flanked the hole in space. A couple of security guards and white-suited lab assistants lay motionless on the deck around the pool. I'd seen Daiyu's handiwork already. Josh didn't want gunshots to attract attention. Besides, other than Sayid's, I'd never seen many firearms in the Cult. Daiyu tensed to rush the door when I opened it but fell back as the view of my face caught up with my feet. We exchanged nods. It was a queer sensation, being a member of a family.

Josh glanced up as the door shut behind me. The tense lines of his forehead relaxed and his face lit up. Just then, Vilja tossed aside a plastic tube and Gwen opened her eyes. "Josh!" Her enthusiastic gasp mimicked my own relief.

I moved to the side of the door, stun gun ready to present the first line of defense once the security guard made his way down the hall in front of the Pusher. "They're coming! Vlad is with them. He's wearing some high-tech bracelets and a crown. He might be supercharged."

"*Merde*! We didn't see that coming. Ready, Vilja?" He stole a few seconds to brush the soaking hairs from his sister's face, kissed her forehead, and then asked, "Did you get him?" I was sure he meant Cardinal di Castoria. The Word's sovereignty was going to need mollifying after this concerted, unauthorized rescue mission.

Exhausted, Gwen nodded.

Vilja tossed aside one last node. "Let's go!"

Josh and Vilja lifted Gwen out of the pool to Eli. The poor girl couldn't even walk. It took both him and Vilja to support her to the rift. Eli stepped through first, and Vilja passed Gwen through to his waiting arms.

As soon as Eli had carried Gwen away, Dr. Singh leaned through the rip and yelled above the rushing din, "Where is Sagar?"

Josh turned a panicked look in my direction. Sagar was supposed to be with me.

"He's fine…" I wasn't sure if I was lying and wondered if I'd made the wrong choice in sending him after Yana. "I knew this was a trap. I sent him somewhere safer…"

"No!" Josh hopped out of the pool. "The trap was for the Guild. They focused all their security to protect the cardinal. They have no idea we're coming for Gwen and that she would grab him from the in-between."

This was where I was pretty sure that the Josh I'd seen outside the door just before I came in was a Josh from farther in the future than the Josh I was speaking to now. "I don't think so. I just saw Vlad and it looks like they knew."

The knob twisted and the door flew open. The guard that kicked it charged through with such force that the door hit the wall on the other side and slammed shut behind him.

Forewarned by his colleague and the doctor, he was expecting the stun gun and deflected my attack. Daiyu and Josh both skirted the pool from opposite sides, racing to my aid. This guard was much more experienced than the one in the stairwell. We grappled, his fist around mine until he shook the weapon from my grasp. It skittered across the tile deck as I resorted to my rudimentary YouTube self-defense and directed a head butt backward to his nose. The guard grunted and then maneuvered a bulky arm around my neck, strangling me in a chokehold. Josh arrived before Daiyu. The guard, still wrestling me, pulled his gun and pointed it directly at Josh's head while shielding his own body with mine.

"Stay back! The chancellor wants to protect this asset, but *you* are disposable."

Daiyu, dashing toward us from the far side, hesitated when Josh stopped.

"Sagar?" Dr. Singh peered through the opening. "Sagar, the door is closing. Sayid cannot hold the rift indefinitely!" As if to prove his point, the static inside the blue-rimmed rip shivered and split, like a television losing its signal. "Where is Sagar?"

In the standoff, Daiyu inched forward.

"No Daiyu! Get out, now!" I yelled. "Go! You and Josh leave. Go! I'll be fine." My eyes begged Josh.

Now that Gwen was out, he didn't have to choose between us. He shook his head.

"Trust me! I'll be fine." My confidence was about as solid as my trust in my 7-second drifts.

The door rattled maniacally beside me, distracting us all. With a nasty grate of ripping metal, it blew open and careened into the pool.

Water splashed the entire room and doused us. Instinctively ducking, the security guard loosened his grip and dropped his gun. Scrambling out of his grasp, I recovered my stun gun and tossed the real one from my belt to Josh. He'd have a better idea of how to use it. The puddles between us stopped it from sliding.

Pivoting, I stabbed the stun gun in the guard's face. He stiffened and fell to the floor. Vlad stepped into the room. Shifting bolts of blue lightning streaked between the bracelets and the crown he wore. Dipping his hands in a wide arc, he targeted Daiyu with his eyes. She schooled him in the tower courtyard and now he was looking for revenge. He swung his arms back up. "No!" I yelled, sprinting to stop him. The guard recovered and grabbed my ankle. I face planted. The stun gun clattered away just beyond my reach.

Daiyu's body vaulted to the ceiling. The protective field she raised around her couldn't block the bulk of Vlad's supercharged kinetic force. He dropped his arms dramatically and the force reversed direction. Daiyu's body plummeted into the pool. High-speed splashes peppered the room. Her body floated below the surface, uncertain if it could rise again. Josh dived for the gun. The security guard hauled me up in a choke hold.

Dr. Petrov appeared at Vlad's shoulder, adjusting the pins in the tight knot at the back of her head as if the fight were now decided. "Did you really imagine, 521, that the Guild's resources were not sufficient to quell the uprising emboldened by your measly 7-second glimpses into the future?"

Josh stood slowly, dripping more heavily than the rest of us, his gun pointed at Dr. Petrov.

"304, how good to see you again. You, at least, should have known the folly of such an expedition."

Dazed and gasping, Daiyu broke through the surface of the pool.

"It wasn't folly. Gwen's out and she abducted Cardinal di Castoria. He's trapped in the in-between. I'd say it was a success, all around." Josh's sang-froid under pressure shouldn't have surprised me. I'd never actually seen him lose his cool—except during that drift where I was dying. Fleetingly, I wondered if he really didn't care whether he lived or died—as long as his sister was out of the monster's lair.

Me, on the other, I cared—more than I cared to admit. To me, he was the difference between static and clarity in my drifts. He was the force that stood against the exploitation of the Guild. We needed him for the very reasons they hated him. And, as far as I knew, the dead didn't travel.

The guard, knowing he couldn't use his gun on me without serious repercussions from the chancellor, targeted Josh. Daiyu paddled to the edge of the pool. Vlad tensed, prepared to destroy her. Dr. Petrov touched his arm and immobilized him with a glance.

"Is that what you think, that we planned all of this to safeguard your sister and the cardinal?" Dr. Petrov chortled disdainfully. "Bread crumbs. 521 is the true goal. She is the future. And we knew she would lead us to the elimination of an annoying obstacle. Did you think, 304 that we would let Dr. Singh defect?" She turned her gaze on the rift.

Dr. Singh bellowed insistently for his son, his voice growing more and more agitated. He could only see through the rift's direct line of sight. "Sagar? Sagar! You must come through now! We have only minutes before the rift closes."

"The boy is still here?" Avarice gleamed in Dr. Petrov's eyes. She accosted the security guard that helped her escape, dragged him into the corridor, and pointed him in the direction I sent Sagar. "Find the boy. Bring him to me."

*Merde*! Why couldn't Dr. Singh keep quiet? Dr. Petrov might have assumed Sagar was already out through the rift. I would have found a way to sneak him out, even if it meant staying behind.

*The roof.* The Josh of my drift, who knew more than the Josh in this room, told me to go to the roof. I had to get Sagar and Yana there. But first, I had to make sure Daiyu and Josh got out through the rift—or the Josh that sent me to the roof wouldn't exist.

Daiyu crawled out of the pool, splitting the focus of the guard who held me throttled. With the doctor's back turned, Josh, who obviously knew his way around a gun, fired at the most volatile threat, and the one most likely to strike at Daiyu with little or no provocation—Vlad. The Pusher dived for the deck. Tile shattered behind him. When the security guard moved to return fire, I dove for my stun gun and hit him with it again. His shot hit the pool as he convulsed and dropped.

The fire brought Dr. Petrov storming back into the room. Of course, true to his unhinged nature, Vlad pulled himself up in a rage. Ignoring the doctor's frantic orders, the Pusher reacted like the maniac he was. Grunting, as if lifting it himself, he directed his kinetic field toward the water in the pool and heaved. All the water began flowing toward the ceiling. Daiyu, already near the rift, hesitated. "Get out!" I yelled. "Go back, now!"

The tidal wave loomed above us.

Daiyu wavered. Josh shouted, "Go!" Ignoring us, she sprinted to offer him the cover of her energy field.

Josh didn't understand that he, too, needed to leave me to the future we'd arranged. "No, Josh! Run! You'll be crushed. Go! I'll be fine!"

The churning of the rushing torrent mingled with the gale of the rift. The room roared in the convergence of nature's most powerful elements. Vlad's intentions obvious, Dr. Petrov retreated, sprinting to the safety of the hallway as the last of the water rushed upward into the mushroom blooming at the ceiling.

Vlad shoved his arms downward.

# CHAPTER 48

Freed, the water plummeted. Daiyu sprinted, slammed into Josh, and wrapped him in a protective embrace. The swollen wave crashed down on their heads. When it hit the wall, the force of the backflow rushed toward the doorway, overwhelming the security guard and sweeping me and Vlad to the opposite side of the room.

For minutes, the water churned and rolled me, filling up my nose and seeping down my throat. The bulk of the wave followed the slope of the deck back into the pool. Choking and spitting, I hauled myself up.

Vlad's head and arm bracelets crackled intermittently. Puddles of water rippled about his body, sprawled against the tiles. His own rashly unleashed force had knocked him out cold.

Josh floated face down in the pool. "Oh, Goddess, no!" I jumped in after him. Daiyu bobbed to the surface at the opposite end, dazed, but conscious. The water was less than waist high, now that half of it had sloshed into the hallway. Holding my breath, I flipped Josh over. "He's still breathing. Help me get him to the rift!"

We hauled him to the edge of the pool and then hoisted him onto the deck near the rift. It rippled and cracked, the hurricane-force wind muffling to a storm.

Dr. Singh's face peered through. "Where is Sagar? The rift is closing! The Guild must not have him. You have no idea what he is…"

Paying little attention to the doctor's ranting—because I knew that somewhere in the future Josh and I saw the rift shut, stranding Sagar and me. We had made—would make—

arrangements for it. *The roof.* Daiyu and I dragged Josh's limp body to the waning rift.

Over the wailing siren message, "Security Breach! Security Breach," the howling wind, and the sloshing of water into the pool, a vague scuttle of feet, bare, heeled, and leather-souled, wafted up the corridor. I could deal with that later. At the moment, the most urgent goal was to get Josh to safety, otherwise, our plan for the future might never come to be. "Go!" I shouted to Daiyu. I'll hand him through to you. He has to get out to make the future happen."

Nodding, she lifted her leg through the shuddering rift. Grunting and heaving against the dead weight, I shoved Josh, feet first, into Daiyu's waiting hands. Dr. Singh helped thread him through, more to unclog the space between him and his son than to help Josh. Josh's body shivered as his chest passed through the field. His eyes opened and he startled, realizing I was sending him away. "No! Stop! We didn't see this, Ivy. We didn't see Vlad."

"Yes, I did—we did." I kissed his forehead and whispered in his ear the time and date I saw on my mother's dresser when he told me about the roof. "*The roof.* That's what you told me in the drift. Thank you—for everything, Josh."

"Ivy, no, let me stay!"

"I need you to go more."

Dr. Singh tugged on his feet and I pushed him through.

When his body had disappeared into the space on the other side, Dr. Singh's face reemerged. He glanced back and forth between the machine and Sayid. Our Rifter's hand trembled violently with the strain of maintaining the field.

"The machine is functioning beyond maximum. Where is Sagar?"

"I'm going to go get him now. Please, Dr. Singh, trust me. We have a way out." I said it as if it were a reality, even though I knew it was only a possibility that I just barely set in motion. Sagar hadn't come through the blown off doorway yet, with or without Yana. I rushed to make sure that happened, but Dr. Petrov emerged from the hallway, blocking my path.

Two security guards, guns drawn, followed her in as I cautiously retreated through puddles. One thrust a squealing and writhing Sagar into the room. The inept guard I handcuffed to the railing in the stairway trailed a docile, pink Yana through the door. Behind them, an olive-skinned girl, about my age and height, stepped quietly into the room.

"Well, this was truly unexpected." Dr. Petrov grinned triumphantly at Dr. Singh. Her pride in victory over the competition bloated her chest and oozed from her eyes. "Now, we have *both* the seers when we hoped to procure only one. You chose badly, Dr. Singh. After your many years serving the chancellor, you should have known better how to protect your assets. Do not fear, though, we will learn from your mistakes."

"That is my son!" To my horror, the doctor lifted one leg through the blinking field. He'd never get back out in time. Sayid's face strained with tension, his arm falling as he fought to hold the rift open.

Perhaps as her superior, Sagar's father never truly saw the monstrously sadistic side of Dr. Petrov. I feared he had no clue about the depths of her perversity and her lack of humanity. He still believed she would respect his talent and honor their professional bond. I knew better. "No! Dr. Singh! Don't!"

Only half of Dr. Petrov's face smiled. "There was a time, Dr. Singh, when you would have been untouchable. Unfortunately, you are no longer a high-value asset." She turned abruptly to the guard holding Yana and assumed possession of the girl's hand. "Shoot him."

The man strode quickly forward, gun outstretched to the rift.

"Papa!" Sagar squirmed and struggled against his captor.

"Dr. Singh! Get back!" I launched myself toward Sagar's father as the security guard fired. The shot rang hollow through the pool room and pierced my shoulder. I crumpled to the floor, grasping the burning wound. Blood oozed between my soaked fingers.

"Ivy!" Sagar screamed.

My blood diffused in cloudy skeletons through the puddles around me. The guard shot again, over my head. Dr. Singh groaned above the roar of the rift's wind. From the ground, I watched a crimson splotch spread across the white robes on his chest. Astonishment spread across his face. His foot receded through the tear in space, and he fell back into Sayid's room.

"Paaapaa!" Sagar's cry, long, drawn, and feral, shivered the room. The same sound burst from my own chest when I knelt beside my mother's dead body. Only Sagar's wail was born, not of regret for time wasted in ignorance, but of lament for moments not yet lived.

Sayid howled, stretched beyond his capacity, and the rift snapped shut.

# CHAPTER 49

"Papa! Paaapa!" Terror, horror, pain; each one sculpted into its own mold the muscles of Sagar's face.

My shoulder, bleeding and throbbing, I kicked the back of the guard's knees, toppling him to the floor and releasing the gun in a clatter of metal on tile.

Dr. Petrov straightened her shoulders. Inhaling and exhaling deeply, she dropped Yana's hand and strolled toward the pile that was me and the guard struggling for possession of his weapon. Apparently, she thought the scene was over. She kicked the gun out of reach, grabbed the guard by the collar, and tossed him away. "I SAID, 'protect the asset'."

"521, you've damaged yourself." Recovering her proximity to Sagar, she widened the gap between us. The guard struggled to contain the boy's tantrum. "Protect that asset. He's only a boy. Secure him!"

"Papa! Papa, no!" Sagar's whimpers echoed around the walls. He pulled away from the guard and reached for the empty space where he last saw his father's slumped body. My heart cringed for him.

Fog forming in my head blocked the signals from my brain to my feet. My hand clutched the wound in my shoulder. Blood seeped through my fingers and congregated in little puddles along the wrinkled skin. Nauseous at the sight of it, I crawled toward Sagar.

"Papa!" His screams pelted Dr. Petrov's back like so many feathers, but they bit right into my soul.

"Why waste your strength?" A thrill of vengeance had crept into the doctor's voice. "You'll need it, you know, once we begin testing again."

Tears welled up in my eyes. Anger welled up in my veins. The insecure guard who shot Dr. Singh was more susceptible to my rudimentary self-defense training than his more experienced colleague. Already crouched on the ground, I gritted my teeth defiantly against the stabs of pain that rippled from my shoulder and launched my foot at his nose to release the ankle he had throttled. My heel crunched bone. Blood seeped from his nose and mingled with mine in the puddles.

"No! No, Papa! No!" Crazed with grief, Sagar kicked and strained. The officer yanked and twisted his body, trying unsuccessfully to subdue him. He had lost all sense. The portal to his father had snapped shut. His emotion kept escalating and had nowhere to go. The room vibrated around him.

Dr. Petrov signaled the dark-haired girl with the deeply bronzed skin standing at her side. "427, could you convince 513 that he should curb his resistance and follow you back to his room? I'm afraid this officer's battering will damage the asset. Your methods are so much less barbaric." The girl stepped toward the officer grappling against Sagar's violent mourning. The doctor redirected his attention to me. "Escort 521 and 517 to the 11th floor. Our little drama here is done. The chancellor needs some information about the future ASAP. 521 is not a reliable source. We'll need 517's services to process the information she foresees."

"No! Papa!—Let me go! Let me go!—Papa!" I wasn't sure if I was just more sensitive than Dr. Petrov—well, obviously, I was emotionally—but physically, I didn't think that she was aware of the tremors subtly building beneath our feet.

The girl, 427, rather than taking charge of the squirming and screaming boy, took possession of his wrist, held it high, and closed her eyes as if meditating. For a brief moment, enough time for Sagar's guard to make his way across the room to confront me, the tantrums abated to low murmurs and the trembling in the air and the floor stilled.

"427 is a Controller." Dr. Petrov explained. "The skin to skin contact allows her to synchronize her brain waves with Sagar's and influence his thoughts and emotions."

The young woman, having calmed the storm to a mild breeze, turned to lead Sagar out. With his free arm, the boy grabbed his head and refused. “No!” he shouted. His eyes, full of burning rage, focused on 427. Confused, the girl started as if she’d never been contradicted before. She grabbed her own head. Her chest inflated before she spewed her cry into the room. Frantically, she shook her arm in a vain attempt to release Sagar’s wrist. “He’s burning me! He’s burning me!”

“No! Papa! No! I need you, Papa!” As Sagar’s cries gathered steam again, 427 joined in, mimicking his laments, as if he had reversed the flow of her gift. They both reached their hands toward the spot where the rift had disappeared.

This time, the tremors in the floor spread to the walls. The tiles shivered.

Dr. Petrov’s eyes grew wide with an expression that mingled both fear and awe. We were about to see what Dr. Singh meant when he told us we had no idea what Sagar was.

The security guard, distracted by the tremors and the united wailing of the two assets, fell easy prey to my stun gun. It sputtered its last store of energy into his chest. He slumped over onto the body of his bleeding colleague. The weapon was now nothing more than a short stick.

Sagar’s mourning chant stopped abruptly. “He’s dead!” he whimpered in chorus with 427. Tears blobbed and trickled down his face. A stream of snot ran unchecked to his lips.

Dr. Petrov, consumed in a gleam of conquest, ignored the insignificant plight of her security guard and knelt in front of her prize. I stepped cautiously forward, my head and hand silently protesting, urging her to back off. The doctor failed to sense the depth of power behind Sagar’s tirade. His father must have had good reason for concealing the magnitude of his son’s unleashed neuro-kinetic fury. “Sagar, sweetheart, your father was holding you back. Look at what you can do. We can help you. Wouldn’t you like having such power?”

The doctor drew Sagar’s forlorn gaze from the spot where his father last beckoned. “He was not supposed to be here,” he explained, more to himself than to her. “I never saw him here. I only came because I knew he was not in danger…I brought him here…” He stared at the doctor blankly, bewildered by his lack of foresight, unhinged at the realization that pursuing this course altered his visions so catastrophically.

"He was not supposed to be here. I never saw him here." 421 took up his chorus.

The doctor, sensing weakness, resorted to her natural tendency to dominate forcefully what wouldn't come willingly. Grabbing his shoulders, she shook him. "Stop! Stop this now! Release 421."

"You killed him," Sagar responded weakly, his voice tiny and timid.

Dr. Petrov misread, as an acceptance of her power, Sagar's dawning realization that his father's death was not his fault. "Enough of this! You will release 421 and you will follow me back to your room."

"You killed him. *You killed him.* YOU KILLED HIM!" As the boy's rage grew, 421 mimicked his chant. The tremors reemerged. Cracks serpentined across the floor. Tiles shook free from the walls and crashed into jagged shards.

"Sagar? Sagar!" Limping forward, I tried to stay the rising tide. "Come with me, kidlet, I'll get you out of here." Casting a warning glance at Dr. Petrov, I approached the boy as she retreated. But the trembling of the floor followed her. The security guards wobbled, trying to stand. The bulk of the shaking centered on the ground around the three of them.

Yana scuttled to the doorway where she huddled, her arms protecting her head.

Perhaps for the first time, Sagar became aware of his own power. He and 421 both stretched out their arms, focusing the shivering in the air and the walls and the floor around the doctor and her guards. "You killed him! YOU killed him!" The tremors shook the floor beneath Dr. Petrov so violently that she stumbled and fell. She and the guards ducked and covered as tile shards sprang up from the floor and launched themselves at their huddled bodies. Machinery, medical tubing, wires, plaster from the ceiling obeyed Sagar's will. The drawers and cupboards at the back wall flew open. Bandages, syringes, plastic bags, and bottles of medication hurled themselves at Petrov and her accomplices.

The focal point of Sagar's rage began to widen. The floor cracked beneath us. 427 screamed and fell to her knees, drained or overwhelmed by the flow of Sagar's power through her mind.

"Let her go! Let her go!" I had to free her before he killed her. She was only an innocent bystander, maybe a prisoner, maybe a loyal operative, but either way, Sagar would never forgive himself for murdering her. I knew this because he and I were made of the same weave. Desperate, I seized his wrist.

His power, recognizing a fresh spring of energy, relinquished the dead source and ricocheted up my arm toward my brain while 427's arm fell limp to the floor. "YOU killed her! YOU killed her!" Against my will, compelled by the energy surging through my brain, I chanted with Sagar.

The entire room shook with the amplified power of our gifts combined. The throb of the gunshot wound disappeared. The bottom of the pool cracked and the water emptied into the void. A large rift opened in the ceiling above us. Sagar's rage poised to crush us all. But, the very fact that I was still aware, that he had not completely appropriated my will, suggested I might still have some control over his.

"Sagar! Your mother!" Those few words, forced through gritted teeth, required enormous effort. They pierced the flow of energy between our minds and the bind between us loosened. "You can't leave your mother. She needs you. She needs you now."

The trembling softened, imperceptibly to the Guild trio perhaps, but the tether around my mind slackened, allowing the burning sting in my shoulder to reemerge. "Let go, Sagar." I winced. "We have to get back. Your mother will need you, now more than ever."

"They killed my father! They shot him!" His anger and despair were inconsolable.

At least, I'd opened up a dialogue. The rage melted into mourning. "I know, kidlet, but your mother still needs you. You can't destroy them without destroying yourself. Your mother will have no one if she loses you."

The trembling subsided substantially as his shoulders fell and slumped. Yana glanced up and then checked the hallway for safe, unobstructed escape routes.

"Good boy, Sagar. We have to get you back to Narbonne."

“How? The rift is gone.” Tears welled up in his eyes.

The shaking beneath her body subsiding, the doctor recovered. Her tight bun hung in dusty tendrils around her blood-stained face. Red splotches stained her white shirt, arms, and legs. Still, she was all ambition, assessing her assets. One of the guards lay inert—knocked out cold. The other held his head. 427 cowered and whimpered on the floor at our feet.

We couldn’t allow the doctor enough time to summon reinforcements. “C’mon!” Grabbing Yana’s gloved hand as we passed through the empty doorway, I led the two of them down the hall to the elevator. My right arm numb and dripping trails of blood, I held it close to my body.

We didn’t get 10 yards before we encountered a guard who had taken shelter in the doorway of the next room.

Pulling up abruptly, with a dead stun gun and a bleeding wound in my shoulder, I tried to stuff the two children behind me and stared down the guard. I had nothing—no plan, no recourse. Goddess! I was going to fail Sagar at the last minute. Why didn’t we see this? Because this was the redo.

Dr. Petrov’s walkie-talkie crackled and her sharp, somewhat deadened tone insisted on reinforcements. The guard’s hand hovered warily above his holster. Knowing the same tactic couldn’t possibly work twice, I assumed the role of victim. “You have to help them,” I pleaded, pointing to the room. “There was a horrible earthquake. People are injured! Can you call for help?”

Sagar, still traumatized with the sight of his father being shot to death, watched the man’s intentions from behind my leg. The guard wasn’t buying my act and went for the gun. To all of our surprise, Sagar’s hand shot out faster. The force that he channeled rippled the air as it flew past. The guard’s body vaulted backward, slammed against the wall at the end of the corridor, and slunk down into a heap.

My mouth dropped open and I looked down at my new bodyguard. He wrinkled his nose. The astonishment wore off and I figured I needed to bring him down a notch. “Show off.”

He shrugged, grinning sheepishly, the little boy resurfacing.

At the end of the corridor, we called the elevator. It was already on the 8$^{th}$ floor. I hustled my two charges around the corner and waited out of sight. While the elevator rose, I probed the wound on my shoulder. It was deep and bloody, but I couldn't sense a bullet inside. It must have only grazed me or gone clear through. Given my limited experience, I thought that must be good.

Around the corner, the elevator dinged. The doors whirred open. Sagar moved forward, but I grabbed his shirt. Boots hit the tile floor and rushed off toward the disaster and distress calls in the pool room.

When the elevator was empty, the three of us rounded the corner and slipped inside. "The top one. 12! The roof access will be located up there."

Sagar pushed the button. Nothing happened. "It needs a key." I pulled Dr. Petrov's ID card from the tight-fitting top of my Spandex suit. Streaks of blood smeared the picture and words, but it still worked.

Realizing I was betting on a plan whispered in the last second of a 7-second capsule, that may or may not have been erased, little beads of sweat formed on my forehead as we ascended. If Josh lost consciousness again, if I didn't make it out alive, the roof would hold no foreseen rescue. We'd be trapped with nowhere to go. My palms grew clammy. On the $12^{th}$ floor, the doors pinged and opened on a corridor similar to the one we'd left behind.

"C'mon! There must be stairs to the roof." Taking Yana's hand again, I raced down the hallway. Dr. Petrov's key gave us access to the roof stairs. At the top, I threw open the door, not sure what to expect, wondering if the other side of the building offered a secondary access—just in case.

The raging wind that whipped our hair and struck our faces did not emanate from a rift. A helicopter dominated the space. Powerful rotating blades on the roof whirred and roared. The door opened and I prayed this was Josh's doing, not part of the Guild's trap. I had no other plan.

A leather shoe attached to a suit pant leg ducked toward us from the passenger cabin of the helicopter. I gasped. "Barry!"

"Come on! Run!" He gestured us into the helicopter. Ducking low, we fronted the wind. It shoved us back and tangled even my short hair. With my good arm, I hauled Yana, shivering, into Barry's hands. He settled her in the far seat as I hoisted up Sagar.

The door to the stairwell swung open and Dr. Petrov, rumpled and disheveled, marched through. Half a dozen soldiers poured onto the roof behind her. She yelled and pointed. I practically threw Sagar into the helicopter. He rolled between the seats and started to scramble up as gunshots cracked through the whirring roar of the blades.

"Go! Go! Go!" Barry yelled at the pilot. He reached for my hand to help me in. My wounded shoulder made that arm useless.

The blades gathered speed as I clambered up, propelled by Barry's grip on my one good wrist. The helicopter left the ground. My feet dangled. Shots cracked the rushing wind. Bullets clanked off metal and shattered glass.

Dr. Petrov's screams pierced the cacophony. The shots stopped abruptly and one of the guards rushed forward and lunged for my feet. My good hand had reached the steel bar that bolted the nearest seat to the floor. The guard's hand grasped my ankle. I kicked my foot frantically as the helicopter lifted away from the roof. My hand was slipping from the bar. Barry threw his other arm over and grabbed my forearm. He and the guard tugged as we rose. I was going to be pulled in half. There was no other plan. This was the plan that had replaced what happened before and was clearly not going to work. What did that mean? That we didn't get another chance? That we botched the do-over?

"Do NOT lose the asset!" Dr. Petrov threatened. The guard's feet left the roof. A volley of shots riddled the helicopter with chinks. A thundering impact in my back exploded into pain that ricocheted through my body. I screamed and slid. My hand relinquished the bar. And then blackness.

# CHAPTER 50

My eyes flickered, stuck, and then opened. The world spun and undulated all at the same time. I was used to waking up like this: bewildered, on my guard, ready to spring or run. Beneath numbness, my body throbbed and ached—two holes in my back. What the…? I gasped, lurching forward, adrenaline flooding my veins, fortifying me for quick defense.

The sudden pitch strained the neatly bandaged wounds in my back. This was…a lab. A lab! Oh, Goddess, I'm back in the lab! The Guild pulled me off Barry's helicopter! I thought the nightmare was over.

I couldn't breathe. I couldn't move. No. Wait. No straps, just numb unresponsive muscles. My eyes blinked and refocused on the colors around me—not antiseptic blue and white, calming green and beige. No observation windows. A hospital. My head fell back on the pillow and an enormous sigh of relief deflated my chest. A little side table held a plastic bottle full of water. There wasn't much hygiene or hydration going on at *Génétique*. My mouth felt like wood. I grabbed awkwardly at the container, jostling the bandages, and rewarding myself with a cutting jolt that rifled across my neurons.

Barry strolled past the doorway, engrossed in a phone screen. Glancing up, he saw me sipping voraciously, smiled, and walked in. "Spencer's not going to like this. I promised him, if he went to the cafeteria, you wouldn't wake up while he was gone."

"Who cares about being here when I wake up. I want food, not friends. I'm starving. The food service at the *Génétique* hotel is definitely sub-standard."

"You're in luck then. He only agreed to bring it back and eat here. You know Spencer. The quantities he consumes could feed a whole village."

"He's hollow. Hope he'll share."

"You look pretty pathetic. Your chances are good."

"Thanks. They're not big on hygiene in the Guild either. More ice baths than hot showers."

Barry's jaw clenched. I'd never seen anger on the tree man before. "You'll be sore for a while, but you're lucky, nothing permanent—except scars."

"Definitely not lucky…" I struggled to sit up and he offered a supporting hand to my back, "…more like, I have a guardian. Sagar." I didn't put it past the kidlet to be able to deflect bullets. The little *merdeux* was full of surprises. "He and Yana are here? Right? Nice helicopter, by the way. Didn't know you had one. Glad you do."

"I have many things you don't know about—not yet. Yana's been staying at your house. Spencer gravitates between here and there."

"Spencer babysitting. That's new—and a little scary. His goldfish died—who can't keep a goldfish alive? What about Sagar?"

"I found a safe house for him and his mother. They'll stay in the states with us, of course."

"You don't trust the Word?"

"Do you?"

Too tired for explanations, I leaned my head back and enjoyed the luxury of breathing freely. Adrenalin receded from my veins and the wound on my shoulder screamed.

"How did you know where I was?"

He wagged his eyebrows. "There's very little I don't know. But you have Josh Morgana to thank for this…and I suppose your future drift. I was in negotiations with the Word when he burst in, half-drowned, by the way."

"That's an interesting story about Sagar you might not know already."

He grinned and shrugged. "He insisted I leave immediately on this rescue mission."

I smiled, relieved I'd had the presence of mind to relate back to Josh what he'd told me about the roof during one of the drifts the Guild had induced. "You were in France the whole time?"

"Who do you think settled the mess with the kidnapping charge?"

"Why didn't you tell me? I needed your help."

"You seemed to be doing just fine on your own."

I sniffed, but the self-reliance felt good, all except for the throbbing burn in my shoulder and back. "And did you get what you were after?"

"Did you?"

Biting my lip, I weighed the question. "I got Sagar."

"And, just so you know, you really have no idea what exactly it is that you have there in that boy."

"I'd say I got a pretty good preview."

"You don't know the half of it."

The point was arguable, but I was too exhausted for a robust debate with a kickass lawyer. Besides, Barry would get around to filling me in. He always did—eventually. "I met the boy from my drifts."

"Oh?"

"But you already know him. Josh."

He raised his eyebrows, nodding appreciatively. Apparently, it only made sense. "So, he's been seeing you secretly…"

"…for a couple of decades." I rolled my eyes. "It's not like that."

"I'm a lawyer. I read people for a living. It's like that."

I deflected. "What about you? Did you get what you were negotiating for?"

He rummaged in his pocket and produced the amulet he'd shown me earlier. "You mean your free will?"

"You got it back!"

"Whoever holds this, controls your gift." He handed it to me. "The choices should be yours." That was why I trusted Barry. He held my money, he knew the story of my heritage, he knew my power. He could have manipulated that for so many years, any way he wanted to, but he let me choose. My hand closed around the medallion. "I'm going to have a security guard outside your door until I can get you back to my house. You're a high-value target for the Guild, now."

"I wish people would stop talking about me as if I were a stock commodity."

"Well, I suppose you should know. Seers are rare."

"Yeah, so I discovered."

"They follow a feminine bloodline. You're the unofficial Crone of the Coven. It's your birthright, but only if you want it. The Guild has an interest in seeing the post remain vacant and the Coven loosely aligned."

"And the Guild killed my grandmother with this?" I handed the amulet back to Barry. He'd kept it safe for years, a couple more months wouldn't make any difference. Frankly, it frightened me.

"Not sure I want to go there, Barry. I know I should be more heroic, do something with my gift, but what gives me the right? I can change the future, but who's to say what's better?"

Barry sighed and helped me readjust my pillow. "It will certainly complicate your life if you decide that the Coven should convene once more. But then, you've already gotten a taste of the risks."

"So, all of this. It wasn't just about Dr. Singh defecting? They weren't targeting Sagar just to blackmail his father?"

"His work was crucial to their influence. He was a gifted neuroscientist. They'll miss him."

"Especially if Dr. Petrov is their next in line."

"She's a bit prickly, isn't she?"

"That's kind."

"Sagar was their target. Like the amulet, he is a key element of your power."

Frankly, what had happened to Sagar in the lab at *Génétique* frightened me. "You should have seen what I saw, Barry. His powers are dangerous."

"He's young. It has always been so with a young Protector. But where a Crone is given, a Protector comes as well. Sagar is yours."

Fitting. He'd always been this odd mélange of advisor and child—protector and protégé. That explained the odd sensation in the lab when he took my hand. He'd been usurping 427's gift, wringing it from her, but with me, it was more like we melded, and in the end, I had ultimate control. But the real clue was the number of times Sagar had saved my butt even though I was the one supposed to be saving his.

"How long before they come for us?"

"The Guild is much stronger along the coasts in the States. That's how you've managed to avoid their all-seeing eye for so long. The imbalance that is rocking the European continent has not yet reached our western coast, but it's coming." Barry's phone buzzed. "I have to take this. I'll leave you to Spencer."

He turned to leave and I called, "Will he come?"

Barry knew who I meant.

The thought of leaving without saying good-bye weighed on me. I had imagined that meeting me and visiting my past had been a choice. Somehow, I had hoped that the possibilities that our gifts combined offered would draw him to me. But the images of Vilja and his sister, of everyone he'd rescued from the Guild's exploitation, made me believe that perhaps I was only a necessity of the moment. "Will I see him again?"

"That choice is his. The Cult is not as confining as the Guild, but it will require some subtle negotiating for him to leave. He risks much."

I nodded, attempting to look brave.

"And yet, he stands to gain more." Barry winked and stepped into the hall.

# CHAPTER 51

Spencer and I slouched on the grey couch near the hearth. Dany snoozed at my feet. She was happy to have me back, wouldn't let me out of her sight. Spencer wasn't nearly the dog lover that I was. She looked a little thinner and danced anxiously every time I headed for the front door. She ripped up my mattress two days after I left, a fitting punishment, I guess. I was sharing with Yana in my mom's room until the new one arrived.

The usual remains of a funeral feast cluttered the kitchen table. If I was Ivy, named after the creeping vine, Spencer was the stone wall that I wrapped my tendrils around and used for support so I could reach the sun. He made all the arrangements for a small memorial service for my mom. We were indulging in some cinnamon rolls and coffee to dull the sorrow.

"Sometimes, I think she's not really *gone* gone, you know, like there are pieces of us that float around in all the universes. If one piece leaves the game, it just joins another that is still in play. The idea of the in-between gives me hope."

"Believe whatever you want, Ivy. No one knows any better. It's all conjecture and wishful thinking."

Batting my eyelashes, I thanked him for his profound sensibility. But in the end, I didn't need more mushy sand to squelch around my feet. I needed the frank reality of Spencer to help me find solid ground.

"What still bothers me a little, maybe even tempts me to try to get back in touch with the Cult…"

"You mean with Josh?"

"Well, yeah, I guess." I hadn't seen or heard from my blue-eyed drift boy since I got home, not in my present *or* my future.

It was probably for the best. We didn't exactly see the world through the same lens. I shrugged off the knowing look on Spencer's face. He knew well the scent of unrequited love. "Anyway, during a drift in the Guild facility, he told me we couldn't trust someone, but the drift snapped shut before he could tell me who. I just wonder if he knows, or if I told him after."

"Do you know who it was?"

"No. But I have my suspicions. Sayid's rift sent me to the Guild. Whether or not he calculated that is up in the air." I handed Spencer the amulet I'd been inspecting. "The thing is, when Sayid came for this, it was Vilja that told him he was supposed to get it, not the Hand—the guy that runs things for the Word." I ran my fingers through my now lavender short hair that was pushing back toward shoulder length. When I came home, Spencer insisted I dye it back. He was affronted that someone else had dared usurp his role as Supreme Overlord of hair.

"Are you sure that's not just wishful thinking?"

I shrugged. He was right. The last time I saw Josh, Daiyu was carting him away through the rift at *Génétique*. What I feared was that Vilja was the reason I hadn't heard from him. I was just another "asset" necessary to the success of his plan to liberate his sister. "It just seems like I should have seen him, you know, told him everything that was going to happen so he could show up when he was supposed to—like that drift where I was in some village clock shop. That one never happened."

"You probably did see him after. Maybe you were hiding there *when it first happened*, but now you don't need to because he came back and told you what went wrong the first time and you changed it. Or, it's still in the future."

"You're probably right. My memories of those drifts have that *dream / I'm not sure if it was a dream*, quality now. I just wish I could control it all a little better."

He turned the amulet about in his hand. "So, you don't really know how this works?'

"I know it killed my grandmother. It's not like I'm going to experiment on my own. Dr. Singh he's…"

His eyes narrowed. “What you need is a certified neuroscientist. Someone qualified to do human testing.”

“Oh, Goddess, no! Please!”

“I happen to know the 4.0 child of two neuro-scientists earning his degree right here in Salt Lake.”

My head flopped back on the saggy cushions at the utter absurdity of the idea. We both knew Amr was too much of a pirate at heart to settle down to something so mundane as research. “You know I’m thrilled Amr’s doing so well. I mean, how ironic that *he* came to visit *me* in the hospital. But you’re not seriously suggesting that I recruit him to work with me?”

“No. I’m not suggesting it. I’m preparing you. There’s something I haven’t told you about Amr…”

“Oh, no…”

“Chill, girlfriend. He just, uh…”

“What?”

He frowned and shook his head, “uh…nothing. He’s coming over here…” he glanced at his phone, “…in about 5 minutes—give or take a few.”

“What! Now? I need a chance to think about this. I…”

“Look, Ivy, face it!” He shook the amulet in front of my nose. “You’ve always wanted this. You’ve wanted to figure out how to use your gift. You’re genetically programmed to guide the rest of us.”

“That’s hilarious. I don’t even know where the hell *I’m* going.”

“You’ll figure it out.” He knocked on my forehead. “Hello! You see the future. Amr could help you control this. He’ll jump at the chance. He loves this *merde* and you could pay him more than he’s making as a doctor. We’re rich. It would be totally *lit*. Barry’s all over the idea and he’s got the resources of the Coven behind him.” He leaned over and waggled the amulet in front of me. “Think of it, you and Amr, together—again. The shoulder-length lavender year is coming back at you.”

“You’re so full of shit. You’ve been warning me off Amr since I met him. Girlfriend of the month. Remember?”

“That was before you needed a resident neuroscientist.”

"I think you just want to figure out a way to keep him hanging around here where you can bask in the sunshine of his amazing good looks. You have no morals."

"Not my type. And expediency trumps morality—every time. Maybe he's changed. Maybe he'd liked to settle down."

"Some things don't change, besides…" Saying the words of how I felt about Josh wasn't necessary. Spence picked up on the body language.

"Drift boy? Yeah, that's going to get awkward. Ivy, you have to wrap your head around the fact that a string of 7-second dates isn't really long enough to…"

The knock at the door cut short Spencer's sage advice.

"Oh, shit! That's him, isn't it?"

Spencer shooed me to the door. Dany pranced at my feet as I walked. My hand short of the knob, I stopped and took a deep breath before opening it. I was so torn. Amr was in my future and I knew it. He'd be sitting next to me at the round table. But, Josh would be toasting me on the other side. But, Amr was the one who would be watching out for me at the side of the bed when Josh popped in to tell me about the roof.

"Hey!" I feigned surprise until I realized who was standing in front of me and really felt surprise. My hand flew to my mouth. My mask of bland disaffection warped in the blink of an eye to genuine relief, disbelief, and a deep resounding shudder of satisfaction. "Oh, my Goddess! Hey, Traveler!"

Josh stood on my doorstep. "Is that all I get, Drifter?"

My eyes stung. I threw my arms around him and held him tight enough to squeeze out the doubt, the distance, the ideologies, the intrigues—everything that stood between us. Dany joined in the love fest, dancing on two legs and pawing our hips. "I never got to say good-bye. I thought we were done," I murmured into his shoulder.

"Done?" He leaned back and then did that adorable French thing, kissing me on both cheeks. "We've only just started. You and me, Drifter—we're better together."

FIN

# ACKNOWLEDGEMENTS

Many thanks to Curt, my favorite and most demanding editor. Our romance is clearly more than a 7-second affair. As always, thanks to Josh for his visionary editorial comments, Janie for the artwork on the laundry room wall, and Connor and Sam whose insightful comments guided the course of this story in its early stages. Thanks again to Anna, Norm, Libby, Pat, Janet and John for their invaluable comments.

And thank you for reading. I hope you enjoyed the story. I'd love to read your comments and feedback on Amazon.com. I look forward to hearing from you.

# ABOUT THE AUTHOR

Rachel DeFriez is the author of the award winning zombie romance trilogy WALKING GREY, the supernatural thriller I AM KRONOS, the urban fantasy 'TWEEN OAK, ASH, AND THORN, and her first romance RAVENS AND LAVENDER, awarded Recommended Read in the 2021 LUW Quills Contest. She lives with her husband and Maine Coon in the Salt Lake metro area where she teaches high school French and creative writing and advises the literary magazine. Her four children all found best friends to join their team and moved out to pursue careers in the extreme sport of life.

www.ingramcontent.com/pod-product-compliance
Lightning Source LLC
LaVergne TN
LVHW091122080826
845145LV00008B/2016